Beach Boy

Ardashir Vakil

Scribner Paperback Fiction
Published by Simon & Schuster

SCRIBNER PAPERBACK FICTION
Simon & Schuster Inc.
Rockefeller Center
1230 Avenue of the Americas
New York, NY 10020

Originally published in Great Britain by Hamish Hamilton, Ltd.
First Scribner Paperback Fiction edition 1999.
SCRIBNER PAPERBACK FICTION and design are trademarks of
Jossey-Bass, Inc., used under license by Simon & Schuster,
the publisher of this work.

Designed by Brooke Zimmer
Set in Fournier MT
Manufactured in the United States of America

1 3 5 7 9 10 8 6 4 2

The Library of Congress has cataloged the
Scribner edition as follows:
Vakil, Ardashir, date.
Beach boy / Ardashir Vakil.
p.   cm.
I. Title.
PR9499.3.V34B4   1998
823—dc21   98-21194
CIP

ISBN 0-684-85299-3
0-684-85300-0 (Pbk)

Permission to reprint the following copyrighted material
is gratefully acknowledged:
"Harmony," written and produced by Elton John and Bernie Taupin.
Copyright © 1973 Dick James Music, Ltd. Used by permission.
All Rights Reserved.
"Venus," words and music by R. van Leeuwen. Copyright © 1969
International Music Network Limited. Used by permission.
All Rights Reserved.

To my mother

Beach Boy

Although every man believes that his decisions and resolutions involve the most multifarious factors, in reality they are a mere oscillation between flight and longing.

——HERMANN BROCH, *The Sleepwalkers*

I was eight when I encountered the friendly elephants. Perched on a padded seat, in a theater jammed with human bodies, I watched Rajesh Khanna, lead actor in the film, as he urged his noodle-trunked mates, Rani and Soni, to push his broken-down Jeep. Bodies swayed to the melodious hit song.

> Chul, chul, chul, mere haathi
> O mere saathi
> Chul re chul khatara ki . . .
> Chuliya, motor car
> Dhakka de, mere yaar . . .

As he sang, Rajesh leapt from one end of the open-top vehicle to the other. Sometimes, during the song, he pretended to be driving, tooting the horn and swiveling the steering wheel. Then he would jump up, turn around, arm extended in front of him, and serenade the elephants, while cocking an eye at his lead lady, who sat in her pink sari, eyes laden with mascara, coyly surveying the scene. The packed cinema murmured approvingly, sighed and shifted in their seats. In the darkness, women smiled at their children, and the occasional cry of a baby was swiftly smothered by a melting brown breast. Men wandered into the aisles and headed toward the toilets to smoke beedis. They hawked paan juice on the bespattered walls and emptied their bladders into the tall urinals.

I looked to my left and caught Mrs. Verma patting her oiled black hair, a vacant half-smile on her face. This had been a difficult film to get tickets for. Mrs. Verma had needed to phone one of her filmi friends who happened to know the deputy manager of the Nandi cinema, and he, after some fussing, oohing and aahing, had promised four cheap tickets in the front stalls.

The film had been on release for nine days. Every one of the twenty-two cinema halls in Bombay in which it was showing displayed the familiar black and white signboard on its entrance steps: HOUSE FULL.

As the song faded and the Jeep jump-started into the trickling sunset, my arms pimpled at the prospect of two-and-a-half hours of unfolding drama. Momentarily, I worried about the popcorn and masala chips in the interval, then I allowed all thought, sound, even smell, to seep steadily away from my screen-fixed consciousness. My head settled, as in a comfortable vise, my eyes swam from image to image. The dialogue, the scenery, the minor characters, the clothes, the different voices—I followed them all with painful concentration.

The hero, Rajesh, meets the heroine, Tanuja, at college, little suspecting that their parents are plotting their marriage in the background. The sequence of scenes leads up to the formal visit of Rajesh and his parents to the home of their prospective in-laws. The two sets of parents and one widowed white-sari'd grandmother are seated in the sparsely decorated living room. The heroine's family is respectable but not very rich. As the idle chatter continues, the audience anxiously awaits the entrance of the bride-to-be with the tray of tea. Her mother assures the hero's parents that she is educated up to "intercollegiate," but not interested in pursuing her studies any further. Grandmother extols the virtues of the dead grandfather and sheds a few artificial tears, before explaining that the only mission left in her life is to see her beloved granddaughter happily married to some nice young man from a well-respected family. Just then, in minces Tanuja, having held herself back at the door for a moment. Her father extends his arm encouragingly. "Aao beti, aajao idher." A little sitar music, the hero's surprised face, his parents' immediate admiration. Dutifully shy, tea tray awkwardly balanced in her hands, she meets Rajesh Khanna's eye with a little stutter of delight.

"Kya hai beti? Is anything wrong?" inquires her mother.

Soon after, the happy couple are circling the wedding pyre seven times. Strings of champa flowers, like pretty white curtains, cover their blushful faces. Two songs take care of their courting and their honeymoon in Kashmir. Rani and Soni, the hero's pet elephants, form the backdrop for the first song, the Himalayan mountains for the second. In the log-fire dining room of the luxury hotel in Gulmarg, Tanuja and Rajesh giggle cozily about when to have children, their preferred sex and their names. These were the bits, like some of the song sequences, where I got a chance to look around me, take a break from all that intense concentration. My anxiety about eats in the interval increased. I had sixty paise in the pocket of my shorts, perhaps just enough to get me a small packet of popcorn. My eyes were on the screen, but my head was filling up with Punjabi samosas, Five Star chocolate, chutney sandwiches, Smarties, peanuts, Mangolas, and then—

Prem Chopra appeared. A whisper travels through the crowd, "Prem Chopra . . . Prem Chopra . . . Prem Chopra aya re . . . dekho re Prem Chopra . . . villain number one sala!" On the screen is the man with the most evil leer in the cinema world. Black oily mustache feathery under his nose, tapering to a thin line at the corners of his mouth. His cheeks are puffy and arrogant, his hair is slicked-back black. His suit is vivid purple and his broad tie sits garishly on his red shirt. But it's his eyes that do the most damage: black dots of fire, shining and crackling from hell. He pauses, allowing the audience to recover from his presence, saunters up to Sharmila—the character played by Tanuja, who, despite the warning music, has not noticed his arrival—and hisses breathily.

"Arre, Sharmila! Tum idher? What a nice pleasshuure to see you here." This is the devil himself. He slurs and smirks, and uses heavily accented English words. The crowd loves him. Rajesh suddenly looks forlorn, like a pink-faced cherub. Tanuja tries to speak, but all I can see is the fright in her eyes. Prem strokes his cheek, leans to one side, and asks with exaggerated solicitude: "Arre, won't you introduce me to your young friend?" His tongue flickers and licks his lips like a cobra. Tanuja just manages a reply. "This is my husband, Kamal." Swallowing hard and looking at Prem all the time, she completes the formal introduction. "And this is Dhiren, Dhiren Kapur." On her last word the music rises to a crescendo, "Taaaeh, Taaaeh, Taeh, Taehhh!" As the trio remain frozen in their separate amazements, across them flashes in huge blue letters:

INTERVAL

Everyone stood up and no one could move. Usha Verma turned immediately to her two sons, Navnish and Avnish. Her eldest son, Rajnish, had generously given his ticket to me.

"Avnish, have some popcorn, hain? Shall I bring you a samosa? No? Acha chulo, Fanta pee lo. Navnish, you will have some popcorn, no?" Enviously, I watched this careful display of motherly affection. When my family went to the cinema, to see films in English, I pleaded with my mother, "Please can I have fifty paise for popcorn . . . pleeeze? The chicken rolls here are really tasty . . . I'll only have one." Her stock answer was, "We're going home for dinner. It will spoil your appetite. You don't need it." With my mother, I was always fighting a losing battle. With Mrs. Verma, I had to maintain a balance between embarrassment and anticipation. I knew Usha Aunty would offer me popcorn and drinks, which I would greedily accept, like the cinema ticket, without having the money to pay for them. But first she would take her time spoiling her children, with repeated offers, from which they would nonchalantly pick something. In the end, she would buy them everything anyway. I would have to wait, accompany her out, and accept her eventual offers with a shy shake of the head, as if to pretend that I was not desperate with hunger.

Straightening the pallu of her sari, with a jingle of her bangles, like a graceless Kathakali dancer, Mrs. Verma turned to me and said, "Chulo, Cyrus. Coming with me?"

Mrs. Verma was all color and smiles. She had a plump oval face caked with powdery foundation. She was often to be seen sitting in front of her dressing-table mirror, correcting a tint, dabbing her cheek, or spraying some fragrance on her neck. On her table she had a host of artificial stick-on bindis to choose from, hundreds of glass, silver, brass, and gold bangles that lay on special stands on either side of the mirror. Today she has on her forehead a dark blue dot encircled with tiny petals of white. Her chubby forearms seem strangled by colored bangles. Her hair is tied in a bun and round it is a small garland of fake orange flowers. From her ears hang a pair of gold enameled stars that stand out in the gloom of the theater. Her lips are painted chocolate red. By far the most important aspect of her face, unless caught in a moment of utter privacy, is that she is always smiling. To get to know Mrs. Verma, one needed to comprehend the hundred variants of her smile.

In her company I was horribly nervous. Determined to please, servile in every way. "Usha Aunty, you think Prem is hiding some secret?" I asked. I wanted her to acknowledge me as an amateur aficionado of Hindi cinema. I knew all about Hindi films from magazines like *Stardust*, from song programs on the radio, from the hoardings dotted around the city, and from listening to filmi gossip.

Mrs. Verma's smile broke into a laugh at my question. She seemed amused by my interest, but not amused enough to reply. She surveyed the crowd in the stalls canteen, her smile curled downward. "Let's go up to the dress circle, hain?" I followed her up the stairs, comparing her black and white floral sari to the Western clothes my mother wore. As we mounted the stairs, people stared at us unashamedly. In the dress-circle canteen, I was amazed by the din of voices. I recalled our last family outing to the Sterling, to see *Patton*. The canteen at the Sterling was crowded and smoky, but the noise was whispering, the faces all familiar. Here at the Nandi, the atmosphere was more like Bombay Central Railway Station. The racket of voices, the clatter of trays on the counters, the brutal way in which people pushed past you, the shouts across the room, the open-mouthed chewing of paan.

It all made me feel like a child. Frighted. But Mrs. Verma was by me and there was business to be done. I could see the aerated drinks, row upon row, black, yellow, orange, red, and translucent, stacked on the mirrored shelves behind the frenetic sellers. I could smell the fried samosas. The taste of salted popcorn made my mouth dry. I wanted anything and everything. I knew Mrs.

Verma would buy too much and I would get all the leftovers. The vendors shouted over the tumble of voices. I could see money and food being exchanged at tremendous speed, but the crowd remained clotted around the marble-topped counters. Some didn't buy anything, they just stood around watching the greedy and the rich. They may have been hungry, but this was not the kind of food they ate.

The smile twitched on Mrs. Verma's face. "Acha, Cyrus, yaar. Shall we forget it? There are too many people, no?" I looked pleadingly at her. She took pity and handed me a ten-rupee note, saying, "Okay, go and get some popcorn and masala chips and two Cokes, hain? Will you be able to?" I assured her I would. This was the kind of job I loved. Half the size of those in front of me, I pushed and muscled and squeezed like an oil slick wending its way through the gaps between arms, bums, Terylene shirts, and women's bare stomachs. The gray and white streaks of the fake marble counter came into view. I bawled at the man serving, thrusting my ten rupees in front of me. "Aaaaaay, do Coca-Cola, do masala chips, aur teen packet popcaaarn." The unshaven vendor shot me an irritated glance, as he continued to serve the other hecklers. "Chulo bhai, jaldi karo na, film start hone vala hai," I called out. Eyes fell upon the money and the little hand that held it. I had an audience. I hauled my torso onto the counter and reached out with my hand. The irate vendor rushed up, shouting at me to get down off the counter, "Heeey chokra, kya kar raha hai? Chulo, neeche chulo." I could hear members of my audience laughing. This could get serious, though. The vendor was not amused. Turning to the sulky woman next to me, he politely asked, "Hah, kya chaheye aapko, madam?" I waited patiently. He would get to me in the end.

"Where have you been?" Avnish asked. The two boys looked bored and uneasy. Mummy coddled them. "Are you too hot? Sorry, I couldn't find any ice cream. Here, Cyrus managed to squeeze through and get you a Coke. That's what you wanted, na, Avnish?" I offered up the popcorn and the wafers but they shook their heads. Suited me fine. Mrs. Verma took one of the packets of popcorn from me and lovingly tore open the waxed edge. She held it out to Navnish. "Try a bit of popcorn, bete. Nahi? Kyon, you don't like it? Acha, never mind. Mangola le lo. No? That also you don't want?" Mrs. Verma leaned back in her seat with a wry smile and a shake of the head. Navnish sulkily took a crisp and asked for a Coke but there wasn't any left. "I don't like sitting downstairs," he said. "I only like sitting in balcony or dress circle."

"Theek hai," Mrs. Verma consoled. "Okay, next time balcony, hain? I couldn't help it this time, everything was completely full. Sethi sahb ne kaha hai, pukka, he will get the tickets for next Friday's show."

Wrinkling his nose, Avnish complained, "There's a horrible smell down here."

"Badbu aa rahi hai, Avnish? Hah, I can smell it also," said his mother. From her handbag, Mrs. Verma took a scented airline napkin, ripped it open, and passed the wet towel to Avnish. The hall lights dim and the action on the screen abruptly begins.

At first, my attention is split between the masala chips I grope for in the dark and the faces on the screen. Soon the story sucks me in with its lurid and beckoning colors. A landscape of snow-clad mountains and silvery rivers lies beyond the log-fire interiors of Rajesh and Tanuja's honeymoon motel. Every twenty minutes or so there is a song. A courting song, a honeymoon song, a sad song, a love duet. Most of the songs for women in Hindi films are sung by the tireless nightingales, Lata Mangeshkar and her sister Asha Bhosle. The music is invariably composed by that famous father-and-son duo, S. D. and R. D. Burman. Between them they have produced more than 20,000 songs. All this making music together produced its own happy ending. In real life Asha Bhosle and R. D. Burman fell in love and got married.

It becomes apparent that Prem Chopra's arrival in Kashmir has punctured Rajesh and Tanuja's honeymoon bliss. He knows secrets about Tanuja's past that will embarrass her and he loses no time and wastes no subtlety in painting the picture to Rajesh. Rajesh is desolate. He asks Tanuja for the whole truth. She wails and cries, saying what happened between her and Prem was not her fault. As she recollects aloud, the audience is afforded a flashback of events in which Tanuja appears, sporting a knee-length college skirt and pigtails. A younger-looking Prem manages to seduce her.

When the story is over and Tanuja is kneeling by his feet, Rajesh swears that he will exact revenge. He will tear, limb from limb, the vicious dog who dared defile his holy wife. Then Tanuja begins a mournful song in high-flown Urdu that I found difficult to follow. I could see Mrs. Verma, her chin tilted upward, her eyes aglow with moisture, utterly engrossed by the lyrics.

Sitting in my skimpy blue trunks, I felt the underside of my thighs wet with the sweat collected between them and the cheap plastic covering of the wooden seats. The man on my left was chewing a mixture of betel nut and paan; a heady smell, both sweet and slightly rotting. Across this wafted the flowery perfume worn by Mrs. Verma, not altogether masking the bodily odor from her armpit. Several rows behind us a baby was crying and I could make out the jingling of its mother's bangles as she attempted to rock it back to sleep. I wondered how many babies there were in the audience and what pleasure they were gaining from the film. What a sound it would make if they were all at once to start up and howl.

But it was the elephants and the "deeshum-deeshum" fight scenes that held me in the strongest rapture. Rani, Soni, and their darling baby, Moti. They were the ones who saved Rajesh's life in his final combat with Prem. Rani, who swept him away in her trunk from an onrushing truck driven by Prem; Soni, who got shot between the eyes but delivered the final revenge by crushing the villain under his hoof, accompanied by cheers from the audience. Rajesh, Tanuja, Rani, and the baby elephant shed copious tears at Soni's funeral.

Those were the pictures I carried in my head as we drove home, past the pool of lilies on the edge of Bandra. Women washed their clothes in the blackened water, bare-backed children swam in the brackish soup. I imagined having my own tame elephants as playmates: Moti and Tingoo running to greet me in the garden of our house on the beach, frolicking together in the salty water of the sea, sticking their trunks over the parapet of my bedroom window, nuzzling my cheek with the snail-like flesh on the tips of their snouts.

2

I have been bunking off school to go to the movies. I have stolen money, I have sold things, I have double-crossed my friends and—I can't bear to think the thought—I have been into the bathroom with my brother's friend, Darab.

He said my cock looked like a fish. I was taken aback. What kind of fish was he thinking of? I held it in my fingers and tried to imagine the tail and fins. "Where is the tail?" I asked. He pulled the top, the bit that looks like a Hitler's helmet, and laughed, showing his silvery braced teeth. "Hee, hee, hee, look at that teeny fish mouth." Then he twirled it in his crustacean fingers, as if toying with a gormless piece of plastic, before pulling my hand over to his big Labrador of a cock. It was huge and handsome. He wrapped my little palm around it, and pumped it down and up. I felt it swell and throb like a god. A rill of awe skipped through me. I had never seen a penis so gigantic. Like Jack's magical beanstalk, it was growing in my slowly moving fingers. Darab had dropped his hand away and was leaning his head to one side. We were standing next to one another in the gray bathroom. Our shorts were on the floor. His back rested against the whitish marble of the wall. On the enameled towel rail hung a green bath mat. The seat was up on the pink toilet bowl. Its shapely shanks were gleaming. Everything in the bathroom, the pink bath, the roll of toilet paper, the shiny basin, the chrome mirror, seemed cold. I returned my gaze to the shape in my hand. It was now three times the size of my fist. I wasn't sure which part of it to hold. The deliquescent skin unfurled, revealing a wet rod of flesh. I felt a little sick. Darab held his hand over mine, yanking it back and forth with increasing speed. I gave up my earlier restraint, pressed my fingers tight around the middle of his shaft, and worked it like a piston.

Marvel arose in me as the globe of his cock grew purple. It looked as though it might burst. Darab seemed to relax his body in the confidence that I had got into a reassuring rhythm with my hand. I felt a tautness in my fingers, something new moving inside, a straining at the skin and, incredibly, it was still growing larger. Uncontrollable, unrecognizable sensations, like hunger for food I had never tasted, coursed through my stomach and legs. Darab pushed my hand with his. I went faster and faster, up and down, trying not to think of my aching arm and of how long this would last. Somewhere inside my hand I felt a watery plink. His body jerked, as if in the throes of sleep. Then, to my silent surprise, out of the tiny hole at the top of his cock a thick porridgy liquid came spitting out onto the clean floor. I withdrew. Darab grabbed his penis and pumped it vigorously. His whole life seemed to be wrapped up in this emission. I was suddenly superfluous—like someone who had chanced to walk into the bathroom at that moment. More white slush puddled out of his shrinking penis. His lips stretched wide over his iron teeth, he grinned and pointed at my little fish. It was poking out, skin tight, parallel to the floor.

I SAT ON the chair in front of what my father called the Chippendale furniture. A mirror, a set of drawers, two desks, and six bookshelves, three above each desk. A small cupboard with sliding doors separates the desks. I pictured Darab's tall muscular body, his hard chest, his vulgar laugh, his curly black hair, the wires and hoops of steel that wrench his misshapen teeth, and his phony American ancestry. He'd be round again next weekend luring me into the bathroom. I forced myself to think of something else. I got off the chair and put a record on the player.

> . . . got me on a mountain top
> Venus was her name . . .
> Yah, baby, she's got it!
> I'm your Venus, I'm your fire
> At your desire . . .

I loved the bit where the guitarist gets his solo and thrums the strings like claps of thunder. I turned up the volume and pretended I was strumming the guitar, sauntering up and down my room singing along, flinging my body from side to side. When the guitarist's riff came round again, I jingle-jangled with a floppy, wrist and an imaginary plectrum in my fingers. I glanced sideways at the drummer, then down from the stage, into the screeching hordes, fans throwing their panties at me and baying for my body. I smiled nonchalantly. From behind me, above the noise of the music, I heard someone shouting my name. The voice grew threatening. "Cyrus, Cyruus, Cyruuuuus! Put that bloody racket off!" I bumped the needle off the record. The floor turned cold under my motionless feet. It was my neighbor, the dreaded Mr. Krishnan, so angry that he had come into the house

the back way and was mounting the wooden stairs. I could hear
the hiss of the cheap amplifier as he came striding down the corridor toward my room, bare-backed and barefoot, holding the
front of his white lungi in his hand and breathing heavily. He
stopped halfway down the corridor, eyes bulging, and pointed his
finger in my direction. Like a sage from the Amar Chitra Katha
comics, delivering a curse on an unsuspecting village girl who has
disturbed him in his meditation, he shouted, "If I ever hear you
play that music so loud again, I'll personally come over here and
break the machine in two. Do you hear?" Then he was gone,
pounding the tiles with his menacing feet. In a daze of fear, I
dropped onto the edge of the bed, lay down, and waited for my
heartbeat to return to normal.

Darab in the bathroom, stealing money from my mother,
bunking off school, lying to my neighbors, and now Mr. Krishnan's wrath. I was in solid trouble.

Mr. Krishnan's house was right behind ours, a small box-like
cottage with two rooms upstairs and down. The back window of
my bedroom looked out onto the front of the cottage. My narrow
balcony was less than twenty meters away from Mr. Krishnan's
sons' bedroom. Mr. Krishnan was a Marxist. He had an old Ford
DeSoto, he had rippling muscles which he used to beat his sons
and when his wife got in the way he beat her too, he had black
oiled-back hair, his skin was the color of bitter chocolate, and he
walked fast. Straight as a ramrod, pacing up and down the length
of his living room. His dark feet moving soundlessly over the
speckled tiling of the floor.

Mr. Krishnan had three sons, Ajay, Sushil, and Ravi, all long-
distance runners. They ran on the beach in front of our house.
Saturdays and Sundays the whole family woke at five-thirty,
rubbed their sleepy eyes, shook off their pajamas, pulled on their
swimming trunks, and made their way down to the beach. To stay
close friends, I had to go with them. We walked down the lane

that sloped toward the beach. Mr. Krishnan walked in front, making circular sweeps with his arms, like a windmill, Ajay next, followed by Sushil, and five-year-old Ravi trailed behind. The sons diminished in size behind their father. They copied his swagger and his loosening-up exercises. Ajay and Sushil were tall and thin, Mr. Krishnan and Ravi were short and hunched, like boxers. They all wore neat crew cuts. The dawn was gray and wet, and fell comfortably on their bare coffee-colored shoulders. They were not the only ones awake at this hour. Around them was an assortment of morning strollers: some in white shorts and white canvas shoes with walking sticks in hand were out for the exercise; others in dhotis and freshly ironed kurtas carried flowers as devotional offerings to the sea; some stood as still as rocks, looking meditatively at the rising sun. This was the hour of exercise and prayer, it was a time of calm. Occasionally, a belch or a low-flying early-morning plane punctured the quiet.

The four Krishnans strode out onto the dewy sand, sand that gave way below their feet and trickled up between their toes, and further out to the darker, denser, harder sand that was so smooth to run on. They walked for a mile along the beach, and then Ajay started to run. He ran for two miles up to the creek which stretched inland and disappeared amongst the thatched huts of the fishermen's village. There he bathed and swam in the tranquil waters and waited for the rest of the family to arrive. When the family had had their swim in the brackish waters of the creek, they ran the whole stretch of the beach back to the sloping lane and the concrete lifeguard stand that stood outside our house.

The creek where we swam marked one end of Juhu beach. All along the shore, for about three miles, were bungalows and two-story houses. At both ends of the beach were villages of Koli fisherfolk. My aunt once told me that these were the original inhabitants of Bombay. Before the Portuguese, before the Mughals, before the British, before the buildings and cars, there were communities of Koli fishermen, feeding on the bounteous waterways of these islands. They were still here in places like Juhu, Worli, and Marve. In Colaba their tin and canvas huts were overshadowed by neighboring skyscrapers, in Mahim by a church and cinema hoardings, in Mazagaon by huge ships and dock warehouses. They lived in the nooks of the city or on the margins of suburban beaches, but always within reach of boats, water, and fish.

The Krishnans were my friends. I went running with them, I copied their mannerisms, I spent hours playing marbles with them, sitting in their living room, eating their food, going out with them, meeting their friends and relatives. All day, during the holidays, we roamed around in nothing but our swimming trunks. We ate, drank, played, swam, and slept in these trunks. Mr. Krishnan led by example. During the day he was always to be seen striding up and down his living room, to and fro, to and fro in his black, red, or gray costume.

Early one evening I was sitting in the Krishnan household. The clouds loomed heavy and dark with rain. A wind fanned through the branches of the coconut trees. As usual, I was the interloper. The boys were having their baths. One by one, they descended the stairs looking scrubbed and wet-haired. I sat on a low wooden chair, dusty with the wear of the day we had spent together, starting with the early-morning run and ending with a game of cricket on the beach. In the final sprint, at the end of the three-mile run we had had earlier in the day, I had just managed to pass Ravi after we had been running neck and neck the whole way. The frustration, the pain, the betrayal had all been too much for him and he had burst out crying when his effort to keep up had failed. I felt shamefully triumphant afterward. I was three years older than him and twice his size.

Ajay had joined us now and we were all sitting together hardly able to talk for hunger. Mr. Krishnan had gone for his bath and Mrs. Krishnan was preparing the dinner in the kitchen. With Appa gone, the boys could relax a bit, complain to their mother, and harry her for bigger portions of food. The lights in the kitchen were bright, and tempting smells of frying onion, ground coconut, and coriander stole up my nostrils. Sushil rubbed his thin stomach and licked his lips.

"Aaii aaii yo Amma. Are we having uttapam today? Aaah, lovely, lovely crispy uttapam." He rubbed his hands together and took an inward breath of saliva and air through clenched teeth. I swallowed nervously and tried to change the topic of conversation. The thought of sitting there waiting for an uttapam I might never get filled my empty stomach with apprehension.

"What is an uttapam, actually?" I asked Sushil.

"You mean you've never had uttapams before! Oh, yaar, they are delicious. You dip some in sambhar while it's hot and then you take some green chutney like this." His fingers bunched as if they were holding a chapati, dancing over the condiments on offer, and popping the imaginary morsel into his mouth.

Mrs. Krishnan came out of the kitchen carrying a pile of stainless-steel thalis. She had a scowl on her face, a trademark scowl with which she addressed the burden of her life. I couldn't bear to count the thalis. I knew the chances were my place would be laid. It happened every other night, either here or at the Vermas'. There had been no call from my family. They knew where I was, or my presence hadn't been missed. The sight of the thalis and the sour smell of the simmering sambhar was making the boys ravenous. Ajay urged his mother on.

"Amma, we're so hungry, please come on. Where are the uttapams? When will they be ready?"

"Be quiet," she shouted. "The whole day I have to sweat and slave to feed you, wash your clothes, clean the house. Be patient, another five minutes and you will have your food. And Cyrus will have to wait today. There is only enough for one extra uttapam and your father may want it. I can't go on feeding Cyrus all the time. Where will all the money come from?" I looked away from my friends and tried to pretend I wasn't absorbing their mother's insults. I should have got up and walked out of the house and never returned. I let the hurt roll to one side. There was more to come. This time in Malayalam.

"Why doesn't his mother feed him properly? They've got so much money and they can't even feed their children properly." References to my mother's not feeding me enough, sometimes overt, sometimes snide, had a currency amongst the neighbors at whose houses I often ate. I considered these insults a fee one had to pay for eating their food, for demanding their friendship, for sleeping in their beds, partaking of their quarrels, sharing their holidays, walking their dogs, making love to them, even sharing in their dreams. Generosity is often spiked. Hospitality has its limits. Even Christ could not resist the temptation. At the Last Supper, our morals teacher told us, Jesus knew that the disciples were guilty. I puzzled over this. If he knew, why didn't he do something about it? And why was he sitting around a table drinking wine and eating bread with Judas and Peter and Paul? Incidentally, I also wondered why at his last meal he hadn't asked for something more delicious than plain bread. I would at least have asked for dhan sakh, for a lobster or a crab from the nearby sea. I found out from Aunt Zenobia that at this dinner he told the disciples that he knew that one of them was a liar and another one a traitor, and that he wanted them to drink the wine as if it were his blood and the bread as if it were his body. That's when I understood what Jesus was trying to do. The wine must have burnt like a river of lava down the throat of Judas. What a hunk of bread for Peter to chew. As long as they lived, how could they ever forget such a guilt-ridden meal? Perhaps this is how Peter ended up in Kashmir, as our Indian legend has it, feeding the birds.

My neighbors were like Jesus. They liked to give, they

wanted to share, but they couldn't resist the temptation to make me feel guilty, to make me suffer, to make me feel ashamed of my family, to pretend that I was a deprived child to whom they provided succor. My neighbors had different religions from Jesus, though, and they hailed from different parts of the world.

There were the Krishnans from Kerala, the Vermas from Delhi, the Hussains from Agra, the Ericssons from Sweden, the Maharani from Bharatnagar, the film star from Poona, the sausage dogs from Germany, the one-eyed cockatoos from Australia, the red-plumed parrots from Africa, and us, the Parsi Bawas from Bombay. The Readymoneys. Yes, that was my father's name, the name my great-grandfather earned for himself when he took on the trade of moneylender ninety years ago in the docks of Bombay. We are Zoroastrians, like the Topiwalas, the Bottleopenerwalas, the Batliwalas, the Lawyers (or Vakils), the Boxwalas, and the Ghaswalas, who are all named after the vocation of their ancestors. We pray at agiarys—temples where the same flame has been kept burning for hundreds of years. We have pictures of Queen Victoria on our walls. "B for Bawa, B for British," my non-Parsi friends liked to tease. We offer up our dead to the vultures on the top of Malabar Hill in huge stadium-sized wells called the Towers of Silence. We come from Iran, even though my grandmother hates to admit it. We drink cows' urine to purify our bodies, wear a sacred thread around our waists and a muslin vest with a tiny pocket of wisdom sewn in its breast. People often talk of us as being honest. We build ships and colonies—baghs where poor Parsis can lead a decent existence.

My family lived in a glass house facing the sea. My mother, Mehroo, my father, Minoo, my two elder brothers, Behroz and Adi, my younger brother and sister, Nasli and Shenaz. Over our heads jetliners soared to foreign climes across the Arabian Sea, the water on which, as my father reminded me, our ancestors, fleeing religious persecution in Persia, sailed their boats to the coast of western India. I can see them all those hundreds of years ago, docking their battered boats on the beach, not far from our house, to the amazement of the Koli fishermen who would have been dragging in their fish-laden nets first thing in the morning. I can see their tired, hungry Persian faces, their tattered tunics and turbans, their straggling beards, their eyes half mad with fervor and thirst. I can see the head priest, the dustoorji, wading out in front of his flock, nursing a silver goblet with a candle-like flame flickering inside. The flame he has been cradling all the way from his desert home. Out of the water they come, bowing politely to their naked dark-skinned hosts, kneeling down on the wet sand, kissing the ground and joining their hands in prayer to Ahura Mazda.

There we were, the Readymoneys facing the Arabian Sea. To our right a lane sloped from the tarmacked trafficky road downward onto the beach. To our left was the vast compound in the midst of which lay the crumbling house of the Maharani of Bharatnagar. Behind us, parallel with the Maharani's backyard jungle, were four identical small houses built in a square, each with two floors and a roof terrace. The Krishnans and the Ericssons lived in the two cottages directly behind our house, and behind them were the Hussains and the Vermas, whose houses backed onto the main road. The five buildings neatly squeezed into a space no bigger than the Maharani's compound. By scaling a wall, jumping a gate, or crawling through a bush I could get from any one of these six houses to the other without having to go all the way round to the road and come through their normal entrances.

3

I padded down the spiral staircase in the middle of the night. Except for the rising snores from Scorpio, our undernourished Irish setter, who lay in his customary position in the corner by the door, all was quiet. Bhagwan, the butler, slept on the Persian carpet in the living room. As I passed by him, he snorted, turned around, wrapped an imaginary blanket round his body, then cuddled it up against his cheek. I crept into my father's study and sat in his high-backed black-leather chair designed by Arne Jacobsen. My thick head of hair reached only halfway up the seductively curved backrest. On the polished wooden table lay a paper knife and a leather folder. Swiveling round in the chair, I opened one of the slim drawers in which my father kept his pens and took my time choosing. I liked them all. The gold Cross, the Mont Blanc, and the silver Parker 45. Unscrewing the fat fountain pen with the crest on the top, I placed it on the table. From another

drawer I brought out my two-rupees-twenty-paise Rashna notebook and flicked through the string-bound pages.

In the flap of one of my father's books I had once read about
this artist, a man with a razor-sharp mustache who spent years
recording his dreams in a diary. He used these dreams for his
paintings, and also in a film involving the slitting of his own eye-
ball. That was the kind of thing I would have liked to do.

It felt sticky in the study so I dragged open one of the sliding
glass doors that led into the garden. The salty smell of the sea
blew in, a distinctly fishy odor. Drying, salted Bombay duck left
out by the fishermen. I wrote the date on the top left-hand corner
of the page: 23 June 1972.

The whiff of fish snared me in the memory of an evening, a
few days ago, spent in the kitchen watching our cook prepare for
a dinner party. I decided to describe this in my notebook.

*I am kneeling on a white stool in the kitchen, following the cook with
my eyes. He is examining eight slabs of cold hilsa, a fish found only
in the holy waters of Calcutta's Hooghly River. These have jour-
neyed by air, on beds of ice, to the Crawford Market fish stall where
our barua haggled for them at five this morning.*

*The barua was born in Chittagong. His forefathers were taught a
wide range of culinary secrets by the French colonists. Only his clan,
the Mughs, are privy to the art of unlocking the hilsa from its countless bones. He wraps the raw slices of fish in a folding wire net and
lays them on a smoking brazier in the small porch outside the kitchen.
He prepares the potatoes, slicing them into thin straws for parboiling.
By and by, he turns the smoking fish over (how does he gauge when
the moment is right?) and blows at the coals through the rusty flap of
the burning sigdi. On one side the fish has turned hickory brown. The
fire under it spits and frets. Clouds of smoke blow into the kitchen.
Barua pours the boiling water and potatoes into a colander in the sink.
He drops the steaming straws onto a dry cloth. Bhagwan comes into*

the kitchen and shouts at the cook, berating him for misplacing the butter, "Arre, budha wo makhan kahan rakha hai tune." The old man grimaces. The two of them hate each other. Each thinks the other far inferior in race, rank, and education. They argue viciously about trivialities. Where the flour or salt or butter is kept. Whose responsibility it is to look after them. Who drinks more sugar in their tea. The cook often replies in Bengali or Hindi, knowing that Bhagwan finds these languages hard to understand. He growls at Bhagwan to leave the kitchen and attend to his menial duties in the house. "Dekh nahi sakhta, main kam kar raha hu. Jao, jao under. Mem sahb bula rahi hai." I am on the cook's side, I don't want him to be disturbed. I tell Bhagwan to go and look for the butter somewhere else. He gives us a long look of disgust, mumbles under his breath, and goes away.

The cook stokes the fire, throws some raw sugar over the fish. He wants smoke, not flames. The fish must retain their firmness. He turns them over a few times, then brings them, still smoking, onto a marble-topped surface in the kitchen. His back is bent with care over the hilsa. He cuts horizontally across the length of its soft belly, lifting away the top half on the blade of his knife, deftly aided by his fingers. The open interior reveals a cobweb of bones, many of which are invisible to the unpracticed eye. This skein of treacherous kaatas is the reason why most people don't bother eating the hilsa. The cook runs his blade up and down the body lifting up the needle-like bones, feeling with his fingers for a lurking transparent offender, body, hand, and eye straining to the pleasure of this intense work. I take one of the bones in my hand and test it on my finger. Sharp as a porcupine's quill.

It takes him half an hour to slice through the eight pieces, remove all the bones, and return the two halves of the fish together like the layers in a sponge cake. When each portion has been filleted and reassembled, he lays them out on a large silver platter. Every now and then he salvages a stray flake and pops it into his mouth or into my hand.

The oil, left to heat on the gas stove, has started to fume. Barua

throws in a tiny potato straw. Fat fizzes and bubbles around the hap-
less stick. He transfers the shredded potatoes tenderly into the hot oil,
glances around the kitchen to check everything is in its place, pulls out
a bunch of parsley from a paper bag, separates a few choice sprigs,
and finely chops the rest. He chops like an artist. The fingers of his
left hand hold the bunched parsley, while with the other hand he holds
the blade and the handle of the knife as he cuts through the leaves
with a circular downward thrust. Like an axle driving the wheels of a
steam engine, the serrated edge seems somehow to cut at the parsley
twice in the one action.

The potato straws are ready. After draining the grease, he sieves
them and places them on some brown paper to soak up the excess fat
and absorb some air. A pale yellow mountain of crunchiness. I stuff a
few in my mouth and get scolded. He uncovers the fish, gives Bhag-
wan a warning shout, lays the straws like a golden hedgerow around
the fish, neatly places four parsley sprigs around the border, a little
chopped parsley on the caramel-brown hilsa, and cleans the edge of
the silver platter with his filthy kitchen cloth. Bhagwan is standing by
in his crisp white tunic, the one he reserves for special occasions, with
silver buttons down the front. Like me, he seems enraptured by the
cook's final ministrations, a faraway expression on his face. "Chulo
Bhagwan, kya khada hua hai idher. Le jao under. Hurry up! For
God's sake take it away," says the pitiless cook. I shadow the dish, as
Bhagwan carries it through to the pantry, where he rests it on the side-
board for a second while he steadies himself to bear its weight. I can't
help but imagine the horror if he dropped it on the floor. He places an
absurdly large fish knife and fork on each side of the platter, straight-
ens his tunic, takes a deep breath, and lifts up the salver with both
hands encircling its rim. Gingerly he shoulders open the swinging
door. A throng of voices floods in from the dining room. I catch a
glimpse of coiffured hair, shining saris, and dark suits sitting around
the rosewood table.

•◆• •◆• •◆•

SITTING IN the study, I could taste the spittle gathered in the bowl of my mouth. The night sky leaked bits of gray and red. Voices seeped in through the open window. I ventured out into the garden. The talking came from the lane to the right of the house. Standing on the dewy grass, I could see the silhouettes, their bodies darker than this fading night, of Koli fisherfolk going to work, striding into the sea with their nets draped around a wooden pole propped up between two shoulders. Once, standing at the edge of the water watching them gather in their nets, I saw a body pulled ashore, a pale bloated carcass in black trunks. A few people stood around looking at it. I remember thinking: ten minutes ago he was just having a swim.

I went inside and sat again on the black chair. An hour ago I had been thinking of something—a dream, a story, something exciting to record in my exercise book. I decided to write about the first thing that caught my eye when I looked into the garden. I saw the hibiscus bush, its scarlet flowers creeping along the far wall. I recalled the time Ajay and I were hiding in that corner looking out for lovers. That's where I began.

Ajay and I are crouched down in the dark. Ajay has his Alsatian bitch, Chikee, sat beside him. He strokes the dog to keep it quiet, calming her with Malayalam words. The tide is high and the monsoon waves crash and cruise on the beach in front of us. The sea wall of our house juts out a few feet farther onto the sand than the wall of the Maharani of Bharatnagar's compound. A little corner of rubbish has formed where the two walls meet, a sheltered nook that avoids the public gaze. Ajay has a torch in his hand. He peeps over the parapet for a long time. "What's going on? What can you see?" I whisper. He puts his finger on his lips and grins. "Ssshhhh. Just wait a little, then you can look." The beach is windy and deserted. The breeze leaves salty droplets on our skin. I can hear loud breathing, the sound of saliva and smacking lips. I look over at Chikee; her head is resting comfortably on her extended front paws. Impatience gets the better of me, I poke my head over the parapet. A woman in a sari is lying on her back. A man is leaning over her. His hands are probing her body. Her blouse is unfastened and the thin man is holding her breast. Her gaze is bent over his hand while she grips his neck like a wrestler, fingers furled in his hair. Ajay tugs at my shirt, I wish he would go away and leave me here watching. All the world is in this open shirt, this hand, this head held tight. As night falls and cool gusts ruffle the ribbed leaves of coconut trees, lovers huddle all along Juhu beach, on stairs, in shady bits of broken concrete, the sand getting in their clothes, their bodies in passion wedged. This pair has probably spent the evening mooching around the beach, waiting for the curtain of darkness to drop.

The woman below me arches her head for an instant, wriggles furiously; she pulls at the man's hair. The sweet sickly smell of rotting garbage blows in our direction. Ajay leans over the wall brazenly. He shines his torch at them; in the triangle of light I catch sight of the woman's bare belly. The couple stare blankly into the torch beam. Then the man smothers the woman with his body as if to continue. I notice she is fastening the hooks at the front of her blouse. I'm amazed by their docility. They don't shout or swear at us for causing this cruel interruption. The thin man gives the woman his hand and pulls her up out of the bed of rubbish. They don't look up, but I can tell they know we are watching. He dusts the seat of his trousers and she arranges her sari. From the bowels of the city they came to this hidden corner of sand, and back they go again. I feel angry, angry, angry. All I wanted to do was stay crouched here by the wall and watch their ecstasy unfold. A chance I might never have again: two faces hardly glimpsed, two bodies so nearly naked, so alien, so close. Callously unearthed in the dark. For days, scenes, angles, shots of their bodies, haunt my waking thoughts.

WILTED, for lack of sleep, I wondered why I'd written all that. I had been intending to write about the lies I had told Ajay. The lies he had forced out of me. The sickening lies about sex. The lies about my mother that he kept making me retell. But those lies, those secrets, were too hard to think of now. My eyelids drooped with sleep and my shoulders were like loaded scales dragging down at my neck. I drew two short lines with a cross in between to mark the end of my diary entry.

4

My father owned a lot of books. He signed his name across the front page, and wrote the date underneath. His signature was ornate, like the Gothic front of Victoria Terminus, full of irrelevant flourishes. His handwriting was the same. Illegible but stylish. Every day he made sure that I did two pages of handwriting exercises from a copybook. He checked my lettering carefully and left a bold tick behind.

I've looked at these bookshelves for many years now. Some of the titles form a backdrop to my life. The colors on the spine, the thickness, the size. Sometimes I found things hidden inside them: a train ticket to Hampstead Station in the pages of a volume of poetry by Keats, a sheaf of notes on the essential points of Will Durant's arguments in *The Story of Civilization*, a poem by my namesake great-uncle, who died of consumption at twenty-eight, in the moth-eaten pages of *Thus Spake Zarathustra*. I knew that my grandfather, a merchant seaman, had been in love with Keats's poetry. My father kept up the obsession. There were two shelves devoted to different editions of Keats's poems. In a pocket-sized Buxton Forman, I found a love letter from my dad to my mum. It was dated 4 June 1969.

> *My Darling M,*
> *How happy you have made me today! The thought of you and I so strongly in love, our beautiful house and our five precious kiddoes.*
> *I felt so strong in your arms this morning. It made me think what a fool I have been this past month. Forgive me sweetheart. And know that, as there is breath in this body to love, it reaches out for you every minute.*
> *Your ever loving,*
> *Minoo*

The letter made me tearful. Late at night I heard screams coming from my parents' bedroom. They were both, especially my mother, very emotional. My father could also seem a little distant. Sometimes he didn't seem to hear what I was saying—as when I asked him about inviting Mr. Krishnan and his family to lunch on Sunday. "Daddy," I said, "Mr. Krishnan came over to use the telephone today and he was asking if he could borrow a book." I was worried my father would say no; instead he went on reading the paper as if he hadn't heard me speak. I raised my voice. "Daddy!"

"Oh, sorry, Cyrus, I was absorbed in this article. What was that about Mr. Krishnan?"

"Mr. Krishnan wants to borrow *Khrushchev Speaks* and he was asking if you have *Lenin Speaks* as well."

"I don't think we've got *Lenin Speaks*, but he can have the other one. Bloody Commie that he is."

"And can we ask them to lunch some time?"

"Sure. What about next Sunday? I'll ask Mehroo if that's all right."

I ran over to the Krishnans' with the hardback under my arm. On the cover was a picture of a fat man with a bald head. Mr. Krishnan was very pleased with the book. He turned it round in his hands, caressing it all the while, and placed it gently on the table next to him. He told me that Khrushchev was the greatest statesman the world had seen since Lenin. I didn't know why these Russians seemed to earn so much respect from him, but I was thrilled to be of some use to this man who was so hard to satisfy.

"My father says, please can you and your family come for lunch next Sunday." At last I could extend some hospitality to the Krishnans. I had often boasted about the famous Parsi dhan sakh with its seven different kinds of dal.

"No," said Mr. Krishnan in his summary manner. "No, we can't just come like that. I must have an invitation in person or in writing from your father."

"But my father just told me to come and ask you," I pleaded. "He even said you could borrow some more books when you come over."

"No. I am not interested in any other books, only *Lenin Speaks,* if he comes across it in his library."

He shook his head from side to side, leaned back, and stroked his shiny black hair. "My sons and I will gladly come for lunch if your father asks us personally and that is my final word." Mr. Krishnan's actions were filled with a sense of righteous pride. His statement to the world was, "I may be a simple man, with a small house, an average job, and not a lot of money, but I know what I say is right and I won't let anyone cross me." Nothing could overturn his confidence in the temple he had constructed out of his ideals and principles. Everything he did was endowed with a moral tone. His indulgences were small but he took a hearty delight in them. On holidays, like today, he drank a bottle or two of Golden Eagle beer before lunch. It had to be Golden Eagle; no other beer would do. Sitting on a mattress, cross-legged in his white lungi, he would pour the beer from its ice-cold brown bottle into his glass mug, tilting his neck with the concentration of a chemist in his laboratory. His sons and I watched as he took the first gulp, before he placed the defrosting bottle by his side. Then he settled back on the white divan, took another swig, stroked his gleaming black hair, and ran his hands over his bare back and shoulders with contentment. The afternoon stretched out in front of him. This was the satisfaction of a man who felt that he had earned it, who had worked hard all week, been woken at five in the morning, taken his three sons jogging, done his weights on the balcony at the back of his house, and read the newspaper daily. He sat on his mattress, leaning on a white bolster, keeping an eye on his family, letting out the occasional burp of well-being. His presence was central to their existence. They worshipped him, while petrified of his sudden and imperious wrath. After a bottle of beer, he sometimes called his sons over to him on the mattress. "Ingé va, Ajay, ingé va, Ravi, aa aa." This started as an affectionate call. But the boys and I knew that it was full of dubious energy. He used exactly the same tone of voice and the same words, "Ingé va, ingé va," when he was about to belt them. So, even on a quiet Saturday afternoon when he seemed cheerful, the call sent a chill through us all. He would stroke and kiss one of his sons, a caress would turn into a wrestling hold, and they would laugh in mock struggle against one another. I would smile with embarrassment, wondering whether I was meant to join in with this family game.

"Will we have dhan sakh for lunch on Sunday?" asked Sushil.

"Yes, definitely," I said. "I will tell the barua to make hot chocolate soufflé as well."

"I liked that custard-apple ice-cream that we had the other day," said Sushil.

"I've told you," shouted Mrs. Krishnan from the kitchen. "I'm going to have to hit you if I have to tell you again, not to eat food at their house. There is good enough food for you in this house. I don't want you to go around begging at their house."

LATER THAT day I sat in my bedroom looking at the furniture, staring at the mirror in the corner. On the Chippendale desk lay my Rashna notebook. I had an urge to reread what I had written, but I was disturbed by the need to find a way of getting my father to invite Mr. Krishnan round to lunch. It was going to be difficult. My father was a busy man. He often worked on Saturdays and Sundays, and came home late at night. I picked up the notebook and sat with my back resting against the headboard of the bed. I had left the pen inside the book. It beckoned me to write something. I made two columns. In one column I wrote things about my father, in the other about Mr. Krishnan.

MY FATHER

My father is a partner in a firm called Readymoney & Company. He has his own office with a custom-made desk in polished wood. On it is a gold cigar box, a paper knife, two telephones, one in the shape of a cobra's head, a photograph of my mother, and one of his five children. Behind his desk, below the large windows, are two rows of shelves stacked with buff-colored tomes on shipping law and ledgers bound in leather.

His office mixes the old with the new. In one corner there is a glass

MR. KRISHNAN

Mr. Krishnan is employed by Voltas Air-Conditioning Company as a sales executive. He has a small desk, four-foot-square, which takes its place in a large office along with three identical tables used by the other three sales executives in the Blue team. On his desk is a heavy black telephone with two silver buttons that are used to connect him to the switchboard, a plastic in-tray with a glass paperweight holding down some papers, and another colored glass paperweight lying on the table.

MY FATHER

coffee table, a modern armchair, and a well-worn leather sofa. This is where I sit when I go, on rare occasions, to pick him up at the end of the day. There are three large paintings by modern Indian artists: Hussain, Padamsee, and Raza; and a small one by the Mexican painter Orozco. A piece of newspaper seems to have been randomly stuck in the middle of this painting. On one wall is a glass cabinet with some shipping medals, a few bottles of alcohol, and a safe.

My father organizes the import and export of goods in large container ships. He handles all kinds of cargo from lead pipes to ladies' underwear. He goes on business trips overseas twice a year with my mother, who makes sure that the business is liberally mixed with sightseeing and pleasure.

He has thick eyebrows and dark handsome eyes. His chin is broad and his cheeks are large. His smile is warm, exuberant, brimming with confidence. People admire him for being well dressed and charming. He has close on fifty suits in his wardrobe and at least two that he proudly proclaims to be tailor-made in a famous shop in London called Savile Row. He has a host of ties from Sulka and Company, broad

MR. KRISHNAN

Mr. Krishnan visits business premises trying to sell air-conditioners. This is not a difficult task since Voltas is the number one air-conditioning company in the country. He also encourages existing customers to renew their service contracts. He earns a fixed salary of one thousand two hundred rupees a month plus a one percent commission on all new orders.

Mr. Krishnan hardly ever smiles. His life is strenuous, lived in a narrow corridor. He has been sent abroad once, to Sweden. As a result, he owns a heavy gray overcoat. It lies in his small clothes cupboard, wrapped up and lined with mothballs. Next to it hang a suit, a jacket, three pairs of trousers, and four or five shirts. I rarely see him in these clothes. At home he likes to roam around, torso bare, dressed only in swimming trunks, or, after a bath, in a white lungi wrapped around his legs in the south Indian style.

His life is resolutely simple. I always know what is happening at the Krishnan household. Back from work at five, running time, bathtime, mealtime, homework time, bedtime. Weekends are given over to rest. Twice a year, on a Sunday afternoon, the family and I pack

My Father	Mr. Krishnan

and colorful but rarely garish. His shoes, bought in boutiques in Italy and America, gleam in the Indian sunlight.

Sitting down to enjoy the emptiness of a moment is a comfort my father never affords himself. There is never any chance of a break in his life because he is habitually unpunctual. His business associates like to poke fun at him by calling him "the late Mr. Readymoney." He regularly misses flights, arrives at the end of meetings, and loses important business deals because of his inability to keep time. His unpunctuality is like a natural defect, a sixth finger uncovered at birth.

into their Ford DeSoto and Mr. Krishnan drives us cautiously into town. We take a walk by the Gateway of India, followed by lunch at the Nanking, where Mr. Krishnan, after careful study of the menu, orders four "American Chopsueys" and two bowls of fried rice. The Krishnans' existence is happily circumscribed. I like the routine in their lives—the order it offers, as compared to the chaotic freedoms of my own home.

Mr. Krishnan doesn't seem to want any friends. I can't remember bumping into a visitor. One time his brother from Kerala turned up for a few days.

I turned back a few pages in the diary and read the description of the couple making love on the beach. I smiled with surprise at the details. I shut the book and tried to work out my next chapter. It would have to be something about my life, perhaps my school, or about Bombay. Thinking about it made it seem so easy.

5

I went to a boys' school called St. Mary's, on top of a flyover very close to the Mazagaon docks. Every weekday I traveled from Juhu on the western shores, its lapping waves and sleepy suburban sand, to the eastern side of the city where the tall chapel spires of my Jesuit school stuck their crosses out into the muggy Byculla air.

I set off at seven-thirty in the morning wearing the school uniform: white shorts, half-sleeved white shirt, white socks and black shoes, an ink-blue cotton tie neatly folded into my pocket. I passed through the gates of the house and into the lane which connected the main road with the beach. The sun had risen more than two hours ago and the water sparkled underneath. The heat of the day had begun to make its impression. I turned away from the delicious sea and walked toward the road. At the corner, the paanwallah, Laloo Prasad, sat in his cubbyhole shop crammed with wares: sweets in glass jars, cigarettes, chocolates, chewing gum, supari, balloons, beedis, batteries, plasters, and other household items. To one side of him were all the ingredients necessary for making the different kinds of paan that were on offer.

"Arre, Cyrus baba, kahan ja rahe ho? Where are you off to? When are you going to bring that fifty paise you owe me?"

"What do you think, I'm going to run away?"

"You may not run away, but my shop will definitely run away if I go on giving credit like this."

"Okay, baba. Don't worry, when I come home this evening I will go and get it," I said in a sugary voice. "Now, can I have ten paise worth of those sweets?"

"You haven't yet paid up and you're still wanting sweets."

"I told you na, I'll pay you tonight, I promise." I pinched the skin on the inside of my neck to indicate solemnity. He unscrewed the lid of a glass jar and took out five pink tablets which he wrapped in a bit of newspaper. "This is the last time. Go on, take it. I'm having pity on you. And don't come back without payment."

I put one of the chalky rectangles into my mouth and stowed the other four with my folded tie. With my canvas knapsack full of schoolbooks, I hurried down the road. As I passed the Juhu Parle nursery school I turned around to look for the BEST bus. I could see the red and white single-decker bearing down on me like an angry rhino. I ran frantically to try and catch it. The bus stop was about a hundred yards away. The bus chased me down and hurtled past. There were passengers hanging out of the rear door. The bell rang and the brakes squealed. No one got off, but one or two commuters were trying to squeeze in past the bodies spilling out of the back entrance. "Aaghe badho, aaghe badho," the conductor shouted as he banged his metal ticket puncher on the roof of the bus, urging the passengers standing in the central aisle to move forward. There was a long queue at the bus stop: most of the people had resigned themselves to waiting for the next 231. Being small, I could jump the queue and push in between the bodies at the door, and hang on to the nearest handle or the arm of the person standing in front of me. I stuck my toe into a space I could see on the last step of the bus and squeezed my hand around the waist of the man clinging on ahead of me, jamming my face against his Terylene-clad back. In the crush, something fell out of my pocket: my tie along with the sweets stowed in its folds. The conductor tugged at the rope pulley. Ting! Ting! the bell sounded twice in quick succession. The driver clanked his gear-stick and just as the BEST 231 jolted forward, I jumped off. My tie lay in the dust like a dead snake. I could find only two of my sweets on the broken tarmac. One of the men hanging out of the departing bus was watching me, as were the people in the queue: ladies in sober office saris, patches of sweat under their arms, men in terry-cotton shirts with neat attaché cases in their hands. A rage of shame burned within me. Why couldn't I have done the sensible thing: left the sweets on the tarmac and got on with my journey?

I took my position at the back of the line. A freshly powdered woman came and stood behind me. The scratched face of my Favre Luba watch read five minutes past eight. I shoved the grubby sweets into my shirt pocket. I was sure to be late for my first lesson. Standing at the bus shelter, I felt exposed. The world was now a heartless place peopled by office workers and business-men swishing by in their chauffeur-driven cars.

It was around this time that there began a realization that people looked at me as if I were odd, like a turtle amongst antelopes. My hair was too long, my clothes were out of sync, my features were foreign, I shouldn't be traveling on public trans-port, hanging out of trains and buses, I shouldn't be sitting in the foyer of a Hindi cinema waiting for the film to start. I wished I could hide these telltale signs. Sometimes, though, being the odd one out, the bad egg, the rotten apple, the black sheep or the white sheep, had its advantages. These became my focus of influence and power. The embarrassment of being on display turned into the egotism of showing off, of procuring things I wouldn't otherwise be able to get, of proving myself worthy of recognition, especially by those older than me, while pretending to play the joker.

Afterward there was always the opportunity to tear off this mask and talk to myself. Feed myself with dreams, tinker with fantasies of sport and sex. I entered into imaginary dialogue with another voice that acted as a kind of friendly interlocutor. When I found myself alone—on the bus, walking on the road, waiting for a film to start, in my bedroom, on the roof of our house—I posed myself questions, discussing the different steps I might take in overcoming a problem.

"You don't really want to go running with the Krishnans at five-thirty tomorrow morning, do you? But then they start getting upset and say, 'You're not our true friend,' and they make you feel bad about it. You'd better just force yourself. But what if you come up with an excuse, like you weren't feeling well? Yes, but they wouldn't believe that. They'd say you were lying, or Sushil will say, 'You're just a weakling,' then you'd be really stuck." Sometimes the voice was reflective, sometimes sorrowful, other times angry or cajoling. "I" and "you" both featured in our conversations. "You" tended to dominate when I imagined I was talking to my brother or my friend, "I," when I was clearly addressing myself. Sometimes I let the voice describe to me what would happen when I met someone, or arrived at a certain place.

"What I'll do is wait for period three to be over, make sure that I don't get into any trouble during the class, and then ask Horace to meet me behind the chapel. I'll tell him about my plan to see *Johnny Mera Naam*. If he says he doesn't have the money, I can pay for the tickets. I've got six rupees, thirty paise. Then in the fourth period we can ask Mrs. Carmello if we can go to the toilet. No, she'll never agree to us both going together. I know what, I'll ask her if I can go and see Tickly Father about the lunch coupons and then I can slip out through the back gate and I'll tell Horace to come and meet me outside Queen Mary's restaurant. I can even buy one mutton samosa while I'm waiting." Horace wasn't interested in Hindi films, and was much too scared of getting caught for bunking. As class monitor he had more to lose. So, often these plans I made with the help of my inner voice came to nothing. This was another sad aspect of my life.

"DOES ANYONE know how many islands this city of Bombay consisted in the olden days?" the geography teacher of 3B asked. Four hands went up. One was the clever boy of the class, two were always putting their hands up to answer questions, and I was the joker in the pack. Most teachers know what to expect when they choose a raised hand out of a class. Mr. Machado knew I didn't know the answer to his question but I petitioned him with such vigor, arm stretched out, hissing like a plangent snake, "Sssir, sssir, ssssssirr, please sir." Mostly, to shut me up, he sighed, "All right, Cyrus, what's your answer?"

"Is it five, sir?" I smiled. "Yes, sir, five islands." Mr. Machado ignored my guess. A clever ploy. But I would get him in the end. "Yes, Harshad," he said, turning to the bright spark.

"Bombay was seven islands when it was given by the Portuguese to the British." Harshad added the extra detail without the slightest flicker of conceit.

"Very goood, very goood," Mr. Machado said, stretching out his vowels to steady himself for the next question. It was imperative that he stayed ahead of Harshad. With a gleam in his eye, he raised the stakes, "But do you know why it was given by the Portuguese to the British?" Harshad's hand went up like an automated car barrier. The expression on his face remained unperturbed—it was clear to all of us that he knew the answer. Mr. Machado's bushy eyebrows quivered with agitation. Things were not quite the way he had planned them. He had wanted, with the last question, to launch into a lecture on the origins of the city. The class had heard it all before: his Portuguese ancestry, his deep roots in the history of Bombay, and, finally, the mess that the present municipal authorities had made of this once great metropolis.

"Yes, Harshad," he said after a slight pause. Harshad spoke in the even voice of the knowledgeable and well-mannered child. His mother was a renowned cultural historian. "It was given as a dowry, sir, when Catherine Braganza was married to . . . ," he faltered slightly, "an English king."

"Very good, Harshad, very good," said Machado as he put his hands into the commodious pockets of his gray trousers and walked toward the open window. He stood there and looked out onto the playground. "In the year of 1662, King Charles the Second of England took the hand in marriage of a Portuguese princess." As he warmed to his little lecture, he strode up and down the class, waving his finger and stroking his black locks. Every orifice on his face had a little clump of hair surrounding it or sticking out of it, like curly tufts of pubic growth. These were especially startling in and around his ears, like birds' nests sprouting from the inner folds.

"At that time the Portuguese were in charge of the islands of Bom Bahai, as they used to call it." My hand shot up involuntarily. A tacit understanding existed between Machado and the class that he was not to be interrupted when in full flow. "Sir, how do you know that the Portuguese were in charge of Bombay?"

"It is written in the books, you silly boy. It is all recorded. I am explaining something important and you are asking stupid questions," he said with rising asperity. Titters threaded around the class. "So, as I was saying, it was given by the Portuguese as a dowry."

"Sir, dowry is now illegal!" I shouted. This time some of the boys guffawed. Machado held back the full force of his temper. "Go and stand outside the class!"

"But, sir, I was just asking, please, sir, last chance, sir. I promise I won't do it again."

His nostrils flared, the tufts of hair became increasingly visible. "Don't argue with me, boy, I tell you just get out now!" As I made my way to the door the other boys' eyes followed me with a mixture of fright and delight. I leaned on the wall outside the door. Machado was mercilessly teased by the older boys, but I hadn't got very far in that direction before he had ejected me from the class. Did I really want to be standing here in the corridor on my own, being gawped at by every teacher or student who passed by? Why was I always drawing attention to myself, making people laugh, getting into trouble? Sometimes, on the way home from school, I would make a decision never again to break the rules, but to be like my cousin Jehangir who always stood first in his class and was made the class monitor for his exemplary behavior. But a new day would arrive and I'd have forgotten my resolve to get myself a crew cut or to make sure that my schoolbag was packed with the right books. The Jesuit fathers who ran St. Mary's had got used to picking me out, chastising me for untidiness, lateness, bad behavior in the class, and, most of all, for the long hair that streaked my forehead and fell over the collar of my shirt. The worst of the teachers was an Indian man called Father D'Mello. I was trying at this moment to hide between the wall and the door of the classroom because I knew that this demon, this dreaded Vice-Principal, in his white robes with his wide cloth belt, would soon be on his rounds of the corridors, his tortoise-shell spectacles gleaming on his vulpine nose. He had something of Mr. Krishnan in his demeanor. The same cleanliness of feature, the same color skin, the same slicked-back hair, and the same candid violence in his eyes.

I didn't have long to wait. Hands folded behind his back, he strode toward me. The undisguised pleasure in his eyes when he spied me standing outside the class sent an arrow of fear up my spine. "What a surprise! It's that Cyrus Readymoney again," he jibed, displaying his front teeth and placing his fingers around the back of my neck. "Well, what is it this time, Cyrus? Why are you out of the class again? Something must have happened." There was always this beguiling note of solicitude in his voice, as if he were about to show me some sympathy or try and correct an injustice that might have occurred. I couldn't see any point in lying. "I was fooling around in the class, Father, and Mr. Machado sent me out."

"Fooling around, eh? Fooling around." He turned the words over with different emphases, as if searching for some profundity. I could feel his cruel digits tighten around my collar. "When we get to my office we shall have to see what we can do about this fooling around. What do you say, eh?" I found it impossible to answer his question. All I could think of was the cane in the bottom drawer of his desk.

"Last time it was eating chewing gum, before that it was bullying that nice boy Jamshed Dustoor, then putting pins on Miss D'Souza's seat. I think the time has come for another gray card. Perhaps your mother should find you a different school, eh?" Not another gray card. I couldn't believe he was going to give me another one. Three gray cards and I would be chucked out of the school. I must react. I must show some sign of remorse. I must act like the other boys when they were in trouble: cry and plead and swear. I pushed and the words came croaking out. "I promise, Father, if you let me off this time, I promise I will never do it again." No answer, no reaction. "Father, I thought you were allowed to chew gum in the auditorium. It wasn't my fault. I won't do it again." I couldn't think of anything else to say. By this time he had led me to the area outside his office where the secretaries sat behind a long curved reception desk. D'Mello said something to them, something about typing a letter. They looked at me; I hunted in their eyes for understanding. For a second, I even imagined one of them doing or saying something to rescue me from the clutches of this man. All the while he kept a tight grip on my arm. It reminded me that my father held my arm in the same place when he wanted to apply a mixture of control and affection. But his was a warm, broad, loving hand. A hand I could trust. Standing there, in front of the kindly secretaries, was like the last lick of warm breeze before a plunge into an icy river. I thought I should cry, or at least pretend to cry, but I didn't know how.

He sat down on the chair in his office. Everything was in its place. A glass paperweight, a pincushion, a wooden foot ruler, the two pens taken from his pocket and placed on the table. Then he beckoned me closer. I stood right next to him. We were both facing in the same direction. On the wall opposite me there was a picture of twelve senior boys in football strip, with Father D'Mello sitting in the middle. He opened the drawer on the left-hand side of his desk with exaggerated care. There were two neat piles of cards, one gray and one pink. The pink cards were for minor misdemeanors, the gray ones for major incidents, for fights or repeated infringement of the school rules. Taking his time, he placed a gray card on the table in front of him as if it were the ace of spades in a game of poker. Then he looked up at me and said, "Why are you like this? Other boys don't behave like this. What is wrong with you?" I could see from the edge of my eye that he was taking the foot ruler in his left hand and placing it in his right. Through the frosted pane on his door I saw two boys hovering outside. Then D'Mello raised his arm behind his back. I felt a burning slash against my calves. The first surprise was how little it hurt. He hit me with the ruler across the legs again and again. I could feel a kind of heat building up as the beating went on. D'Mello seemed to be losing control of himself, perhaps it was my witless stoicism that irritated him. He pushed me slightly away from him so that he could get more leverage for his swings. His head and body bent over to one side as he took great swooping hockey-stick strokes at my bare thighs and legs. All the while, I stared in front of me at the light blue paint, the frosted pane, and the soccer photograph on the wall. D'Mello grew exhausted and angry. He wiped the beads of perspiration from his shiny forehead. "You will never learn, Cyrus. Never." Then he began filling in the details on the gray card. He wrote my name in slanted running hand, he wrote the name of my class. Then he came to the line marked Reason, and looked up at me. "I can tell you are not very clever. You know how I can tell that? By the size of your forehead. Your forehead is very small and your hair is always covering it up. Look at any clever person: Nehru, Einstein, even the top-rank boys in your class. They all have large foreheads, open foreheads, clean foreheads." As he spoke he stuck out his glistening pate like an ostrich. Then he took his handkerchief and once again wiped the sweat from his brow. "Go and see who is waiting outside." As I went to the door I could feel his eyes on my legs surveying the damage his hands had done.

6

In the dust-brown playground of St. Mary's my friend Karl Lacedas and I were walking, arms linked around each other's shoulders. It was the lunch break; boys were engaged in games or just strolling around the field. Kites swooped low overhead waiting to pounce on a bit of discarded bread. We had to be careful with our food: they would often use their talons to snatch a sandwich from an unsuspecting hand.

Karl was short, round-faced, and pudgy. He had light green eyes which showed up beautifully against his bronze skin. His thumb was always wet and misshapen with sucking. I rather envied boys who sucked their thumbs, bit their nails, or cracked their knuckles. His white shorts were shorter than mine which gave him a muscular, sporty look.

"So, what did D'Mello do to you, yaar?" he asked.

"He's a bastard, man. He's always after me. It doesn't matter what I do. He must have something against me."

"Shit, look at your legs!" He took a deep inward suck of air.

"Yah, man, he hit me with a ruler. It didn't hurt much, though."

I turned around to look at my calves. There were little red lines, like cuts from a razor, scars that had already begun to heal, all the way up my legs. "Looks horrible, doesn't it? Let's go and see Horace and Glen behind the chapel." Behind the chapel was our hideout, a place that was full of little alcoves and corners. It ran in a narrow corridor between the outer wall of the school that faced the road and the foundations of the chapel. Here it was, next to a grotto with a small garlanded statue of Jesus and Mary, that our gang—Horace, Karl, Glen, Rajiv, Khushroo, and I— would meet at lunchtimes. We would smoke, compare biceps, hand wrestle to see who was the strongest, talk about sex, and share our sandwiches.

Karl and I made our way to the meeting place. We talked in a ragged, haphazard sort of way.

"Did you see Horace practicing in the gym yesterday after school?" Karl asked.

"No. Who was he sparring with?"

"Roberts, yaar."

"Hai cho! Roberts must have given him a thorough pasting."

"Roberts was giving him a chance, yaar. Horace was really quick, huh. He gave Roberts a few jabs in the stomach, thaadaach, thaadaach."

"Did Roberts get angry?" I shuddered at the thought. Mr. Roberts was our sports teacher. His every step was dread-making. He was a well-built, muscular figure with a fierce mustache and a bellowing voice, which he used to petrify anyone who dared earn his displeasure. I was often the butt of his biting sarcasm. He was the kind of teacher who made a lot of jokes, but you never knew when a joke might suddenly end and then you had to endure one of his painful tricks—the Roberts head massage that left your ears smarting red or the bone-crunching hand-shake. He always wore a short-sleeved shirt from which bulged his biceps and a golden box of filterless Charminar cigarettes, the strongest and cheapest brand you could buy.

"What did he do when Horace boxed him in the stomach?" I asked.

"He just shrugged off the punches as if they were little pats, yaar. He danced round the ring saying, 'C'mon, Horace, c'mon, Horace. Left-right combination. Hit me with your right.' Horace was scared, you could see it in his eyes."

"Hey, chutiya! What are you saying about me?" said Horace coming from behind us and clapping me on the shoulder. Horace Lillywhite was my best friend. Like Karl and Glen, he was an Anglo-Indian, with fair skin, bluish eyes, and dark blond hair. He was thin and wiry. It was no wonder that he went on to become the boxing champion of the school. In the first few years he was always made the monitor of the class and it was an essential part of his swaggering pride to sport the red and white plaited cord that monitors wore round their necks. The Jesuits soon realized that Horace, though powerful, was also powerfully naughty. That's when we became friends.

"Hey, Cyrus, let's see your new bag, man. What's this 'SAS' stand for? Bloody shining white, man. Hey, c'mon no, let me bor-row it for one day, man. I promise you I'll bring it back tomor-row," he said, pulling at it.

"What will you do with the bag for one day?" I had sneaked out of the house that morning with this white Scandinavian Air-lines overnight bag. My dad had just come back from Sweden and the bag was brand new. Obviously I shouldn't have taken it, but I couldn't resist showing off to my friends. I knew there was some-thing un-Christian about showing off, and later in the day if I accidentally hit my head on the door of the lift, I couldn't help thinking it was a retributive sign from God. Horace was deter-mined to have the bag. The others took his side.

"He's saying he'll bring it back tomorrow," said Glen. "Why don't you just lend it to him, man?"

"Horace, I've got more bags like this at home, yaar. I'll bring one tomorrow for you. My father will kill me if I go home without this one," I lied.

At four o'clock, when school ended, Horace came over to my desk and snatched the bag from me. Then he ran over to one corner of the class, laughing all the time. I could see from his eyes, his ferret eyes, that now that he had got hold of the bag, there was no way he was going to hand it back. I didn't really care about the bag, but I felt lowered by Horace's methods. I could never do to him what he was doing to me now. When I gave in easily, he seemed a little surprised. We swapped bags so I could take my books home and Horace assured me, "I only want to show it to my sister, man. She loves all these airline things."

On the way to my granny's, where I went every evening after school, I remembered some of the things Horace and I had done together. I recalled that when he had finally discovered through his secret sources the true nature of sexual intercourse, I told him he was talking rubbish because I couldn't believe that our parents could possibly be doing such things. One afternoon we went into the row of smelly school toilets with water fountains outside them. Karl was there too. We locked ourselves in a cubicle and then one by one we took down our scrimpy white shorts and looked at each other's smooth bums. Mine was the darkest color. Even now I can feel the sexual excitement I got from looking at Karl's plump bum. Horace was the last to show his pale, bony behind, and then it was only for a fleeting moment. Powerful people have no arse.

I used to go straight from school, on the rattling blue tin can that was the St. Mary's school bus, to Nepean Sea Road and walk up the steep tarmac stretch that led to my granny's flat in a building called Belmont. There were more buildings starting to be built on and around the hill, and they were destroying part of it with controlled explosions of dynamite. Rocks more than a million years old were being turned into rubble and the noise was frightening the peacocks away from the sparse wood surrounding my grandmother's building.

I walked up the winding road thinking of my friendship with Horace, gazing at the Romanesque statue perched on a pedestal just at the point where the road forked. One road led up another side of the hill to Dubash Mansions, where the older boys played cricket in the compound, a game in which they sometimes allowed me to join. My mother had told me the story of *Great Expectations*. When I looked up at this mysterious castle on the hill, I imagined it held some burning secret like Miss Havisham's.

As I sauntered round a bend, my eyes fell on a five-rupee note lying innocently on the road. I looked up to see if there was anyone around who might have dropped it. It was around five in the evening. An elderly man in a white dhoti was laboring up the hill, a hundred yards in front of me, carrying a large stainless-steel milk container. I quickly decided it wasn't his money.

When I got to my granny's I always had a little talk with her. She told me that a Negro was a person with big lips and that "vexed" meant to be very angry. I used to go to the room at the back of the flat, with its musty mothball-smell, the Parsi Towers of Silence and all the swooping, gorging vultures somewhere in the background. You could sometimes see peacocks from the window and if you were really lucky, a male peacock fanning its feathers. I'd take off my shoes and socks and lie on the checkered bedspread and read old magazines and comics, the ceiling fan whirring above my head. Sometimes I would look at the books in my grandfather's dusty bookcase. I didn't read any of them but I often chose one with an exciting title and gave it to my father for his birthday. I took great care over the choice of book; I expected my dad to believe that I had read the book and liked it.

I'd lie there on the bed while my granny made me hot rotis on which she would spread homemade cream and strawberry jam made by Treeti Aunty in Mahableshwar. I lay there dreaming of those hot chapatis, with their melting cream and great big chunks of sweet fruit, and how I longed for more than the two I was allowed. I also got a glass of orange squash and on special occasions my gran would cook me scrambled eggs. Scrambled eggs were her speciality. I learned from an early age that to make them smooth and creamy you had to have them on the lowest fire possible and constantly stir the egg and milk mixture. When the eggs were almost done, my grandmother would carefully shred half a cube of Amul cheese on top. I gobbled them up with sprinklings of black pepper.

I told my granny about the five rupees I had found. I was surprised by her unfussy reaction. She took the money from me for what she called "safekeeping." Later she said she would give it to charity. I wasn't sure what charity meant, but I didn't think twice about it and went into the back room, lay on my bed, and continued with my favorite *Phantom* comic from old copies of the *Illustrated Weekly of India*. I found out a lot about my body lying on that bed, eating sesame ladoos, waiting for my mum and dad to pick me up, and listening to the occasional cry of the peacocks.

When I got back to school, Horace didn't have my bag but promised he would return it the next day. On the third day, Horace said a terrible mistake had been made: his sister, who had gone on a camping trip, had taken the bag with her. The days went by, I never could find out exactly when Horace's sister was coming back, and I grew tired of asking.

Three months after the bag incident my cousin told me a story. He said that everyone knew that I had stolen this bag from my dad, taken it to school, and sold it for five rupees. I was shocked, not because I was incapable of doing such a thing, but because I felt falsely accused and let down by my granny. The story spread like a disease, and it became a big joke to be recounted at family parties as one more of my outrageous exploits. The other story floating around at the time was about the visit I had made to my father's workplace wearing nothing but a swimming costume. Whenever I hotly denied selling the bag, people laughed. "You lent it to Horace Lillywhite and he's still got it after six months, and on the same day you lent it to him you found five rupees on the road. Ha ha." This was a turning point in my relationship with my granny, who had clearly been responsible for disseminating the story. Never again would I be taken in by her cunning ways. I was "vexed." I tried to explain to my cousin and my brother that if I had sold the bag I would hardly have rushed to give the money to my gran. This didn't cut any ice.

There was nothing for it now but to get the bag back from Horace. I hadn't pestered Horace for some time, and he was acting as if the bag didn't exist, but now I badgered him with renewed vigor. Horace was relentless with his stories, excuses, and promises. So one day in the lunch hour I walked out of school and up the Nesbit flyover that led to our gates, crossed the road, went down the stairs leading under the bridge, and wound my way through the tenement buildings to Horace's flat. It was a very small flat right next to the railway track—one room on the ground floor looking out onto a courtyard with washing hanging on lines and flowering creepers climbing around the door. Yellow and brown commuter trains rattled by every few minutes. Horace had been to my house many times, but I had never seen the inside of his. When I walked back with him after school his mother always spoke to me from the doorstep.

I had disturbed her lunch and she pretended not to know anything about the bag. But I argued and cajoled her into looking for it. It was not like me to be so bold but a lot was at stake. I waited in the courtyard for a while. The smell of frying spices drifted out through the curtained doorway. Then Horace's mother came out and said she would find it by tomorrow and send it with Horace back to school. I could see a chink of hope. The bag was in there somewhere and she knew where it was. I held back my embarrassment and said I was willing to wait there the whole day until she found my bag. Finally, she emerged holding a dusty brown tattered object which reeked of sweaty clothes. So, Horace had been using it for his boxing sessions at the gym. It had been seven months since I had let him borrow the bag.

When I got to my granny's that evening I showed her the bag with a great flourish. The white had turned to dirty beige. It was scratched all over, the strap was broken, and the blue SAS logo was just visible. My gran was unimpressed, she said that Horace was a goonda and had got his five rupees' worth. When I got home, only Bhagwan our servant showed some derisive interest in the returned bag. My family had to be reminded of the incident and when they remembered it, they said I was crazy if I expected this battered object to prove to them that I had not sold the original article.

7

Bombay is not an island anymore. It was once many islands, as Mr. Machado liked to tell us. The sea was pumped out, and rocks and earth dumped in its place. Walls, dikes, bunds, causeways spliced the once separate islets of Worli, Parel, Mahim, and Colaba and finally land ate up the water that separated this city from the mainland of western India. Juhu, where our family lived, on the shores of the Arabian Sea, was part of that mainland. Where the sea had once been, lily-covered tanks of water licked the innards of the city. And yet, the sea is everywhere. Along with the millions in this city, I live and breathe its salty air, mixed in with the fumes of BEST double-decker buses, trucks HORN PLEASE OK, yellow and black taxis, bilious smoke rising from the tall chimney stacks of factories, the honeyed smell of charcoal braziers roasting peanuts, the rotting creeks, the open gutters, and the rows of drying Bombay duck.

Here there are no sunburnt bathers, no striped umbrellas, or paperback novels. This sea is gray, sweating, polluted, flapping against the rocks and walls of countless reclamations. Lapping against the sodden foundations of apartment blocks, leaking into hutment dwellings, bursting its shores when the rains fall down. It's the kind of sea that nobody in the city notices, but without it they would lose their anchor in the world. Walkers and joggers in the early morning, the devout with prayer mats in hand, the fishermen dragging in their nets, the trawlers and huge cargo ships bound for the icy waters of northern countries, the squatters shitting on Juhu beach, the dhobis beating their dirty washing on the boulders of Haji Ali.

In London it's the birds, in Singapore it's the rain, but in Bombay it's the sea that wakes you; the curtain-like drawing-in of a wave or the spray of an incoming breeze. Morning and evening and afternoon and night. Even in the darkness of a cinema, watching Rajesh Khanna dancing and singing his way across the stage in *Apna Desh,* even here in the Citylight theater, there is a sense of water, brackish, dusky, murmuring in the distance.

And in the evening, the sea brings people home. The tired thousands who traverse the city on the Western or the Central line, the overland trains, watching the water come and go below their feet, passing by the cars that creep along the curving causeways of Marine Drive, Mahalaxmi, and Mahim. The overcrowded Leyland buses tearing past queues of waiting commuters. The vacant strollers eating air, the lovers along the beaches, the vendors turning up their gas lamps and primping their snacks. Mountains of puffed rice, yellow sev, purple onions, crisp puris, earthenware matkas full of spiced water. As the light softens, fully clad families amble on the sea front. Men who might roll up their trousers to dip their feet in a wave that obligingly slides their way, pulling the sand from under their toes. Women wrapped in saris, out for a jaunt, not afraid to jump in and wet their heavy clothes. Beggars weaving around the stalls, pleading for a little leftover. Sad camels and their drivers, pony riders, balloon sellers, card-tricksters, sand sculptors, snake-charmers, and bunderwallahs with a mangy monkey in tow. Ice cream sellers and singchannawallahs, carrying their roasting peanuts and gram from a basket around their necks.

The evening sky descends on them all and the tide goes out without a fuss.

After my brush with the elephants, I developed a feverish hankering for Hindi cinema. Mesmerized by its idols, I rushed to see them perform and came out copying their every move. After seeing *Apna Desh, Kati Patang, Aradhana, Daag,* and *Namak Haram* I began to act like Rajesh Khanna. Emerging into the Bombay sunlight, I practiced my heavy-lidded glance on strangers. I walked with my shoulders slightly hunched, leaned to one side, and dragged my feet. I delivered normal speech as if I were handing out an ultimatum. I tried to re-create the rhythms of Rajesh Khanna's speech in English and stroked my cheek as if I were sunk in melancholy thought.

This imitation was not confined to Rajesh. After seeing *Zanzeer* and *Deewar,* I took on the sonorous lilt of Amitabh Bachan's serious lines; after seeing *Bobby,* the playful sing-song syllables of Rishi Kapoor.

This dream world crossed over into real life when people mistook me for Junior Mehmood. Junior Mehmood was the most popular child actor on the Hindi screen. He had long black hair and a naughty but lovable smirk. A lot of the time he was portrayed as a comic character; sometimes he played the part of an important messenger, a smart alec, or a thief who slipped in and out of tiny openings at the backs of houses. My favorite film of his was a remake of the Oliver Twist story in which he played a boy who was part of a criminal gang and robbed people's houses in the middle of the night. The adult hero, a thief with a heart of gold, manages to get him round to the good side by finding enough money to send him to school. When, at the end of the film, the thief is captured and put behind bars, he has the solace of being visited by Junior Mehmood in his school uniform, and then in a college outfit, finally of greeting him outside the prison as a grown man who has done well for himself with smart clothes and a car.

When we stopped at traffic signals, in our huge American car, a blue Dodge that my father had had shipped into the country on the sly, the boys of the street, dirty rags in hand, would weave in between the traffic and come running up to our window. A foreign car was likely to have a film star in it. As soon as they saw me, my long black hair and my light brown skin, they would shout, "Arre, Junior Mehmood, Junior Mehmood! Dekh Harish, Ramu! Hey Chandra! Ye sala Junior Mehmood baitha. Aao idher." They would call out to their friends, who would all come and surround the car and peer in as if in wonderment at some exotic animal. While my parents ignored them, I would beam back at the boys and play along with their fantasy. "Yes," I answered to their questions, "of course I'm Junior Mehmood. Don't you recognize me from my last picture? Hey, *Brahmachari* dekha kya? Usmai mera top role tha."

"Ha yaar. Ye to Junior Mehmood hai na. This is definitely

Junior Mehmood," said one boy with curly hair. His taller friend was not sure. He stood staring at me. "Kya bur bur kar raha hai tum. Junior Mehmood to Andheri mai rehta hai." A discussion would start and I would tell them about the roles I had played in recent years. "Arre *Aao Milo Sajne*, mai mai Asha Parekh ke sath acting kiya. Kya, dekha ke nahi? *Pyar He Pyar* mai maine Dharmendra ko villain se bachaya." Then they would all agree that I was Junior Mehmood and for a few seconds I was transported to the firmament of stardom. I could show off my knowledge of Hindi cinema with these boys. For the children of my parents' friends, whom I was sometimes forced to meet, this world, the world on our doorstep, the world on the street, the world on the hundreds of billboard advertisements around the city, was as alien and as repellent as the underworld of rats in the sewers of the city.

As the lights changed and we crawled away with the traffic, the boys running beside the window suddenly remembered that they had forgotten to ask for money, their main aim in being out here at this time of night. "Hey, ten paise, hey, Junior Mehmood, fifty paise. Humko kuch to de ke jao. Sala gaya, gaya, gaya. Give us something before you go," they shouted out in vain.

I would do anything to get to see another Hindi film. Even though there were seven or eight new films coming out each month, I was always on the lookout for an old film I might have missed. I loved the films about dacoits set in the Rajasthani deserts or in the ravines of Madhya Pradesh, like *Reshma Aur Shera*. Try as I might, there was nothing I could do to keep up with the massive production energy of the Bombay studios. I bunked off school, stopped off on my way home, stole money, went out late at night, traveled across the city to unknown areas, bought tickets on the black market, and scoured the papers for the one theater in the city which was showing the film I wanted to see. Most of these films I saw on my own. There was no other way. Many of the cinemas I frequented were deep in the heart of Bombay and of a kind that Mrs. Verma, for instance, would never visit. She liked to go to the comfortable cinemas in the salubrious parts of town, with air-conditioning and dress-circle arenas, where one could be separated from the sweating mass of cinemagoers, who shouted and clapped and swore, and ate paan and spat out the remains on the walls outside the theater.

To get to a particular movie, I would often take the bus or the train to Sion or Matunga or Parel or Andheri, parts of the city that many of my friends had never seen. I could tell that life was different in these places. The buildings were yellowing, dilapidated, and crowded together. There were more people living on the pavement in tents made of plastic sheets and cardboard, outside which mothers cooked dal and grilled chapatis for their children. There were families who lived in huge wrought-iron drainage pipes lying abandoned on the road. There were no jeans, T-shirts, and suits in this part of town. Rows of yellow-and-black taxis and lots of BEST buses, cycles, and trucks, but very few private cars to be seen. Men on bikes who held on to the chain at the back of a truck for a freewheeling ride.

Often, having arrived early, I would have to wait around outside the cinema for the previous showing of the film to finish. Sitting there in my white shorts and white half-sleeved shirt, I looked awkward, and the minutes passed slowly. There was nothing to do, nowhere to go, and nothing to eat, since I normally had just enough money for the two-rupees-twenty-paise ticket. To pass the time, I indulged in a fad that was popular amongst some of the boys in my school. It consisted of rolling a rubber-solution ball. We bought tubes of rubber solution from a cycle shop, the kind used for repairing punctures, and you spread a thin layer of this paste on the lid of a Bournevita tin. Then you waited for the sticky paste to dry and mopped it up with the inside of your palm, using a circular motion, much like rolling a ball of dough from a flattened-out piece of pastry. With each accretion of rubber solution the little ball grew a tiny bit; soon you could bounce it around like a super-ball. I learned from making this rubber clew that no object dropped from a certain height can bounce back to the same height, however energy-efficient it may be.

People looked at me with curiosity as I spread the reddish gluey substance on the shiny lid of the tin. The task engendered its own obsessiveness. As I squeezed and spread and rolled, I labored with the happy feeling that my ball was growing bigger and bigger, but after I'd worked away for hours and days and used up six large tubes of solution, the super-ball was no bigger than a walnut. And I'd imagined I was going to build it to the size of a tennis ball.

I gave up. But there was something in the process of making that ball that I never forgot. An acknowledgment, perhaps, of the futility of human endeavor. Hours spent waiting for what you want, occupying yourself with activities that amounted to no more than a fraction of a millimeter added to the surface of a sphere. For the first time, while rolling that glue and waiting for the film to begin, I understood the meaning of time passing, of time wasted, of being left behind by time. Until, of course, the lovely face of the actress, Sharmila Tagore, robbed me of all such morose thoughts.

9

My life was all balls. The cricket ball, the dog's hard ball, the squash ball, the croquet ball, the football, the rubber-solution ball—but most of all, the tennis ball. The tennis ball is versatile like no other. With it you can play cricket, hockey, pat ball, catch-monkey, donkey in the middle, football, French cricket, basketball, water polo, even volleyball. We were a family obsessed with tennis. All of us, my father apart, played every day of the week except Sunday. There wasn't a club in the city whose courts we did not know: the Khar Gym, the Bandra Gym, the Bombay Gym, the Willingdon Club, the Cricket Club of India, and the Maharashtra State Lawn Tennis Association, where I learned the basics of the game. My mother and I watched, followed, and played in tournaments all around the country. We scanned the sports pages of the *Times of India* for news from the grand slam tournaments around the world. During Wimbledon we were

glued to the radio following the progress of Margaret Court, Billie Jean King, Rod Laver, John Newcombe, Stan Smith, and Ilie
Nastase. My favorite showing-off story was how Newcombe had
once visited our house for a beer. Being sixteen at the time, he
had to hide behind the curtains to drink it.

In her younger days, my mother had trained at the Queen's
Club in London to try and qualify to play at Wimbledon. She was
seeded second in the All India rankings of the day. But her training was cut short when the drizzling gray and cold of an Earl's
Court bedsit, and the separation from her two-year-old son, got
the better of her ambition.

So much in our family revolved around the game. My
mother's life, her relationship with my father, and her relationship with me, all these could be decoded and deciphered through
backhands, forehands, volleys, lobs, and serves. Particular shots
decided the fate of future relationships, long and bitter debates
ensued about who was better than who: matches that were won
left one with a high for weeks to come; matches lost were cause
for days of introspection and postmortem depression.

ON A HOT afternoon in April, about two-thirty, earlier than normal for tennis, I was due to play Sandeep Gupta in the first round
of the Maharashtra Open, Under 12 Competition. He was seeded
one, I was an outsider. The Gupta brothers, Sandeep and Sanjay,
were of Kashmiri origin and lived in Bandra. Sandeep was ten,
Sanjay eleven. Their father, who was also their coach, was a
serene-faced doctor. Pale Kashmiri skin and unusual green eyes.
His sons had something green, something blue, something
slanted in their eyes. They could easily be mistaken for twins.
They were a spindly limbed, resilient, and cunning duo. Onto
their grasshopper bodies were attached these two huge globes for
heads—round and smiling. The two boys were well-known pro-
tégés of the Bandra Gymkhana. I had seen them play a couple of
times and I knew in my gut that I had the beating of them.

On the afternoon of the match, my mother and I drove from our house in Juhu to the suburb of Bandra. I was dressed in my Fred Perry white shorts and shirt, my mother in a dazzling blue dress. On the road, my mother coached me on the art of match play.

"Now, Cyrus, listen to me. When you are practicing shots before the match, what you have to do is play a few strokes to both sides, especially his backhand, and see which is the weaker side."

"Yes, but what if he doesn't play any backhands?"

"He has to play one or two," she said, tutting irritably. "What I mean is, most players at your level have a weaker backhand. Even Rod Laver attacked Pancho Gonzalez's backhand. So you see . . . and then when you're playing him, don't start hitting everything to one side. Unless it's very weak: then you just attack . . . from the word go . . . and then he's finished." My mother was given to not finishing her sentences. Impatience was one of her chief characteristics. She spoke in half-sentences because she didn't think it necessary to complete a sentence once its meaning had been conveyed, because she couldn't wait to make her next point and, most important, because she didn't want to leave a gap in which to be interrupted. I was trying to keep my mind on what she was saying when two women in saris suddenly walked in front of the car as if it didn't exist. Luckily we were not traveling fast. My mother jammed on the brakes and leaned her hand on the horn. Most drivers would have shouted at the pedestrians. My mother carried on as if nothing had happened.

"Yah, but then what will Sandeep Gupta do? Are you paying attention or not? What do you think he will do when you play on his backhand? What he will do is run round his backhand," she said, answering her own question. I was watching a man dragging along a huge ice block with a hook, his vest drenched in sweat. The block of ice skated meltingly along the baking tarmac.

"What d'you mean 'run round'?"

"Don't be silly now, Cyrus. You know what 'run round' is. If he is standing here," my mother let go of the steering wheel with one hand to give her demonstration, "and you hit the ball here, to his left," she pointed with the other finger, "to his backhand, he runs further to his left and plays it with his forehand. Therefore running round . . ." By the end of these heated gesticulations both her hands were off the steering wheel and the turquoise Fiat we were in careered toward the pavement. A swerving cyclist shouted an insult through the window.

"Hey, akal ka dushman, jara dekh ke chalao gadi."

"Oh, shut up, you bloody fool!" my mother replied under her breath. Hardly stopping to take another, she continued, "So, then, what do you do then? If he runs and tries to play it like that, on his forehand, what do you do?"

Everything was always a test with my mother. Have you heard of . . . ? Do you know how . . . ? Can you tell me . . . ? I was terrible at tests. I always came thirty-ninth out of forty in my class at St. Mary's. There was little chance of me coming up with the right answer. At that moment, I would have given anything for John Newcombe to come and whisper it in my ear. I said, "You keep on playing on his backhand."

"Noooooooo! Oh, my God! How can you go on playing on his backhand! Cyrus, after all these years . . ." And here she let her hands rise from the steering wheel and dropped them down again with a sigh and a wry twist of the mouth. Then she went back to her explaining mode. "If he keeps on running to the left and covering his backhand, then what happens is the right-hand side of the court is left gaping open. Obviously, his forehand side gets left open. So what do you do? Naturally, you play to his forehand. Either you will hit a winner or when he rushes back across the court then you have enough time to play to his backhand. Do you understand now?"

I nodded. I had the feeling that before our journey was up I would hear the explanation again. My mother was fond of repeating herself. It was part of her teaching technique. Drumming it in. I'm still not sure as to the effectiveness of such a method. Did it make me willfully deaf to her advice or did my pretending not to listen signify an acute subconscious absorption?

"You must be patient. Wait for the ball . . . George says you've got good shots. But you try to hurry them . . . you hit them too hard, hit them out . . . You know which turning it is? You mustn't make unforced errors. Never mind if you don't hit winning shots. You mustn't make any," she stopped to gather up her energy for the emphatic repetition, "unforced errors."

I was sitting in the corner of the front seat, wedged between the door and the backrest, like the taxi drivers, with their elbows leaning out of the window. "Can one make an unforced error if one isn't playing tennis?" I wondered. "Are unforced errors a problem in other areas of life?"

I was having difficulty concentrating on my mother's voice. Being in a state of nervous excitement, I wanted to spend these last moments before the match quietly, letting my mind wander to anything but the game in front of me. I thought of the Chinese meal my mother had promised to take me to if I won. I thought of both of us returning to our glass house when everything was over, turning into the lane, past Laloo Prasad in his cubbyhole, past the Krishnans' gate with its black and white notice, "Beware of Dog," glimpsing the coconut seller on the beach, running up the spiral staircase to my bedroom.

Through the car window, I looked out at the tall neon sign for Caesar's Palace. I'd never been into that hotel even though we must have passed it a hundred times. A little farther on, the postbox red of the Frankie stall caught my eye. Mr. Tibbs's original creation: the nan and egg roll filled with delicious mutton curry. Even my father, who was not one for roadside food, liked them. What was that playing at Bandra Talkies? Oh, *Mere Apne*.

I hadn't seen that one. Shatrugan Sinha, trying to be a hero instead of a villain. "Meena Kumari at her very best!" the poster said proudly. I wanted these familiar signposts en route to go on for eternity. I didn't want us ever to get to the Bandra Gymkhana tennis courts, brown and hard in the blinding sun. I wanted to blink and be back in the lane outside our house, the tennis match over, whatever the result. Or back in my bed, where I was lying an hour ago reading my James Hadley Chase novel.

We were stalled in a traffic jam on Linking Road. My mother's voice reached out and grabbed me by the elbow. "Don't be too confident, huh, Cyrus. Sandeep is meant to be very good."

"But Sanjay is meant to be better than Sandeep."

"Yes. But you shouldn't think of that now. Both are very good. Now, c'mon, just grit your teeth. Even if you lose the first few games, don't just give up and start hitting the ball wildly. Be determined, clench your fist, like Billie Jean."

I thought of my mother's pearly teeth. She was always telling us how her dentist said she had such a perfect set. I recalled a match she'd played in last year, in the final round of the Western India Championships. Her opponent was Neeru Seth, a short, dark, dogged-looking woman from the armed forces. I was sitting watching from a round-backed cane chair in the corner behind the baseline. Absorbing the weight of every ball she hit, every forehand she guided over the net, every backhand she speared to the far corner of her opponent's court. Watching her little pattering footsteps as she frisked from side to side. Her eyes bulging as she swung a forehand winner down the line. The drop of her head and the swing of her arms to and fro like a clock, while she changed ends. The occasional smile slung to the corner where I was sitting.

And my mother. I should be watching her play, but I couldn't bear to. When she caught my eye, she didn't smile, her mind hot with the strain of thinking about the next few points. I remember, after the match, how upset she was to be beaten by Neeru Seth, who later became the governor of India's most notorious women's jail. Tears mixed in with sweat dripped like melting fat down her arms and neck; her voice cracked as she spoke to the local coach. "But she behaved very badly, George. She can't behave like that, shouting and grunting and . . . I had three set points, three times I played to the backhand but she got it back. She kept on moving her feet when I was about to serve my second serve, moving her feet like this, pit pit pit, I don't know, maybe that shouldn't be allowed. Are you allowed to distract your opponent like that?" George didn't speak, he just looked at her soothingly through his horn-rimmed spectacles. Impassive as ever. And all through that game I had been thinking, "She's going to lose the match, she's never going to make it."

We turned right at Dawood Interiors and into the main streets of Bandra. There was little time left for idle thoughts. The past couldn't come and rescue me now. But my mother still had her favorite story left to tell. "Don't forget, I've told you so many times about that time in the semi-final of the Davis Cup when Krishnan was three-five and two sets to love down, and Koch from Brazil was serving. Naresh Kumar, who was the commentator, said, 'What a shame India is about to lose the tie.' People were walking away and going home. Everyone had given up. But then Krishnan broke serve and won the next game and you could see him talking to himself and saying, 'C'mon, Krish, you can do it,' gritting his teeth and clenching his fist. He won that set and then the whole match. I was fixed to my seat for three hours, I missed all my appointments, the match was so enthralling. What delicate shots Krish played! What guts he showed! What determination! Really he's an all-round player. At the end, Koch was finished, a broken man, completely finished. The people in the audience gave them both a five-minute standing ovation."

I loved this story but I wanted to know more details. I

wanted her to relive the match so I could see it as if it were a film. My mother was more interested in the moral. As we approached the Bandra Gym, she spun it out. "So you see, it shows you, if you really want to win something badly enough, even if you're love-five down, if you fight back, you can do it. Of course, Krishnan was a great player. Okay, now we're there, have you got everything?"

Mine was the first match of the day on the sun-baked cow-dung court. My mother strode up to some loitering boys, asking questions and demanding service. This was not her territory, but she was someone who could command attention on the North Pole. One of the Gupta brothers trotted over to me, a smile on his globe.

"Are you Cyrus Readymoney?"

"Yup." I smiled back. Was I meant to hate this boy? I rather wanted to be friends with him.

"My brother's just coming. I'm Sanjay," he said shaking my hand, "I think we're playing a match tomorrow in the Under Tens."

"That's at the Khar Gym, isn't it?"

"Where is he? Where is Sandeep Gupta?" my mother boomed. "They should start now, it's already two-forty-five!" Two of the boys hanging around at the edge of the court, I think they were going to be linesmen, ran off toward the clubhouse as if struck by lightning.

"Sandeep's just coming, Aunty," said Sanjay. "Just wait one minute."

"I hope he's hurrying up. Otherwise what was the point of us coming so early? I have to be in town by five o'clock and your father said two-thirty sharp."

Sandeep arrived, running along the side of the court, grinning like a goblin. His father followed after him, tall, avuncular, and bald. He bade my mother welcome and offered her a drink.

Sandeep clutched his wooden Maxply. We shook hands and tossed for service. While we were knocking I noticed Dr. Gupta chatting happily with my mum. I had borrowed my mother's racquet, a Wilson T2000, the same kind Jimmy Connors played with. It was warm and springy in my hand. Sandeep's shots were steady but weak. I responded with some hard-hit drives on both sides. The balls were falling in. After the long car journey, I felt a certain lightness, a pleasant breeze, a relaxation of being. I opened my shoulders and stroked through the ball, watching it closely onto my racquet. I was lost in the effortlessness of this hitting. I didn't have to look, I could feel the balls were landing in. I threw myself into the air and scythed through a smash, punched a few volleys. My backhand felt particularly strong. I looked over at Sandeep when we were practicing our serves. He seemed shaky, like a rickety chair. His serves were dropping in the middle of the box, where I could eat them up for breakfast.

Sandeep won the toss and elected to serve. I remembered too late my mother's advice to observe his shots during our knock-up. But she was right about his backhand—it was weak. He couldn't find enough power in his chopstick frame to hit the ball flat and was slicing it short. I exploited his tentative replies with surgical severity, sailing ahead to 5–1 in the first set. It was all so easy. I allowed myself a smile of triumph. I was serving more accurately than ever, lunging for volleys on my forehand and hitting smashes into the backhand corner of the court. And Sandeep obligingly made some terrible mistakes. Out of the corner of my eye I could see my mother conversing with the doctor, though I could tell they were both following the score and occasionally watching a rally.

There is almost nothing equal to the feeling of bliss when you are on top of a game, playing well and beating your opponent. Your shots get better, the ball speeds to the appointed corner, or depth, or stops dead where you want it to. Your serves come effortlessly: ball, body, and racquet all swinging in one harmonious motion. Your volleys dip and angle and slide away from the reach of your flailing rival. If you miss a first serve, you can afford to take a chance and hit the second one. It tends to fall in. When your adversary finds a good stroke you reply with an inspirational one. Great players talk of playing out of yourself, as if the weight of your body floats away and you are left with an ethereal essence of stroke, hand, and eye. You move fast, you see things early, reaching balls generally unreachable. It's like passing the fifty mark in a game of cricket: you bid goodbye to caution and a full-length ball on your middle stump is nonchalantly half-volleyed to the boundary. You can be polite, languorous, even slipshod. When the tide is swimming for you, you can be sure your opponent will be floundering in the waves.

Having won the first set by 3–15, I was in a buoyant state of exuberance on court five of the Bandra Gymkhana, humming my favorite Elton John song from the album *Goodbye Yellow Brick Road*.

> Hello, baby, hello, haven't seen your face in a while . . .
> Harmony and me, we're pretty good company
> Looking for an island in a boat upon the sea.

The second set resumed where the first had left off. I was three games to love up, strolling around the court like someone on holiday, thinking of the Chinese dinner my mother had promised she would take me to, sprinkling the green chilies on the sweet corn and chicken soup. Already counting on trouncing the elder Gupta brother in tomorrow's match. Going up to the podium to collect the Under 10 and Under 12 winners' trophies. I was four–love up in the second set, receiving serve, and Sandeep was 15–40 down. I hit a couple of overambitious forehand returns, one even bounced onto the bamboo-and-rattan backing behind the baseline.

From deuce, Sandeep managed to claw back the game. I heard my mother's voice from behind me. She was sitting at the back of the court.

"Now, don't fool around, hah, Cyrus. You can lose the match from anywhere."

"Quit worrying, Mom," I thought to myself, pretending I was Jimmy Connors. I smacked the aluminum frame against my calves, I fingered the strings of my racquet, I looked at the crowd, and snarled. I lost the next game.

"Oh, for God's sake, get on with it," I snapped, as Sandeep bounced the ball in front of him for the umpteenth time before serving. Impatience overcame me. I tried to force a couple of backhands down the line. One hit the tape at the top of the net, the other missed the sideline by a fraction. I stared hard at the umpire, as if I were Ilie Nastase. In the next game I had a point to go 5–3 up and I made a double fault. I crashed my racquet to the floor. It was a hallmark of my game that I never committed a double fault. I couldn't believe what was happening.

My mother's voice grew urgent. "Cyrus, you can lose a match from anywhere," she hissed. "Stop fooling around. Pancho Seguira had nine match points against Pancho Gonzalez and he still lost. The main thing is . . ."

I couldn't believe she was telling me a story in the middle of a game. What would the people think? I turned to her and said, "Be quiet please, Mummy. There's no problem. I'm fine."

I sauntered back across the court and thought through my position. I must turn the heat on his backhand. I must focus on each point. Keep the ball in play. The set was now at four–all. The ninth game went to plan. I didn't try anything special, just keeping the ball deep on his backhand. It wasn't easy. His game seemed to have improved and my shots had to be more accurate to prevent him from running round and hitting them with his hungry forehand. In the tenth game he made a couple of nervous errors and that was enough to give me two match points. Fifteen–forty, on his serve. A smile escaped my lips.

"Oh, please shut up, Mummy," I said under my breath. I could see her clenching her fists, urging me on to win the next point. Sandeep served to my backhand. I sliced it low across the court to his backhand and rushed up to the net. I saw him struggling with the shot. I've seen it a hundred times after that. A pathetic half-lob floating pitifully toward where I was waiting at the net. The easiest shot in the game to play. I could have closed my eyes and hit a winner ten times over, in twenty different ways. I swung at the ball with all my strength, there was a strange tinny vibration in my hand, I saw the ball fly out of the court, I saw Sandeep Gupta looking at me with his mouth open, I saw sadness and pain stretching out in front of me for the rest of my life. The ball had hit the rim of the racquet and flown over the baseline. Any other day, a mishit smash would land on the line or on some awkward part of the court. I couldn't bear to look in the direction of my mother.

While I watched Sandeep lunge hopelessly at my vicious slice, I'm sure I had a vision of shaking his hand across the net and saying, "Well done." After that squandered match point, ·Sandeep Gupta also had a vision, a vision of winning the match. From that moment onward he fought like Arjun in the *Mahabharata*, not just with strength but with a force of mind that ran from his head to the steady bend of his elbow as he rained down arrows of woe onto the army of his helpless cousins.

When competition is fierce between two rivals the winner is the person with the greater control over his or her emotions. The blood must remain cool; the hand must keep its balance; something at the center, perhaps even on the edge, in the ball of one's foot or the lobe of one's ear, must nurse a cruel quietness, a consciousness of the life that exists outside the terrible struggle that one is straining to overcome.

After that dreadful smash, Sandeep managed to win three games in a row and stole the second set. At the start of the third set his eyes had acquired a reddish tinge like someone drunk with longing. We exchanged a couple of games. One–all. Then his forehand started to flow. It was a lovely cross-court shot that came from nowhere and disappeared before you had time to take a step toward it. Where had he been hiding it all this time? Having found his rhythm on that shot, the harder I tried to play to his backhand the easier he found it to run round and hit a winner with his forehand. My mother was all passion overflowing onto the court. Haranguing me with different bits of advice, cheering when I made a good shot, desolate when my opponent sent another ball whizzing by me. I could feel her voice as if it were someone shaking me. I flung my racquet on the floor in disgust when Sandeep went 4–1 up. "I don't care," I thought. "I'm going to lose now." I just couldn't get the match point I'd squandered out of my head. The picture of that missed overhead haunted me through every point of the final set. I stopped listening to my mother. "C'mon Cyrus! Don't give up now. Show some determination."

I had lost my will to win or to fight. My opponent swallowed the points like a caterpillar. Larger and larger morsels. As the afternoon wore on to evening he became more voracious. My mother's voice was hoarse by now. I had points to reduce his lead from 5–3 to 5–4. Endless deuces. My spirits revived momentarily when it was my advantage, but he never lost his lean and predatory look. We had been playing for two-and-a-half hours in sunstroke heat but only in the last game did I feel fatigued. The lifeblood had left my game. My mother had gone suddenly silent with resignation and shame. At the end, when we shook hands, I was still half thinking of the vision in which I had won the match after putting away that simple smash. I almost thought Sandeep was going to walk over to me and say, "You won the match really—this rest was just a joke, a bad dream."

My mother and I didn't speak to one another. I should have said sorry or something like that. Normally she would have been analyzing the game by now, telling me what I had done wrong. She bought me a drink. It was cold, but I didn't enjoy it. On the way home, in the car, my mother laid open the corpse of the lost match. Postmortem, she called it.

"The problem with you, Cyrus, is the same in tennis as with other things in your life. You just don't have the staying power, the perseverance. One minute you want this, then you don't like it and you want something else. You thought you had won when you had that match point. You didn't concentrate and then see what happens, you missed the easy smash. I told you in the car before the match, don't be overconfident, but you never listen properly. Your teachers say the same thing . . ." And I salivated with anguish at the thought of a lost banquet of fried rice and sweet and sour pork, of king-size prawns and Singapore noodles, of beef with chilies and lychees with ice cream.

10

And now I must tell you about the Maharani of Bharatnagar. The sedentary queen, the solitary divorcée cocooned in her crumbling mansion on Juhu beach.

For many years she remained a mystery. None of our neighbors really knew her. She was not unfriendly, but she made no attempt to talk to anyone. We had glimpses of her—in her bedroom window, leaving in her car, walking the dogs in the afternoon. We heard rumors and we passed rumors on. Her husband had left her. They hadn't had any children. She had adopted five young girls from villages in Rajasthan. The oldest of them had escaped in the middle of the night back to her village. She got drunk every night. Sometimes screams were heard coming from her bedroom. These, it was said, were cries of pain from her adopted daughters, whom she was beating. She loved animals. Her house overflowed with dogs, cats, fish, parrots, and other pets kept in cages. She had upward of ten servants. Bands of royal relations dressed in Rajasthani clothes of pink and red trooped in and out of the house. In her cupboards she kept pistols and rifles. Sushil Krishnan said he saw her standing at the window, gun in hand, aiming at a crow. One room in her house was full of gold.

I asked my dad, "What is a Maharani doing on Juhu beach? Why doesn't she go and rule her kingdom?"

"Well, they don't really have kingdoms anymore. Mrs. Gandhi went back on her promise and abolished the privy purse."

"What kind of purse?"

"It wasn't a real purse. You see, when the British left in 1947, the Maharajahs lost most of their power. But to keep them happy they were given a certain amount of money every year, depending on the size of their kingdom. This was called the 'privy purse.' Last year Mrs. G. took that away from them. So now they have nothing. Some of them have fallen on hard times. They've had to sell their palaces to people who want to turn them into hotels."

"So, then, the Maharani next door is not a real Maharani anymore? She could be really poor even?"

"I don't know about that. People still call them Your Highness. In their local areas, where their ancestors ruled, the villagers especially treat them with a lot of respect. She must have enough money, her husband is still quite rich and it's his responsibility to look after her."

"What happened that time when you asked her about Behroz's Navjote?" I knew this story but I wanted to hear it again.

"What happened? Oh, yes, we had to ask her if we could borrow her compound because we found that we had invited too many people for the dinner and almost everyone said they would come. We were nervous, we thought she might say no and then we would be stuck. It would have been impossible to fit all the guests in our house."

"How many people had you invited?"

"About seven hundred."

"How did you manage to feed so many people?"

"We hired Mr. Booth, the famous Parsi caterer, and we had three or maybe even four sittings. Anyway, we asked her to come over for lunch, but she said no, she would come over for a cup of tea. And then she came over and she was really polite, and very cultured. She said yes, we could borrow her compound on one condition, that we didn't expect her to have to come to the party in the evening, although she did come to the initiation ceremony in the morning. She didn't like going out, especially at night. We offered to pay her but she wouldn't hear of it."

"So, then, what did you say?"

"We said, of course we didn't want to impose anything on her but we hoped she would change her mind and join us in the festivities."

"Did she come?"

"No, she didn't, but Mehroo says she saw her sitting out on her balcony watching the guests and listening to the band."

"Well, I don't know about that," intervened my mother, who was sitting on the sofa reading the newspaper. "What happened was we sent her a present, some flowers or chocolates or something, and a card to say thank you for allowing us to use her garden and all that . . . So, then, she wrote back this letter saying how beautiful the music had been, how they had played all her old Rajasthani songs, songs from her childhood, and how she was moved to tears and all. Can you imagine? You know we got Grandpa to use his influence to get the police band to play at the Navjote—you know that, don't you, Cyrus? It was meant to be a very special thing. And how many people in the police band? You don't know? More than fifty players! So we thought this would be something unusual. I mean, most people just said get Goody Servai and his players, but I thought we should do something unusual. Anyway, they were the only thing that completely flopped during the Navjote: everything else went off very well but no one liked the police band. All mournful songs they played, and no one knew the music, so obviously there was no dancing. This was the funny thing. The one person who didn't come to the party—and can you imagine, that bloody stupid Mr. Krishnan came and had his dinner in the first sitting and then went home and started complaining about the noise—but the one person, the Maharani, who refused to come to the Navjote, was sitting in her room, loving the music."

I had an urge to meet this Maharani. Like the Hindi movies that had me in their thrall, this woman's life represented a hidden world outside my own, a world in which I might play a part. This curiosity was added to by the fact that my bedroom and hers looked directly into one another. I've already said that the house I lived in was built of glass. Two sides of my room were sheer walls of glass, in the form of big sliding doors. The aluminum frames were shipped in from Hamburg by my father. The Maharani and her companion—there was always another woman in there, a red veil drooped over her face—could see into my room as if it were a giant aquarium. Just as the Krishnans could look straight in at me from the back of the house. The Maharani's bedroom had a little balcony onto which she sometimes came and I could see her moving around in her room. At night her friend (or was she her servant?) drew the curtains. Then the lights stayed on till the early hours of the morning. I looked carefully from the darkness of my room to see if I could catch any action in the cracks of light between the curtains.

I asked Rajnish, the eldest of the Verma boys, to introduce me to the Maharani or to one of her adopted daughters. Rajnish was a bit of a playboy. He had a glamorous way of putting his arm round girls that made them laugh and feel reassured at the same time. I knew I would never be able to develop that skill. It made me envy and hate him. He said he would take me to meet Meera, the adopted daughter with the long black hair who walked the dogs, but it was always the same: "Maybe tomorrow."

I began to watch Meera in the morning. At seven-fifteen a door at the front of the house would open and out would rush a frenzy of yapping, barking, howling canines. As I lay stretched out in the morning glare, in pajamas too short for my ever-sprouting legs, parts of me hanging out everywhere, bolting out of that front door of the Maharani's house would come two golden Labradors, three Alsatians, two golden retrievers, four dachshunds, two poodles, and a host of miniature dogs, some the size of large rats. Tongues lolling, tails wagging, bawling, barking, and mauling one another, they burst out of the door and scampered to different corners of the compound, sniffing at coconut leaves, muzzling bits of overturned soil, sticking their noses in pieces of shit, ferreting for anything that might liven up their hypersensitive olfactory canals. From behind them rang out the plaintive cry of the voluptuous Meera. "Chulo, chulo, Chocky, chulo, Mimi. C'mon you twit! What are you waiting for? Get outside! If you dare do your tutti inside, I'm not going to bloody clean it up. C'mon, yaar, Dinki, it's time to go walkies. Come here, you stupid mutt!" Her disapprobation was directed at the reluctant dogs—the ones who were ill or depressed or injured, or simply too lazy to want to run around in the dirt.

I knew the routine well. The dogs were exercised four times a day. Meera, or one of her sisters, would allow them about twenty minutes out in the open before they herded the dogs back into the house. During that time the girls would stroll up and down in front of my window, from one end of the compound to the other, chatting and laughing. In the morning Meera was often on her own, and from the comfort of my bed, through the huge glass panes, I watched her amble up and down the tarmac strip in front of their house. Every morning before I went to school, before she had had her bath, before she went to college, I gazed at her with concentration so clear that I could melt in with her movements, disappear amongst the folds of her petticoat, be a tiny pebble smoothed by the gentle brushing of her inner thighs. Unnoticed, on the side of her belly or even holed up in her navel, watching, waiting, smelling her different needs.

I can see her now, glowing with health. Her brown skin, her bare arms barely swinging, her hitched-up petticoat, the streaming black hair. Then again, was there something sorrowful in these slippered feet sloping toward my window? She looks at the ground, then to one side, examines her hands, flicks back her hair, yells across at an errant dog. She stops right below my window, glances upward, then turns and lazily walks away.

I can look at her better now. No chance of meeting her eye. I can see the things she wouldn't want me to see, the parts she assumes are hidden. Her slender ankles, the few inches of bare calves, the rounds of her rising and falling buttocks, and the cascade of hair, black, black, black.

Meera and my morals teacher at school, tight-skirted Miss Rosie Castello, became the source of torment and delight during my waking hours.

At night I watched the lights in the Maharani's bedroom. In the morning I watched Meera with the dogs. So many sounds came out of that crumbling house. Yelps and barks from the dogs; bloodcurdling squeals from the cats, like babies crying for their mothers; screeching from the red-plumed African parrots. And then the human noises, a hoarse authoritative voice bellowing commands, the unmistakable cries of wailing, the servants conversing in Marathi, and sometimes, late into the night, a yearning high-pitched voice singing mournful Urdu ghazals.

And all through the night, from eleven to six in the morning, the Maharani's watchman circled the pink house in his brown uniform, marking out his territory by banging a heavy wooden stick on the floor. Each bang was made at an interval of five or six steps and resounded like a rifle shot traveling at least half a mile into neighboring houses on the beach. It was a welcome disturbance for their inhabitants: the comforting expression of good against evil, the sound that confirmed for them that out there in the world things were all right, someone was looking out for thievish rogues.

All along the beach, in the bungalows and houses, there were watchmen fast asleep. Heads wrapped in woolen scarves, arms folded around their bodies, huddled up in a corner, they were snoring the night away. Save Bahadur Shah, the Maharani's stalwart Gurkha watchman, whose stick, thick as a grown man's arm, spoke out for all those comatose chowkidars and drowned out the collective rumble of their snores. This was no mean feat, for there can be little doubt that the loudest snores in the world emanate from the guilty dreams of slumbering chowkidars.

11

I want to be older than I am. I have read Kafka's Diaries, *edited by Max Brod, the first fifteen pages at least. I have read Keats's poems and I have copied passages from Will Durant's* The Story of Civilization. *My cousin has told me about Freud and Spinoza. He says he has read Spinoza's* Ethics. *I know little boys want to have sex with their mothers and little girls with their fathers. I travel the trains and buses of the city and go to films all by myself. I visit Irani restaurants and eat plates of dal fry and keema pao.*

I have written three poems: "Sea Breeze," "Dog," and "Horse." The last one is accompanied by a drawing. I am writing bits of my life story in this notebook. I have drunk half a bottle of rum and I smoked twenty 555 cigarettes the other day. I have stolen money, killed cockroaches and pigeons, and hung around with people who are older than me: my elder brother, Behroz, his friends, Rajnish and Ajay. I am going to find a way of getting to know Meera and the Maharani.

I know what sex is. I have watched people do it on the beach. I frig but nothing comes out. I have read a porno magazine. I have seen a girl naked. That time with Sofie Eriksson when I was beaten by Tangama.

I was very young. The Erikssons lived next to the Krishnans in an identical cottage. We used to be friendly with the two girls Sofie and Natalie. Now they have gone to school in Sweden and we only see them during the holidays. They had two nannies, who wore starched blue and white check pinafores, a bit like nurses' uniforms. The nannies were very strict in a Christian way. They never let the girls out of their sight and always spoke to them in English. They looked down on our ayah, a fat south Indian lady called Tangama. Tangama was bold and brassy and loud. She chewed paan heavily laced with white chuna, a limestone mixture that burned a hole through the inside of your mouth. Her lips and teeth were red with betel-nut juice and on the left side of her swarthy cheeks she had a permanent lump which had developed from years of sucking and hoarding the paan. She wore plain saris but was fond of jewelry. I loved the big gold rings and studs she wore in her nose. She had nightmares about thieves and ghosts stealthily removing her gems in the middle of the night. Unlike the Erikssons' nannies, she let us roam and play unattended, but would always materialize miraculously at a moment of danger.

When I was five or six, about the same age as Sofie, we used to play in a sandbox in the Erikssons' tiny garden. We were captivated by the sandbox. Playing in this tiny enclosure was like being in a foreign country. I had never been abroad, but this chest of sand smelled like my father's freshly opened suitcases when he returned from foreign trips. All that sand on the seashore not ten steps away, and yet we craved for an hour of pleasure in this dream-like casket. The sand was soft and fine and light, almost blond, like the curls in Natalie's hair.

It was a breezeless afternoon. The nannies had disappeared into the house to make cups of tea and prepare dinner for Sofie and Natalie. Behroz and I were playing sand castles with the girls: filling the blue pail and turning it over to examine its smooth walls, spading sand out and making holes, pouring a tiny cup of water into the hole, trying to build a wall around the little castle. Behroz, being the eldest, far too old for a sandbox really, was masterminding operations. He said to me, "Stick your foot in that hole." I put my foot in, it was cool and watery. Then he ordered Sofie and Natalie to cover my foot with sand. Sofie enjoyed the game while Natalie toddled around the box gurgling baby words in Swedish.

Natalie was clad only in her white knickers, the rest of us were in shorts. We dragged Natalie onto the floor of the sandpit and started to cover her up with sand. She babbled, wriggled, shrieked, and giggled. We started to tickle her, she kicked and screeched with laughter. The nannies called out from the balcony of the house. "Now what's all that screaming about?" said Rita, the one with the black bun. "I hope you all are behaving yourselves out there. Sofie, make sure you don't throw sand out of the box or into Natalie's eyes."

The frenzy died down for a minute, then the nannies went back to their tea. We resumed our game with Natalie. We covered Natalie's body with sand, then Behroz ordered us to fill up her knickers. Sofie and I spooned spadefuls of sand into Natalie's knickers. Natalie went silent at the sight of her bulging underwear. She surveyed her weighty deformities with puzzlement. The sand trickled down the insides of her legs. "Fill them up again! Fill them up again!" Behroz enthused. I noticed that though he was encouraging us and watching the outcome with amusement, he was taking no part in the proceedings. Sofie and I were piling the sand in again, thrilled with the strange power we were able to wield. Natalie's behavior alternated between delight at our frenetic filling of her pants and trance-like fascination at the runnels of ticklish sand streaming down her legs. Over and over we scooped and poured the sand into her crotch, prized open the elastic on the inside of her legs, and watched with glee as the sand cascaded down. All the while, the two of us were shouting, "Fill her up with sand. Fill her up with sand." Our enthusiasm finally snapped the *elastic on her knickers. Her face crumpled into a frown and thence to an openmouthed wail. The nannies came running out and looked dumbfounded at the sand-filled pants around her ankles. They glared at Behroz and told him to take me home and not to come and play with the girls if we were going to do these "dirty things." Rita cuddled Natalie and Theresa gently chided Sofie. I had the sense that the children of these foreign neighbors of ours were deserving of better treatment than us.*

And then there was the time with Sofie in her narrow bathroom. The time Rita, the pinafored witch, beat me with the flat of her hand and Tangama caned me with a twig. How did I get there? What was I doing inside Sofie's bathroom? All I can see is both of us standing naked on the cold bathroom floor. I am soaping her back, her lovely white back, burnished to the color of honey by the Indian sun. Her little glistening bum. So soft, so smooth, soap suds, Swedish soap suds, a yellow sponge, we never had things like that in our house, a flannel, vivid strawberry red.

I remember getting wet. I remember the tiny size of the bathroom compared to my one at home, cockroach-infested and large enough to sleep in. Gray tiles I recall, specks of white and black and brown, the fogged-up oval mirror above the basin. The more I imagine myself in Sofie's bathroom, the more I can see around me. The towel rail, the white towels, the toilet-cleaning brush behind the loo, the animal stickers on the wall, red teddies and yellow ducks, the foreign toothpaste that tasted like Double Bubble. I was in there with Sofie, who was having a bath. I was getting wet. I took off my shorts to join in with the bucket-bath. I soaped her, up and down her back, round her buttocks, and down her legs, down the backs of her legs. She stopped moving while I did this; for a minute or two she even stopped talking. She just stood there not minding it at all. Soaping her, I was just soaping her, soaping her. She turned around and I ran the laden sponge down her tummy. Her belly button, unlike my little hole, was tight and sticking out like a sweet. I looked down at the little wrinkle of pudgy skin. Horace must have the wrong information—you couldn't fit anything in there. Sofie saw me staring and turned around. What happened next? Someone must have come in. Why didn't I scream when the nanny burst in and started to lash me with her forehand strokes? The pinafored nanny dragging me with that awful clutching, clammy, sure-grasping hand of hers. Dragging me out of that bathroom, Sofie looking on. Why didn't she rescue me, say something, tell the truth, speak up for me? Soaping, I was just soaping.

"Shameless boy!" Rita screamed. "Going in a girl's bathroom all nanga panga! Putting your dirty hands on her. Cheee, cheee, cheee! Shameless goonda. Just you wait. Wait till Mrs. Eriksson gets home. You won't be coming back here again. No, my boy, never again."

She pulled me down the stairs and into the backyard, letting go of me contemptuously when Tangama came into sight, shouting at Tangama in her broken Hindi, telling her to keep me locked up in the house. Tangama, with her paan-drunk bloodshot eyes gleaming, picked up the nearest stick she could find, any old stick lying on the dirty floor, and thwack, thwack, thwacked me over and over again. I was sure some of the neighbors were looking in on my humiliation. Was Sofie watching? Was the Maharani?

12

I sat in my room looking at the different objects around me. The brass door handle, the miniature Dutch doll next to the mirror, my tennis shoes under the bed, the patterned curtains, the ripped pillowcase. If I looked at any of these objects hard enough they turned into something else. This happened in various stages. At first I just stared, with unblinking concentration at the door handle, for instance. I began to see a shadow. Two door handles appeared before my eyes. At this point the image was fragile, it had to be held loosely. The contours became inchoate, illusions flashed by—an iron, a coat hanger, a range of mountains. I liked the range of mountains. My eyes held them in focus. Now and then the backs of the mountains were tinged with the brass of the door handle as if hit by dazzling sunlight.

Looking up from my range of mountains, I saw the Maharani standing in her box-like balcony. A statuesque, resolute, royal figure. Standing there on her balcony with her short curly hair, her stern eyes, her brown cheeks, and her masculine fingers. She gazed into the distance of the afternoon. The trees blew their breeze at her. She seemed to be smiling. She was wearing a short-sleeved, sky-blue man's shirt that hung loosely around her torso. She stood still, without apparent purpose, listless, unharried. And then, as if this were a scene from a film, she waved, she waved again, perhaps knowing that I was nervous. I went over to the window and stepped out onto the narrow balcony.

"I can see you reading in the night," she said.

"I know," I answered. "I don't like the curtains." There was a gap in our conversation which she made no attempt to fill. "I see Molly and Scotty going for their walk," I said. She seemed unimpressed. I divined that this might be the end of our encounter. She was looking at something in the trees. Then, with majestic abruptness, she beckoned. "Come over and see me." Not so much a request as an order. For the Maharani, the distinction did not exist.

"How do I come?" I asked.

She laughed, showing her teeth. "Arre, just jump over the wall and walk round here," she said, pointing me to the back of the house, "and then ask one of the servants to bring you up. Savant or Bibi should be there."

I sprinted out of my room taking the steps two at a time, my bare feet thudding on the wooden planks. As I ducked under the banister and dropped onto the marble floor, I remembered that, as usual, I was without a shirt. "The Maharani won't be used to it, I'd better show her some respect," I thought. But I carried on regardless. That's what I'm like. I think of a good reason to do something, and then I don't do it.

I climbed over the three-foot wall, rounded and friendly at the top, and circled the pink mansion from the left. At the back of the house I passed the servants' quarters. From my bedroom I had seen the Maharani's neat-limbed Maharashtrian servants clamber in and out of their rooms through the windows. A couple of disused wooden crates served as makeshift steps. Half an acre of rank vegetation grew from the rear of the house down to the main Juhu road. On one side of this unkempt kitchen garden was a tarmacked lane that joined up with the one that encircled the house. A rickety gate at the bottom of this road kept trespassers out. I walked slowly, hoping to be spotted by a helpful servant. The structure at the back was similar to that at the front of the building. A porch in the center with three sets of windows on either side. A dull-green Morris Minor stood in the driveway. Apart from the idle cawing of crows, an afternoon stillness hung about the place. On one side of the porch the windows were firmly shut, layers of dust had settled on the panes, but on the far side they lay wide open. A set of smooth steps led up to one of these rooms. I ascended them and entered gingerly a room that could be a kitchen. It had a stone floor, a little tiled enclosure with an old-fashioned tap, a pump-up kerosene stove, and a few pots and pans high on a shelf. I couldn't see any point in calling out: it was obvious no one was about.

The next room was narrow with a table and a wooden cupboard with glass-fronted doors. Inside it were ordinary plates, cups, saucers, and bowls. I saw bottles of pickle on one shelf. In the dining room my eyes lit on two large fridges. The height of luxury. My mother would never countenance such unnecessary expense. In one corner was a small square table with a faded chessboard design on top, and three wooden chairs. The room extended to the left into a much larger space in the center of which was an enormous rectangular dining table, around which at least twenty guests could be seated. A white tablecloth covered it. All along the walls of this room were glass-fronted cupboards with ornamental silver, cut-glass bowls, and porcelain crockery.

I could hear the squawking of parrots coming from somewhere inside the house. A cat poked its head round the door and looked at me quizzically. I didn't know what to do with cats. I wasn't sure I liked them. I surveyed the vast dining room. Where should I go next? Through the next door? Should I go back? Shout out somebody's name? I worried that I would be caught standing in the middle of this empty room clad only in my shorts. And there were the dogs, who didn't know me, the Alsatians who were trained to bite.

Disoriented in these deserted rooms, I searched for clues to the lives of their inhabitants. After all these months of imagining, of fantasies about the Maharani, about Meera, of watching them in the early hours of the morning and last thing at night, I was at last in their house, picturing their lives through their furniture. I had visions of royal banquets on the long dining table, served up by liveried servants: sumptuous Rajasthani dishes steaming forth, the Maharani's beautiful daughters sitting before me, in between us a leg of lamb baked in the hot spices of the desert. The spices make my eyes water, while the gorgeous Meera strokes my instep with the sole of her foot. The Rani sits at the head of the table presiding over the meal.

My reverie was broken by the sound of scuttling claws descending the stairs. A hefty Alsatian loped into the room. I could tell by its lazy walk that it was not awake to my presence. I had to make a quick decision whether to flee the spot or stand my ground. Before I could move, the dog snagged on my alien scent. It lifted its head, perplexed for an instant, then it bounded toward me, barking. Benumbed but not afraid, I held it in my stare. Three feet away from me the brute held back. It growled and sniffed the air. Then it began its woof again. "Jilly! Stop that. Stop making such a racket. You silly girl," a deep voice called from the other side of the door.

The owner of the voice came striding into the room surrounded at her rubber-slippered feet by a host of yapping

Pekinese and chihuahuas. Her gray-haired companion followed softly behind her. "Hello, Cyrus. Wasn't there anyone to show you the way?" How did she know my name? "Those damn servants. They must be all sleeping in their kholis. Anyway, come upstairs and I'll ring for them and get you something to drink." She shooed the dogs away and I followed her up the stairs, through a couple of empty rooms that smelled of shit, into her bedroom.

I sat down.

"Have you told your mother you're coming here?" she asked.

"No, I don't think she's at home," I answered lightly. Along the wall to my right were two huge fish tanks. A plastic boy was standing amongst the goldfish peeing air bubbles into the water.

"How does he do that?" I said, moving up to the tank.

She explained that it only had a decorative purpose.

"What's that round fish called?" I asked, pointing to a large orange and turquoise chap.

"That's called a discus, because its shape is similar to the discus that athletes throw."

"I know, my mother used to throw the javelin. She came first in the Maharashtra junior competition," I boasted. "And what about that long black fish with the funny whiskers?"

"The one with the silver spots? That's a catfish. It's also known as a pictus," answered the Maharani.

"How do these fish breathe in the water? What do you feed them? Do they ever fight with one another?"

I asked a stream of questions, partly from nerves and partly wanting to please her with my curiosity. She answered patiently. Her companion smiled with benign amusement but did not speak.

"How many dogs do you have? Have you always had so many? You had forty-two dogs before! Fourteen different breeds. Now you have more cats than dogs. Oh, I see. What's the difference between Siamese cats and Persian cats? How come they can jump so high and dogs cannot? Where do you get all these dogs and cats? What do you do with their babies?"

Most adults answer questions out of a sense of duty to the young. They tend to betray lack of interest or mild irritation. This did not occur with my friend the Maharani. On rare occasions when she thought the question too boring or too personal, she gracefully sidestepped the topic or introduced something equally interesting into the conversation. Sometimes I got the impression that no one had asked her these questions before. She showed genuine enthusiasm for our exchanges.

"Do you always smoke these cigarettes?" I asked as she tapped out another fag from the green and white softpack.

"Yes, I like the menthol taste."

"Where do you get them from?"

"I have a man near Gwalior Tank, and if he doesn't have any fresh ones, I go to another fellow in Churchgate. If I'm lucky, someone will get me a carton from the duty free when they come back from abroad."

Legally, foreign cigarettes, like other foreign products, were banned from sale in India. But there were paanwallahs and small cigarette shops everywhere that stocked smuggled goods. Mystique surrounded these imported items. They looked so bright, smelled so new. I used to peer at the cigarette advertisements in *Time, Newsweek,* and *Life*: Marlboro men on their horses, women smoking Virginia Slims in Victorian underwear, with the logo, "You've come a long way, baby!" and Salem girls, dark-haired, blue-jeaned, healthy women, romping around with some tanned muscular jocks. The women laughed while training a hose pipe on the men. These were clean, fresh, fun-loving, minty-breathed Americans. I stared intently at these modern gods, trying to catch every detail and motion of their bodies. White, foreign, but so within reach on the page. One day, I told myself, I would be there. In those green New England woods in the background of the picture. With my striped shirt and my colored backpack, gamboling with that dark-haired girl who looks like Ali Mac-Graw and smoking Salem cigarettes. In the meantime I honed my knowledge of which paanwallah in Bombay stocked the freshest brand of smuggled American fags.

"Acha, now you stay there. I'll show you something," said the Maharani suddenly. She rose off her haunches like no ordinary person. Jimmy Connors had a way of getting up from a cross-legged position without using his hands, but the Maharani made his effort look gormless. She rocked to one side, rolled her hips forward, and in a trice was on her feet and holding the front of her wraparound lungi in her hand to avoid tripping over. There was no hint of effort, no jerk or hesitation. Just one fluid propelling movement, like a drake drifting toward the bank. She put her feet carefully into a pair of clean blue and white Bata rubber slippers waiting for her at the edge of the carpet. Then she went to the walled cupboard at the far end of the room. She asked for the keys and Papu, her companion, produced them. My eager eyes swept over the contents of the open cupboard. Rows of toilet paper, green and white cartons of Salem, neat piles of clean sheets and towels, a small safe, pink and red saris. She pulled out a couple of square objects covered in white muslin. I hoped for a present. Chocolates, sweets, anything edible would do. She unwrapped the muslin carefully. Two photo albums were uncovered, bound in black. She opened one of the albums onto her folded legs: black and white photographs stuck on dark sugar-paper pages. They reminded me of the pictures of my parents' honeymoon. Their arrangement was immaculate, each photo dated and annotated in a flourishing hand.

I jabbed my finger at one of the photographs and started to ask a question. Her voice stopped me.

"Uh-huh," she said, shaking her head. "Don't touch the pictures, Cyrus." There was something instantly chilling in even her tiniest remonstrance. I shrank back.

This was not a quick survey of her life through pictures. She intended to show me particular shots of her childhood. There was a rather stately one of her with her mother. A wan look in her mother's eyes, a mischievous glow on the child's round face. I marveled at a snap of her aged six or seven with her arm around the neck of a leopard.

"That was the one whose ear I bit. Chinky he was called. There were two of them, but one had to be shot very early. There," she said, opening a new page of the album. "That's Meherangarh, the palace where I grew up."

"Which, which one?" I asked excitedly. She pointed at a picture, larger than the usual size. It showed the front of a vast building with an ornate front, little windows and turrets, and a dome at the top.

"How many rooms in the palace?" I asked.

"More than a hundred. There must have been at least twenty rooms for guests. But many were not used. When we played hide and seek as children we would often get completely lost." She closed the album with a wry smile. I wanted to see more pictures. I wanted to ask more questions. But I had an instinctive sense that this was the time to stop. Papu wrapped the muslin round the albums and the Maharani asked for the time, even though I could see a watch on her wrist. She said something about Meera. They spoke in Marwari, a language of Rajasthan that I couldn't understand. You can always tell when someone is losing interest in you. I should have left, but I had a tendency to overstay my welcome. I sat there patiently, not saying very much. I was good at that. She looked at me from the corner of her left eye. Hardly a raised eyebrow, but the look was crystalline. She was amused by my temerity. This was a woman, so she told me, who when eight years old was playfully nuzzled by a leopard who lived in the palace. Her response was to grab its ear and bite a chunk off the end. She knew about insouciance, she knew about daring. She had shot big game and flown small-sized planes. She had been to school in Switzerland and knew how to race down mountains on a pair of skis. This woman, who sat upright on a wine-red carpet in her airy room by the edge of the sea, counting the hours with Salem cigarettes, this same woman had once been the queen of a vast domain.

13

A jingle of anklets announced the approach of one of the Maharani's daughters. It was Meera. She stood at the door with her head slightly bowed. She was dressed in green. A dark green cotton sari and a pale tight-fitting blouse. She came toward the now imperious Maharani, touched her feet, mumbled "Hukum," and receded to one side of the room. The lightness had vanished from the face of the Maharani. In its place was something stern.

Out of the corner of her eye she saw me looking wide-eyed at Meera. "I asked Cyrus over," she said to her. "You know him, don't you?" Meera lifted her eyes from the red carpet and looked at me, sitting there cross-legged on the floor next to the Maharani. "Hukum. I've seen him in his bedroom and I've seen him . . . I've seen him near to the Vermas' house." This was a slip: the Maharani did not like Meera mixing with the Verma boys.

Later on I learned why Meera kept her head bowed in the

presence of the Maharani. It was seen as an act of insubordination to look the Maharani in the eye, behavior that could result in an immediate beating, though this would never happen whilst I was around. It was an offense which, try as she might to avoid it, Meera often found herself committing. She had a curious way of fixing people with her black eyes, from whose stare there was no hiding. She spoke to the Maharani with the necessary formality, but there was a piggish note of defiance that caused her to be beaten far more frequently than her adopted sisters. And when the others were thrashed, with a hockey stick on occasion, they yelled with anguish while Meera remained resolutely dumb. This infuriated the Maharani. Like D'Mello, my hated Vice-Principal, she would double the strength of her strokes to try and drag a response from her silent victim. Both the Maharani and D'Mello required remorse; when they didn't get it, they beat and beat and beat. It seemed to me that all these adults were after was tears and sadness. Toothing away at their hearts was a sadness of their own which they dare not admit to, a pain they could expiate only by flogging someone. There was one lesson to be learned by the victim: display the correct emotion at the right time. Say thank you when someone gives you a present, cry when you are beaten. Even though the sight of an adult thrown into angry convulsions by having to whip some little boy could produce in the victim uncontrollable fits of laughter.

Like the time Glen Lobo, Rajiv Munshi, and I were summoned to D'Mello's office. I can't remember what we were meant to have done. Glen was a tall, thick-set lad, Anglo-Indian like Horace. He had honey-colored hair and a beautiful husky voice that ranged from falsetto crying to baritone shouts.

D'Mello had been promoted to Principal for a spell of four months and he had a new weapon: a leather horsewhip with a little thong at one end which he used to finger while he talked to you. On the way to the office Glen was telling us about his plan to pad his shorts with exercise books. I suggested a hardcover notebook.

As soon as we were inside D'Mello's office, Glen began pleading. "Please, sir. Pleeeeze, sir. Just listen to me for one second, sir. I promise, sir, on God's name, on my mother's name, sir. I'm begging you, sir, please don't hit me." His voice climbed higher and higher, tears rolled down his face as down a misty windowpane, he bent his knees and bowed his body. It was ham acting of the highest order. Rajiv recognized that it would be sensible to follow suit and started his own variety of bleating. "One last chance, sir. Never again, sir. I admit I made a terrible mistake. You can give me a pink card but please don't hit me, sir."

My laughter came bursting out like a cataract. But I managed to hide it by covering my face and spluttering. I would be caned to death if my amusement were discovered, just when D'Mello had reduced my friends to gibbering supplicants. He knew me well by now and didn't expect any show of emotion. Turning to Glen, with a knife-like smile he said, "I don't like you. You tell lies. I know your sort—dishonest boys, telling me lies. Bend down, now, bend down, over here."

"Please, sir, please don't do it. I'll do anything for you. I'll never do it again, sir," howled Glen.

D'Mello raised his voice and his face darkened. "Bend down, my son, or you will get three extra strokes." The laughter was breaking out of me again, even though the humor had ebbed away as I noted Glen's genuine frenzy. He moaned as the whip came down on his backside. At the point of contact he threw himself into the air clutching the seat of his shorts, then tearing at his face with his hands. He gasped for air and between each gasp came more oohs and aahs: I'm not sure how D'Mello got him to bend down again, but after the second blow Glen turned around, limbs flailing, and accosted the priest with his grief. "No more!" he threatened. "I can't take it anymore. You can't hit me like this." There was a new note of anger in his voice. Even D'Mello found it hard to proceed.

That scene has always been dominated, for me, by laughter at the sight of Rajiv and Glen's absurd histrionics, at the challenge to D'Mello's authority from Glen's admirable outburst of rage. But Meera and her sisters, Mr. Krishnan and his sons, their defiant silences and yelps of agony were a different matter. Their pain was that of some monsoon river overflowing its banks. I think of an uncontainable misery that pours from person to person, the need for humiliations to be transmitted from adult to child. Like that time on the Krishnans' farm in Kerala.

I was playing with Sushil in the bathroom. We had all come back from a long walk and were covered in hillside dust. There were stainless-steel buckets of hot and cold water on the stone floor. Water was rationed. We soaped ourselves thoroughly and then began to pour water onto each other to rinse ourselves off. It turned into a splashing game. Sushil warned me we would be in trouble if we wet the bathroom floor—he warned me but he kept on playing. Soon there was water everywhere and the soap was still on our bodies. The noise attracted his mother, who came in and started to slap Sushil all over his face and head and back. He whinnied, "Amma! Amma! Amma!" I stood there wishing she would hit me too. But instead she turned on me with vicious satisfaction. "It's all your fault. You knew he would get beaten. You made him get beaten. This is not your house, you know, where you can waste water whenever you like. Look, look how you have made my son cry."

That time the glum-faced Mrs. Krishnan managed, with one hand, to spread her misery in two directions.

"SEND UP some tea with biscuits," the Maharani ordered Meera, "and some of that fruit cake that Perin Aunty sent."

"Hukum," responded Meera.

"And don't forget to take the medicines down for Choki and Molly. Make sure you see what they eat and if they do any stool outside, examine it properly. Check on Timmy's wound. I don't want it going septic."

"Hukum. Shall I send Babu Mali up to clean the cages?" The Maharani nodded, a look passed between her and Meera. "You want to come down and have a Coke, Cyrus?" Meera said in a kind voice. "Come on, come and help me take the dogs out."

I followed her down the stairs. The dogs were bundling past us. I couldn't think of anything to say. When we got to the bottom of the stairs she turned left into the room with the big dining table and her character changed abruptly. She shouted for the servants, opened cupboards, threw the dog bowls on the floor, slammed a Coke in front of me, rushed in and out of the kitchen, grabbed Rufus, the golden retriever, by the scruff and spooned some red liquid into his mouth. "Swallow it you stupid mutt! Babu Mali!" she yelled. "Babu Mali! Where is that clown?" A tiny man wearing blue shorts and a mischievous grin came jogging into the room. "What are you smiling for? Go and get the food for the fucking dogs!" Another servant, the end of her sari tucked round her waist, came bustling in. Meera asked her, "What have you made for dinner tonight? Same old rubbish, I expect. Dal, bhat, and egg bhurji." The woman sniggered and her eyes twinkled. "I only make what you ask me to make," she said.

Tea was ordered for the Maharani. Dog food was ladled out into tin bowls on the floor. The room stank of boiling bones. The big dogs sucked and scraped and gorged, their noses plunging in and out of the brown slop. The sausage dogs, of which there were at least five, ate with restraint whilst the miniature dogs sniffed with disdain at the mess they were being offered. Meera dropped down onto her seat, jammed between the chessboard table and the cupboard. In front of her was a loaf of sliced white bread, a bottle of mango pickle, and a chipped plate. On the plate she laid a slice of bread, spooning some of the oily green mango bits onto its absorbent surface. She responded to my questions with the irritation of someone too busy to answer idle inquiries. I could remain if I wanted to or go home. She didn't care. I sat on one of the dining-room chairs, watching as she dragged her teeth across the tart kernel of the raw fruit, and sipped my Coke.

14

Now I'd found my spot beside Meera, I wasn't going to let go. I could be tenacious when I wanted to. I didn't acknowledge her displays of contempt. I never thought about the consequences any more than I did when I bunked off lessons and crossed the length of the city to visit an unknown cinema.

When I got home from school I would change as fast as I could and rush over to see the Maharani. We sat and talked and I told her all my latest news. Then Meera came home from college and I clung to her like a limpet while she fed and walked the dogs. As the evening wore on, I would most likely go over to the Krishnans' just in time for dinner. Later, under cover of darkness, I would jump over their wall and into the Vermas' tiny garden. Mr. Verma had normally had a few drinks by then and the whole family would be in cheerful mood. Food was served after nine. I would join them at the table.

Wherever I was, regardless of plans, if one of my neighbors asked me whether I wanted to go out with them, to the movies, to visit their friends, into town for a meal, even on a holiday, I always said yes. Sometimes I smiled demurely to cover my embarrassment, sometimes I feigned reluctance and hung my head to one side as if considering their invitation. "Actually, I have to go and do my homework, but . . . actually, I wouldn't mind coming to the film," or, "Actually, I'm really full, but . . . maybe I'll try just a little bit of that fish. I've never had it before."

During this period of my life I was often in my neighbors' houses for eight hours at a stretch. They worried about what my parents would think and sometimes forced me to phone home to let them know where I was. My parents were working or busy enjoying themselves, and had got used to the fact that I was happily ensconced in one of my friends' houses. My neighbors thought that if they said, "You're welcome to come with us as long as you ask your parents for permission," this would settle the affair. For some years they remained unaware that my parents were frequently not at home and that all I had to do was tell our servant, Bhagwan, I was going out for the next few hours. If he said no, I would interpret this as yes, and return to my friends with a beaming smile. Complications arose, but I was never afraid of a bit of scolding or shouting. D'Mello's cane had inured me to any subsidiary stricture.

On occasion, though, when I had to get my parents' permission, I engineered these communications in subtle ways. For example, when Mr. Krishnan succumbed to the cajoling of his children and invited me on their family's annual holiday to his mother's farm in Kerala, I sought the right moment to approach my parents with my request. They had to agree to my being away for six weeks and missing four days of school. The journey was long: forty-five hours on a train and a half day's bus ride at the end. The farm was remote. The Krishnans had told me about their life there: hunting and camping in the woods, eating the birds that were shot on expeditions, cooked in special ways by their grandmother, fishing and swimming in the nearby lake, long treks into the leopard-infested hills.

After dinner one night I clambered onto my mother's lap, put my arm around her neck, and snuggled up. It was one of those rare occasions when the whole family was sitting together round the table. "Mummy," I said, whilst I stroked her hair and kissed her cheek.

"What is it, my darling? You've become so heavy." She jogged me up and down on her lap. "You're no more a baby, you know. Hah, Minoo are we going to dinner on Monday at the Trivedis' or not? I don't really want to go, they always serve dinner so late."

"Mummy, why do you always have Cyrus on your lap? You never let me sit your lap," complained my sister.

"Come on, Shenny. You come and sit on my lap, and then you must go to bed," my father said. "You better decide Mehroo. I'm quite happy to have a few nights in. I'll have to work late on Monday, so I could meet you there straight from work."

"You're always going out," I moaned. "You never want to stay at home with us."

"We're going to Panvel on Saturday. We'll be together the whole day."

"Can we stop at that biryani place?" said Behroz.

"No, that's in Taloja, on the way to Poona," said my father. "We better ask the cook to make us sandwiches for the journey."

"If there are ghats on the way," giggled Adi, "we better remember to give Shenny travel pills, otherwise she'll be sick all over us." My brother knew there were no steep roads on the way to Panvel. He got the response he was looking for.

"Shut up. You stupid boy. You're the one who needs pills.

You're the one who takes those brain tablets every morning," she said, pointing to a yellow and red bottle on the table.

"Now stop it!" said my mother. "I've told you not to joke with Adi about that. Those are iron tablets, not brain pills." The cook came in through the swinging door. Adi looked crestfallen. Just then my mother seemed to me the most beautiful woman in the world. Her rich black hair, her smile, the warm brown arms with which she encircled my waist, the tilt of her neck, and the light in her eyes. These were ecstatic moments: sitting on my mother's lap, watching her talk, knowing that an evening of plea-sure was spread out before me in the shape of those visits to neighbors, the food, the conversation late into the night.

Whilst discussing plans with my father and the cook, my mother spooned out the dirt from under my nails with her thumbnail and flicked it away. She checked the cook's account book, talked to him about the success and failure of dishes pre-pared in the last week, and canvassed opinion from all of us on what we should eat the next day. The cook stood quietly in his food-splattered apron and his narrow white trousers, his face passive: like an ancient hillside, it had deep wrinkles running down it. He nodded or shook his head from time to time when we shouted for each other's attention. Once my sister threw a sil-ver spoon across the table at me; it missed the target and hit the cook on his balding brow. Blood poured, but the barua spoke not a word.

These after-dinner conversations, with the cook standing by, were a family ritual that made sense of our lives. There were end-less arguments about food: the height and consistency of the cheese soufflé, the hotness and flavor of the pulao, the stickiness of the meringue gateaux, the rising price of mutton, the proper way to cook spaghetti. "When will the cook learn to make fish saas the way Granny makes it?" my elder brother would ask.

"He'll never learn from her, because Granny refuses to tell

him any of her cooking secrets," my mother would answer. "I've told her so many times but she just won't listen."

"But then a lot of great chefs are like that," my father would respond. "They can make elaborate dishes but they can never write down the recipes."

There were discussions about school reports, about tennis matches—who could beat whom—about holidays—where we should go as a family—about home improvements—when the holes in the roof were going to be fixed. The voices rose, simultaneous but separate spats developed between parts of the family and then tessellated into one large volley of words. Everyone was in love: we were in love with each other, but also with the sound of our own voices. Visitors sat openmouthed at our thunderous decibels. Some of them enjoyed the spectacle and came back for more, others left shaking. When our emotions got the better of us there was violence, bloodletting, and tears. Food was overturned, chairs thrown back, cutlery flung. Once a placatory kiss my mother tried to plant on Adi's cheek turned into a vicious bite, the marks lasting for months.

All through this the cook stood in his customary position, in the corner by the door, between my parents, hands folded behind his back. His notebook lay open in front of my mother, the accounts for the day neatly laid out on a fresh page. It was the same sort of exercise book—carrying on its cover Rashna, the smiling rosy-cheeked schoolgirl with long eyelashes and white skin—that I used to record the story of my life. And the same book lay in the slim wooden drawer behind the desk in my father's study.

The book lay open on the edge of the table, the date written large at the top of the page: 16 June 1972. While my mother dissected these accounts with the cook, Adi, my brother, in need of some attention, was pulling and pinching my sister's sleeve. She in turn was trying to ignore him and attract my father. "Shenny,

Shenny," teased Adi. "Shall I tell what you were doing with the pictures in Mummy's drawer? Shall I tell Mummy, hah?"

Shenaz turned in his direction, twisted a lump of his fleshy arm in her fingers, and dealt him a swift punch on the back with her tiny fist. Adi squealed. "Aaiiii, you mad girl. Look what you have done. How can she behave like that, Mummy?" He reached out and tried to pinch her back. She pulled away and started taunting him with her most hurtful chant. "Brain pills, brain pills, brain pills." Soon I joined in. Adi sat there seething. "Stop teasing Adi!" my mother said. "It's very unfair of you two to gang up on him like that. So, anyway, Minoo, if we can't have Urmila and Ravi Seth on Saturday, we'll be left with thirteen at the table and foreigners don't like to sit thirteen at the table."

"Brain pills, brain pills, mad boy, brain pills," my sister and I chanted. I could see Adi's face crumple into a tablecloth of pain. I had seen that look before. He leapt up from his seat, frenzied and tearful. "I'm not mad . . . I don't take brain pills." He flung himself at Shenaz. His hands blundered into her thick black hair; she wailed and tried to dig her nails into his arm. My father intervened. Both Adi and Shenaz were crying hysterically, my sister in huge sobs, punctuated by a long whine, like a steam train leaving the station.

"Shenaz is very tired. She should have been taken to bed a long time ago," said my mother in exasperation. "Where is that Tangama?" Our ayah arrived as if she had heard the question. She took Shenaz in her arms and cuddled her. "Don't cry," she said. "Don't be silly. Everything will be all right." Then, to my brother she pleaded, "Arre baba, why do you hit your sister? She is only a small girl."

"But Shenaz shouldn't tease him like that," my mother said. "You know it's wrong to make fun of him and call him mad and all that." This brought forth another bout of crying from my sister. "You always take his side, just because he's your son." My mother sniggered involuntarily. "All right, all right, don't cry now. Come and give me a kiss goodnight."

"You're always horrible to me," cried Shenaz, declining her offer.

Fixed to my mother's lap, I watched Tangama take Shenaz to bed. The cook was given his latest orders and my father handed him the money for the next day's shopping. Adi and Nasli sloped off to play carom and Behroz left to meet Rajnish Verma. As the cutlery was being cleared from the table and the cook took his leave, I was left on my own with my mother and father. It seemed so quiet after the commotion of the last hour. The rosewood table was empty. Outside, the air was murky. The almond tree that bore no fruit stood serene in the darkness, its flat veined leaves unruffled by the breezeless night.

I kissed my mother on the cheek, breathing in her lightly perfumed skin. With my arm around her neck, I looked over at my father's broad face. "I'm going to marry my mother," I vowed. My mother laughed, "You can't marry your mother. What about your father?"

"One day he'll go away somewhere and then I'll marry you. I don't care what anyone says." I looked over triumphantly at my father, who was only half paying attention. He had a newspaper in his hand and was scanning the pages.

"Listen to what your son is saying, Minoo. He says he wants to marry his mother, like Oedipus. You're a crazy boy, you are." She gave me a squeeze. "My little Oedipus, that's what you are. You know who Oedipus was, hah?" I shook my head. "He was the one who killed his father so he could marry his mother."

"That's what I want to do!"

"Oedipus or no Oedipus, I'm going to bed," said my father.

"Mummy," I said. "Can I go with the Krishnans to Kerala for the holidays?"

"With the Krishnans to Kerala? What do you mean? Have

they invited you? You've never mentioned this before," said my mother.

"Mr. Krishnan asked me. It's his mother's farm and they go every year. They want me to ask your permission."

"How long are they going for?"

"Six weeks."

"That's far too long," my mother said.

"Why, they'll look after me properly. I really want to go, Mummy."

"Let's see, we need to talk about it properly. Minoo, what do you think?"

"It could be a good idea, but we need to ask Mr. Krishnan if he's serious. Maybe Cyrus can go for two or three weeks. Anyway, we'll discuss it later. It's way past your bedtime now. Off you go."

I jumped off my mother's lap and gave my father a peck on his stubbly cheek. That was enough. The seed had been planted. The details would sort themselves out later. That night I lay in bed and imagined bright green forests, hills crawling with leopards, partridges shot and transformed into spicy curry by the able hands of Mr. Krishnan's mother.

15

I lay in bed with no clothes on. An air-conditioned breeze floated out of the vents on one side of the wall. The curtains were drawn, my pajamas strewn on the floor. The sheets swaddled my body, the weight of the blanket tucked in at the sides kept me warm. I let my hands rove over my hairless chest, pulling my stomach in, running the tips of my fingers against the outlines of my ribs. How many times could I do it in one night? Three had been the limit so far. Do other children my age do this? Do they rub their cocks against the hard mattress and imagine congress with a woman? I recalled broaching the subject with my cousin Jehangir. He told me he had first discovered the pleasures of masturbation by rubbing the bristles of his toothbrush against the tip of his penis.

I thought of Meera. I could see her in her bathroom in the morning. I imagined her with one leg propped up against the windowsill shaving her calf. I imagined my cheek resting on her thigh. I saw everything. The black panties on the floor, the protruding navel, the surprising bulge of stomach, her nipples quivering like the tops of medicine droppers, and her pubic hair. I run my hand through this dankly odorous mat of curls, unfurling the knots.

I imagined her calling to me, from the edge of her compound. I slide open my sister's bedroom window and see her standing in the light from the sea. The night is wet. I skip down the branches of my almond tree. All the malice she feels against me is drained out of her face. "I need to get out of here," she says, climbing over the wall. I notice the inside of her thigh. I help her up the tree, watching her every movement from behind. She enters the room through the window, her long black hair falling down her back. She sits on the edge of the bed. I kiss her around the neck. Something wet sprayed onto my stomach. I breathed out with shock. This was the first time I had had an emission.

Meera evaporated into the darkness. The puny stiffness in my hand turned to mush. My body found its curve in the sheets. I closed my eyes in an effort to bring Meera back to where she was sitting on the edge of the bed. I tried to forget the damp around my waist. My hand moved, but my brain refused to provide the desired pictures. Perhaps if I backtracked a little to the build-up. Once more, I am helping Meera up the tree. This time I notice her fat ankles as she climbs, my finger catches on a splinter and blood runs out. I look again for the inside of her thigh, her flowery nightdress. I kept losing the focus of my fantasy and my penis remained resolutely limp in my hand.

Then I heard the bedroom door squeak. Someone was pushing it open. We have had burglars come into the house at night. I shut my eyes and pretended to be asleep while thinking of the embarrassment of this pretense, should the thief attack me.

Nakedness added to my anxiety. I turned onto my stomach. I could tell the person was moving over to where my sister was sleeping. I sneaked a peek and recognized the shape of my father's head. He pulled the blankets over her shoulders and whispered, "Sleep well, my darling little girl, sleep well." Then he approached my bed. I lay still, fearful that he might uncover my nakedness. "Cyrus," he said softly. "Are you sleeping?" He sat down on the bed. I wondered what time it was. I could hear the distant voices of the servants talking outside the kitchen. With his fingers, my father combed back the hair that fell around my face. I felt like a bird ruffled by the wind. He spoke soothing words in a disembodied voice, "Sleep tight, kiddo, my tough cookie, my little badmaash, rascal that you are. How fast you run at tennis, huh? All that chasing after the ball must make you very tired."

I could tell he knew I was only half asleep. I noticed a far-away quality in his voice, a bit like the voice I used when I talked to myself. I imagined his eyes were closed like mine, in contemplation. The hand he laid on my head was also a balm for his own troubled life.

There was trouble in my father's life. For years his past had lurked underground. Now it was beginning to claw its way to the surface. An old ugliness was dragging him down, forcing him to revisit his former lives: the death of his father at the age of nine, the years spent in an orphanage in Poona, the poverty of his mother, his unsuccessful marriage, his deceptions, his affairs, the two daughters he had abandoned.

I remembered a black and white picture of his father dressed in naval uniform, looking proud and austere, the father who had taught him to love ships and worship Keats, the man who had collected more than a hundred volumes of the poems and letters. The lowly sailor who knew every poem by heart, who visited Keats's house in Hampstead whenever his ship docked on the

English coast, who loved English literature and died too young. I thought of my father's favorite lines of poetry:

> *My heart aches, and a drowsy numbness pains*
> *My sense, as though of hemlock I had drunk,*
> *Or emptied some dull opiate to the drains*
> *One minute past, and Lethe-wards had sunk.*

Yes, he would like to forget, to drain away the sins, to keep them hidden, the way they had stayed for so long.

But it was all cracking open in the late hours of the night. There were screams from my parents' bedroom. Screams only a wife could utter. There were other noises. Noises of objects being broken. Crouched outside their door with my mouth open, I heard it all.

"How could you be so heartless? How could you?" my mother wailed. "After all these years." My father howled like a tree lashed by a tornado as my mother tore into him with her fists, her nails, her teeth, her tennis-playing arms. "What a bitch!" I heard her say, hoarsely. "What a low-down Punjabi bitch!" I was shocked to hear her swear. "You bastaaard!" Every word threatened to split her body in two. It was as if she were willing herself to implode, to unleash something uncontrollable, cataclysmic. It made me think of those apocalyptic weapons stowed away by Hindu gods for the ultimate battle. I wanted to put such a weapon in my mother's hand. "Ten years of marriage ruined by that ugly twopenny cow-faced air hostess. I should have known not to trust you. You were always like that. And now, you dare to tell me that I have to change!" Then came the sound of pounding, struggling; someone fell on the floor. My father's stricken voice, "Mehroo, Mehroo, Mehroo!"

I stood outside in my pajamas, not knowing whether to run back to my room or barge into the maelstrom. My parents had always had arguments. We'd got used to their duels. But I had never heard my mother scream like this, and I had heard her scream a lot. This wasn't the last time either; night after night this war raged on. My sister, Shenaz, was too frightened to get out of bed, though the voices kept us both awake. When I got back to our room she would ask, "What's going on?"

"They're still fighting," I would answer and pull the sheets over my shoulders.

MY FATHER'S hand was still there, it rubbed over my blanket. It half awoke me from my vision. It spoke of hurt and doubt, and of his indiscretions. His fling in Bangkok with Asha, the "Punjabi bitch," with Rosie, his long-legged Anglo-Indian assistant, and that final peccadillo with the beautiful Italian in her husband's study. Now Mehroo was seeing another man. He could see the telltale signs in her eyes and on her cheeks. Thinking of them together juddered his neck. His temples bulged.

I WAS WAITING outside the tennis courts. The setting sun sent flames of red and orange across the sky. My mother was in the changing rooms having a shower. She often disappeared for ages, emerging from the curtained doorway in a great hurry to get home. I was playing with my walnut-sized rubber-solution ball, bouncing it against the wall of the dressing room, when I saw my father coming down the cement path, striding toward me in his impeccable dark suit and his wide-striped blue and gold tie, an agitated expression on his face. He kissed me with his light evening stubble and asked where Mummy was. I said she was in the ladies' dressing room. He went off to look for her and returned a few minutes later with furrowed brow. He took me by the hand tightly as we walked toward the car park. I was excited because I knew he had brought the Herald with the soft-top turned down. I suggested places we could look for my mother.

His grip was hurting me but I dared not mention it. I dragged after him as he searched different areas of the club. All the time I sensed a heat rising in his face.

We ended up at the swimming pool. "But Dad," I said. "She never goes to the pool." None of us ever went to the pool. He wasn't listening. He pulled me toward the covered area under which people sat eating snacks and drinking tea. He seemed to know where he was going. The next thing I saw was my mother sitting in her tennis skirt talking to a gaunt gray-haired man. My father must have seen them before me. We got to within five feet. They saw us. "Mehroo, we're going." His voice was curt. The man next to my mum looked pale. There was a white pot of tea and some cups and saucers on the table. I remember wondering if they were eating sandwiches. My mother leapt out of her chair, a smile withering on her face; my father whipped around, holding me firmly all the while, and we strode away from her. "Minoo! Minoo, wait!" she called. "Listen to me. You don't understand . . . I was only talking." She stuttered as she chased after us. My father, grim, stony, silent, my mother babbling plaintive words. "I didn't know you were coming, Minoo. I was just having a cup of tea . . . just talking, that's all." Words, words, words. I was hearing things I couldn't understand. I wanted to stop them both and ask for an explanation. I wanted to enjoy my drive home in the open-top car.

I got into the tiny backseat. My parents sat silently in the front. My father drove recklessly down the left lane squeezing past the cars on his right, pedestrians jumped back onto the pavement. There were shouts of surprise and anger. We turned right into Marine Drive. The fluorescent street lamps of the famous Queen's Necklace had just been turned on. My mother's jaw was trembling with the emotions she could no longer keep in. "I told you what would happen," she cried. "I told you that if you went on behaving the way you were, then someday I would also have to go and find someone else. What can I do? What do you want me to do?" I wished she wouldn't shout so loud. People were looking at us. "I'm not one of those servile wives who is just going to sit at home and wait for you to finish your affairs and still be smiling at the end. At least this man is kind and tender. He listens to me."

My father replied in a voice devoid of feeling. "I don't want to discuss this with Cyrus in the car. All I can say to you is it's all over between us. I've had enough. Either you or I is leaving the house tomorrow."

"Yes, why don't *you* go! It's all your fault!" she screamed. "It's my house and my children. Why should I go?"

We were stuck in the traffic opposite the aquarium. People stared at us from every direction. Two young men on the pavement holding hands and gaping, a man in a white dhoti peering through his bottle-glass spectacles, a fat lady in a sari sitting in the back of a green Fiat, a foreign couple in a Mercedes, a shoeshine boy holding his box in his hand. I stared back at him. He must have been the same age as me. I thought of the time in Churchgate when I paid fifty paise to have my black shoes shined. My mother was crying in the front seat. I wanted to climb over the seat and comfort her. I wanted her to stop. My father's knuckles were white, his fingers wrapped around the gearstick.

Some of the kerosene lamps on Chowpatty beach were aglow. I wished the evening sky would fall like a shroud and cover us up. As if he'd read my mind, my father stopped at the side of the road. With cars honking at him from behind, he unbuttoned the back of the slot where the rain hood disappeared, pulled the soft-top out and over our heads, flipping in the levers that secured the hood to the front windscreen. Usually I helped him with this task. But on that day all I wanted was to get home quickly, jump over the wall, and seek refuge at one of my neighbors' houses.

With the hood up we crawled in gloom through the traffic bound for the suburbs. As darkness descended on the city I looked for the familiar landmarks through the front window: Haji Ali Mosque, Lotus Cinema, Siemens tractors, City Bakery, Dunlop and Glaxo, Century Bazaar, Kismet Theatre, Shivaji Park . . .

AND STILL my father's hand moved absentmindedly up and down the blanket, as if smoothing away the pain. His fingers trembled with adulterous thoughts. There was something special between him and me. He recognized a similar vagabond, vulnerable spirit in his son, a recklessness rushing toward ruin. In the sleeping cage of juvenile bones, he could feel a kindred heart beating. That was why, as the minutes slipped away, he remained there, on the edge of the bed, pressing down the past.

I SEE MYSELF in the doorway of my parents' bedroom, my eyes still blinking in the harsh tube light from the adjoining bathroom. Standing in the open doorway, this is what I see. My father is holding a white towel against his cheek. My mother is crying and dabbing her arms with cubes of ice. When she sees me she rushes forward and grabs me by the wrist. "Listen to me, Cyrus, listen to me." Then her voice breaks off again. My father tries to shepherd me out. His shirt is torn.

My mother's face is haggard and riven by tears. It has gullies through which the tears are falling. She pulls me into the bathroom with the deep blue Italian tiles: as if for the first time, I see them reflected in the mirror. "For ten years, Cyrus, your father and I had a wonderful marriage. Everyone used to envy us. They used to say, look how happy Minoo and Mehroo are." My father bangs on the bathroom door. "Let the boy out, Mehroo. He should not be up at this time of night." But she has locked the door.

"For ten years," and here she pulls at my arm to make sure I am listening, "we were happy. But now your father wants to ruin, he wants to ruin everything because of his pride, his bloody thick-headed stubbornness!" My father is still rapping on the door. "Open the door. Don't do this to the boy, Mehroo. Open the bloody door."

"No, no, no! I'm going to tell him the truth. What a selfish, brutish, horrible creature his father is." My mother's nails dig into my arm. Something makes her unlock the door at this point. My father is standing there and I can see his bottom lip is swollen.

"But what has Daddy done?" I ask my mother. I am shocked to hear myself speak.

"I'll tell you what he's done, Cyrus—"

"C'mon, Cyrus. Go to bed," interrupted my father. "We'll talk about it tomorrow."

"No!" screamed my mother. "I want to tell him. He is my son. You won't listen to anything. So I'm going to tell him." This is a scream like no other I shall ever hear from her again. It's a scream that strikes terror into us, both my dad and I are rooted by its force. From that moment on I knew everything, everything my mother knew, everything that happened in her life, and in my father's. And a lot happened very quickly.

My mother packed her bags and took the five of us to a flat in Bandra. My father remained on his own in our glass house by the sea. A week later my mother was offered a flat in a building near Peddar Road. I didn't see my father for three months.

IN THE fog of sleep a faraway hand stroked my hair, I felt a last loving clench around my neck, a mystic massage with the fingers. A voice falling from a cloud, "Sleep well, little darling, sleep tight," and the tiny click of the lever as it slipped into the lock.

16

All my life I had wanted to live in a high-rise building. At last this wish came true. My mother, my brothers, my sister, and I moved from Juhu to the twenty-first floor of the tallest building in town. Bombay had grown into a city of apartment blocks. The very rich bought two flats at the top of a building, knocked a staircase through, and called it a duplex. The only people who had houses in the center of the city were embassies, the governor, and two Parsi dowagers who refused to vacate their dilapidated mansions and refused to die.

Elsewhere houses were bulldozed, rocks blasted with dynamite, the sea reclaimed. Hutment dwellers shifted to make way for the high-rise building. No square foot of earth was wasted: twenty-story blocks reared up on thumbnail plots of land. There were twin blocks and triplets, buildings hugged each other so close that friends could pass each other messages from the windows of their eleventh-floor flats. Each building had its own character, its own number of floors, its own color, its own balconies, its separate garages, its garden, its compound, its lifts, its association, its clubs, its games, its swimming pool, its groups of boys and girls, its watchman, its back stairs, its servants' lifts, its stains, its crows, its garbage dumps, and its name.

In Bombay all the buildings have names. Even if they are crumbling and unlikely to survive another monsoon, they have a name. If you want to find out where someone lives you don't ask them which street they live in: you ask the name of their building, and failing that, the name of the nearest well-known building.

I envied my schoolfriends who lived in these buildings. Rajiv in Aquamarine, Hormuz in Dolphin, Hoshang in Gulmarg, Khushroo in Sea Spray, and my cousin Jehangir in Hill Park. Every evening they returned home to their flats, had their biscuits and tea, or milk or juice, then ran down the stairs to play games with the building boys—cricket or hockey or marbles or itty-kitty or hide-and-seek. If they weren't playing a game, they wandered around the compound as one big gang, laughing and making a racket. Jehangir's building had a round fish pond with a fountain and goldfish in it, where all the boys and girls used to congregate. As an outsider, I wasn't talked to much, but I hung around and tried to join in. The boys were especially lucky, I thought, in being able to be friendly with so many girls. Girls who wore Western clothes and were not afraid to show off their legs.

When I went to stay with my friend Khushroo, we would stand against the front wall of the compound and watch the waves roll up and crash against it, a thin salty spray collecting on our hands and faces. To one side of the wall stretched a telephone wire on which little sparrows sat. Boys from the building would try to shoot them down with their air rifles.

Around five in the evening the bhelpuriwallah would arrive.

Sometimes one snack seller would service three or four buildings in the area. He always stood at his appointed spot. Surrounding him would be a group of hungry customers.

One Friday after school, I went with my friends Hoshang and Rajiv to Aquamarine, where Raju lived. His mother fed us with bhajias and orange squash. Downstairs we joined a collection of boys playing cricket in the driveway. When it was my turn to bat I surprised everyone by scoring thirty-four runs in no time at all. I hit the ball all over the place. I achieved this by pretending the bat in my hand was a tennis racquet. When I got caught, Raju came and put his arm around my shoulders. "Well done, yaar. You hit some damn good shots. That six you sent over the garage, man, that was choko!" I smiled with pleasure. The other team were going to find it near impossible to catch up with our total. Raju said, "Hey Cyrus, chul yaar, the bhaiya will have come. Let's run and get some bhel. I've got solid amount of money, man, my mother gave me."

"If we go now, won't they shout at us to give them their batting?"

"Let's see, I'll ask Hoshang. Hey Hosi!" Raju shouted across. "We're just going to get some bhel, we'll be back soon."

"Ja, ja," said Hoshang. "You give us our batting first and then you go. You can't just take your batting and then run off like that. I'm telling you, hah, Raju, that's not fair. I'm not playing with you otherwise."

"Arre baba, we'll run there and back, no? Rashid will start the bowling and he'll get your whole team out in two overs." We began to move off, but Hoshang was not happy.

"You see, hah, we'll not allow you to play again if you don't come back."

We ran out of the gate and onto Gamadia Road. To our left, we could see a group of boys milling around the bhaiya. He had a cane stand shaped like an hourglass on which he rested the various ingredients of his trade. These were kept in a large tin container the size of a car tire. He walked, balancing the container on his head, with a cotton cloth to support it. The cane stand fitted neatly under his arm.

When he arrived at his spot he removed the polythene covering of the container and checked that all the ingredients were in order. There were plastic bags and stainless-steel receptacles full of food, all neatly placed in concentric circles. In the three thick plastic bags he kept the airy puffed rice, mamra, the crispy yellow vermicelli, sev, and the tiny brown biscuits, puris. These foods had to be kept airtight or the damp Bombay air would make them soggy.

Raju and I were standing amongst the hive of hungry boys and girls bunched around the bhaiya. Bhaiyas come from a particular caste of traders in Uttar Pradesh. They dress in kurtas and dhotis and often have a distinctive twirled mustache. I asked Raju once, "But why does the bhaiya come all the way from UP to sell bhelpuri in Bombay?"

"Arre, what are you talking? They are specialists, no. They know all the secret ways to make the chutney and cut the kanda and all."

"That's true. Your bhaiya's tikha chutney is superb, yah, makes my eyes water, man."

My eyes fix on this man's fingers. His nonchalant air as he peels another purple onion and slices it in half. He wipes the knife. No chopping board, so the whole operation has to be performed in the palm of his hand. He makes horizontal slits across the onion half, then vertical ones tilting the flaked onions into a stainless-steel box. Again he wipes the knife with the cloth. He unwraps a steaming potato. When and how was this potato cooked? He peels the spud with the blunt edge of the knife, then eases the blade through a pattern of yellow-white cubes. Once again he cleans his knife.

Boys and girls shout at him from all directions. "Hurry up,

bhaiya. I want three bhels and four sevpuris. Two of them tikha, and one mild. Don't put any onions in one of them. Please, bhaiya, I've been waiting for fifteen minutes now. It must be my turn. I told you my order, no?"

How can they harry the man like this? I swallowed hard on the saliva that had gathered in my mouth. Flies buzzed around the food, my eye was caught by the large bosom of a girl in a blue frock. The bhaiya cuts a lime in half, he chops a green mango into tiny squares, he shreds some coriander leaves, he lifts up a box and slides out a sheaf of pages torn out from a magazine. The paper is thick and durable but not glossy—perfect for the food it will hold. He folds one sheet over and makes a wide cone-shaped vessel. Now comes the delicate throwing together of ingredients, dry and wet, that delights the heart.

He takes a fistful of mamra and drops it into the paper cone; this is followed by fingerfuls of sev, onions, and potato. There are requests for extra ingredients from the customers, "More onions, bhaiya! Don't stint on the potatoes! Bit more raw mango!" The bhaiya continues at his job with serenity. He gives each of the chutneys a rattling stir: a red one with chilies and garlic, a brown one with tamarind, and a green one with chilies and coriander. He pours a spoonful of each of the chutneys into the paper cone and mixes all the ingredients together. The final additions come according to the customer's taste. A squeeze of lime, a few coriander leaves and a sprinkling of raw tangy mango, a last fingerful of sev.

I was never sure when he was making my bhelpuri because the bhaiya rarely spoke except to tell his customers how much they owed him at the end. Unlike the others, I was slightly disappointed when my bhelpuri was ready since I had no reason then to stand around watching him prepare the dish. As long as I was hungry I could have stood there all day long, mesmerized and my mouth watering.

Observing the preparation of food, in the kitchen or on the

street, is a lesson in patience. Each cook has his or her method of chopping, sorting, stocking, spicing, stirring, mixing, melting, beating, fingering, and tasting. I learned this early, from sitting in our kitchen watching the cook at work, from watching Mrs. Verma or Mrs. Krishnan, and from asking questions of my granny. I couldn't cook anything myself and knew nothing of the pleasure a cook gains from seeing someone tucking into their handiwork. But I often wondered whether a certain sadness might not accompany the eating. To be appreciated, unlike a book, a film, or a painting, food has to be destroyed, consumed, transformed into waste.

My life too had been transformed. My parents had split up. I was nearer my schoolfriends, and the building boys, but I missed my neighbors in Juhu. We were high up in the night air of Bombay, an air that smelled of people and cars and hot tarmac streets, so different from the beachcombing breezes of our sea house. I lay in my new bed, on the twenty-first floor, and listened to the echoing steps of late-night people hurrying home to their beds. I dreamed of miraculous things happening to me.

Someone offers me a deal. If I am willing to sacrifice my left hand, they'll give me the power to swim like a dolphin. I agree. I see myself winning nine gold medals and standing on the Olympic rostrum, like Mark Spitz, waving to the crowds and appearing on the covers of *Time* and *Newsweek* with the medals round my neck. Then I am dreaming of playing tennis like Rod Laver. Winning all the junior and senior tournaments in India, winning Wimbledon over and over again. I am kissing the trophy on Centre Court and the crowd is throwing their hats off and teenage girls are squealing in delight.

Someone was walking around our flat. A door slammed shut. It must have been my mother returning from her visit to Naresh's flat. She was seeing this other man: a mysterious man I had only glimpsed once, sitting on a cane chair at the edge of the swimming pool, but whose appearance my mother had described to me in detail. He was from Cochin but had lived in Bombay for twenty years. He was handsome, silver-haired, and some years older than her. He had a company flat and a house in Lonavala which had a tennis court. I knew when and where she met Naresh. I knew what they talked about and what they did. Meanwhile, I was also aware of conversations going on between my mother and father. I had become a master at overhearing telephone calls and placing my ear against doors.

I thought of Naresh's tennis court. Perhaps if we moved in with him, I could practice every day and really turn into a champion. I indulged in visions of living in his mansion in Lonavala, going to south India to meet his family. He had two daughters in Cochin from an earlier marriage to an Italian woman. Thoughts of the south reminded me of the friends I had left behind in Juhu. The Krishnans must imagine I had left for good. What about going on holiday to Kerala with them? They must have forgotten that idea. We lived in such different parts now. Juhu felt so far away, like somewhere in the country. I resolved to go there on the weekend, visit all my neighbors and remind the Krishnans that I was still counting on their invitation. It struck me that I had not seen my father for six weeks. I had kept myself away, knowing that he was angry with my partisan attitude. I thought of him sitting in the garden looking out to sea with only the dog to keep him company—the thin Irish setter who spent the day curled up in his marble corner.

A battle ensued between my sleep-starved body and my waking mind full of plans for the weekend. Seeing Meera in her green blouse. The lunches I would eat. If I went to the Krishnans' at twelve, the Vermas' at one-thirty, and the Maharani's at two-thirty, I could manage to have a bite at three houses. I was drifting off on trays of food: mutton korma, thick gravy full of cardamom, poppy seeds, tender slow-cooked meat, mangoes, onion uttapams, cheese toasts with tomato and garlic, shriveled baby brinjals that look like mice, aloo parathas flaky with ghee, mint chutney, cool milky curds . . .

ON SUNDAY I went to see my father but he wasn't there. I was pleased. I wouldn't have to worry about being kept from the meals awaiting me at my neighbors' homes. They welcomed me like a lost friend, someone who'd been away and returned safely. I felt wanted. But their generous offerings of food were tinged with pity. I could tell they were being solicitous because of the break-up of my parents. I wanted to tell them that the separation was not permanent, that there was a chance that things could be patched up. I knew: I was the mediator, the advisor. Then I thought of the house in Lonavala, the half-Italian children, the tennis court. Would they be irredeemably lost? My neighbors were tactful. The Krishnans were expecting me to go with them on their holiday, they talked of what we would do on their grandmother's farm. I sat down to lunch. Paper dosas, coconut chutney, potatoes, and sambhar. I ate hungrily and Mrs. Krishnan made no sarcastic comments. After lunch, Sushil and I played marbles in the backyard. I won three of the five games. Normally, as boys of the same age, we competed edgily. But on this day I felt Sushil extending an intangible grasp of the hand, a quiet arm around my shoulder. Perhaps I was imagining it, but I felt a pang of love toward him. After our game I had to tear myself away, lying that I was due back home. I was on my way to the Vermas'.

While I was away, Mrs. Verma had complained to Mrs. Krishnan that Ajay and Sushil were climbing over their wall and into the garden. Mrs. Krishnan retorted that Mrs. Verma was a liar and that her sons would never cross into a neighbor's property—least of all Mrs. Verma's tiny front yard—without permission. Mrs. Verma was not used to the venom of Mrs. Krishnan's tongue and recoiled into acrimonious silence. The two families no longer acknowledged each other when they passed in the street. I would have to be careful. To be seen at the Vermas' might mean the cancellation of my trip to Kerala.

The Vermas were sitting round the table at lunch. The scene was so different from the Krishnans'. It was like entering the hub-bub of a mosque after the seclusion of a chapel. Sunday was a day of calm at the Krishnans'. Lunch was eaten with silent enjoy-ment, each person getting their fair share on their shining thali. Extras were rare, conversation was sensible. At the Vermas' lunch was raucous and crowded. The table seemed too small for the large, round members of this family. The furniture was loud and comfortable: high-quality plastic flowers, big soft cushions, and beanbags in red, white, black, and yellow.

"Arre yaar, Cyrus!" Mr. Verma shouted. "Where have you disappeared to?"

"Pull up a seat," said Mrs. Verma. "Avnish, let Cyrus squeeze in next to you, hah." Then she called out to their ayah, "Arre, Cyrus has arrived. Can you get him a plate and make one or two more parathas?"

"Three parathas, baba, he will eat at least three and then I won't get any," shouted Rajnish.

"No, no, Aunty," I said politely. "I've already eaten. I'm full up, really."

"Actually," said Mr. Verma mimicking my lilting voice, "actually, I'm sure you can eat one or two mouthfuls." Everyone laughed and just to keep them merry I said, "Actually, I would love to taste a little bit."

"They are delicious today, hain na, Avnish?" Avnish nodded his head while scooping a little envelope of aubergine-filled paratha into his mouth. "So, have you seen any new movies, Cyrus? In Bombay there are so many big cinemas. Have you been to any of them?" Mrs. Verma asked.

"Yah, I've been to Lotus, Ganga Jamuna, Opera House," I

lied. "I went to Alexandra Talkies, but that was horrible. All rats running around the floor and bugs in the seats and all." My paratha arrived. Golden and crispy on the outside, stuffed with delicately spiced potatoes.

"Have you seen *Namak Haraam?*" Navnish asked. "Damn good film, yaar. Rajesh and Amitabh star in it."

"Hah, Amitabh is very good. Brilliant dialogue scenes and what fantastic songs!" Mrs. Verma said, shaking her flower-decked head. When I hadn't seen a film I hated to admit it, so I just kept quiet.

"What about *Dum Maro Dum?* You must have seen that, Cyrus?" said Navnish.

"Hah, yaar! *Hare Rama, Hare Krishna,*" shouted Mr. Verma. "You must see that. Rajnish was totally smitten by Zeenat Aman."

"You mean that new young actress who looks like Ali Mac-Graw? They say that Dev Anand found her somewhere in a village," I said.

"You must have read that in *Stardust*. It's all false rumor, all 'Neeta's Natter' buqwaas. Zeenat was a commerce student at Sydenham College, and Dev Anand gave her a minor role in one of his movies."

"How do you know all that, Aunty?" I asked.

"You know my friend Tabassum? The one who presents *Phul Khile Hain Gulshan Gulshan* on the TV."

"The program where they show all the film songs?"

"That's the one. I'm sure you've met her, no? Anyway, she knows Zeenat and she took me to the shooting of Dev Anand's latest film."

"You went to a shooting! I've always wanted to go to a shooting."

"Hah, I went last week," Mrs. Verma said casually. "I might go again this week. You want to come, you can come." There was a note of hesitation in her voice that I found easy to ignore. "I'm sure Tabassum won't mind. Or, if you can't come tomorrow, then I can ask Sethi. Maybe he can arrange something." She was wriggling out.

"I can come tomorrow, Usha Aunty. What time will it be?" She didn't answer. Instead she turned to her favorite boy. "Navnish, shall we go to the shooting tomorrow? Do you want to come?"

Once again I had to wait and hope that the mollycoddled son would accede to his mother's wishes. I knew that if Navnish declined to go, the whole trip would be put off. I leaned forward toward him. He shook his head in a noncommittal way. "There are too many people there, Mummy. You can't see anything. Haven't you been to a shooting, Cyrus?"

"That's why I really want to go. Come on, I'll keep you company. I just want to see what it's like," I pleaded.

"Acha, chulo, we'll go then. But not for too long, hah. Two hours maximum."

17

On Monday afternoon I ran down Nesbit bridge to catch the 4Ltd bus to Santacruz. A cruel brightness reflected off the cars. You had to be careful not to touch any shiny surface for fear of being scorched. My underarms dripped like broken taps. The white school shirt had turned transparent on my back. On the double-decker bus I sat upstairs to dry off in the hot breeze.

Mrs. Verma and Navnish were waiting in the front of their white Fiat. A small fan fixed to the dashboard spun pointlessly in the sultry air. Mrs. Verma kept glancing in the super-large rear-view mirror to check the state of her makeup. She was clearly agitated by the heat. Tiny cracks in the thickly spread foreign foundation appeared on her face. I jumped into the backseat, apologizing profusely for my late arrival.

We were heading toward the Sun 'n' Sand Hotel to see the shooting of Dev Anand's latest film, *Heera Panna*. The Sun 'n'

Sand was the only four-star hotel on Juhu beach. A three-story building painted in broad strokes of white and orange, it was where all the visiting foreigners stayed. From the beach, you could see them lying on their sunbeds in front of the swimming pool. Slim white women, mostly air hostesses, in bikinis and sunglasses, pot-bellied businessmen, and pilots reading the papers. On the other side of the wall that separated the hotel lawn from the beach, an array of beggars, snake-charmers, monkeywallahs, and sundry performers tried to amuse the hotel guests. The sunbathers tried to ignore the hucksters, but there were tricks they always fell for: the bedraggled monkey scampering up the wall; the cobra rearing its head at the underfed mongoose; the little girl, barely four years old, perched on the end of a bamboo pole, held up by an emaciated man who was probably her father, her arms extended outward, the end of the pole digging into her empty stomach, looking as if at any moment it might impale her. The child looked with her big black eyes, head bobbing above the wall, at the reclining white figures. The foreigners peered back from behind their airport thrillers. Who could deny her a few paise? To make matters worse, there was always a gaggle of locals watching the performers, sometimes laughing at their forlorn antics.

On days when the hotel was booked for shooting, the swimming pool and the area around it were closed to the public and the foreigners. Only special guests—relatives and friends of actors and the crew—were allowed into the hotel to view the shooting.

Sat in the back of Mrs. Verma's Fiat, I wondered, Will I get to see anything? Will we be able to squeeze into the inner cordon? Won't it be amazing to see the fight scenes from the movie in real life? I felt inappropriately dressed in my white shorts and shirt. Navnish was wearing Wrangler jeans and a multicolored T-shirt. He clinked the steel strap of his bulky watch around his wrist.

"Mummy, will Tabassum be waiting for us at the entrance?"

"Hah, bete, she said she would be there at four-thirty. Acha, Cyrus, have you seen the picture of this new girl Dev Anand has pakroed? Her face is on all the posters. Sixteen years old she is meant to be, and Dev Anand is how old?"

"He must be in his fifties. Do you know what scene they will be shooting, Aunty?"

"I think it's a song sequence, maybe even some dancing on the beach. Kishore and Neeta from *Stardust* should be there."

Oh no, I thought to myself, I was hoping for a fight scene.

"Don't worry, Cyrus, there'll be lots of film stars," said Navnish.

"Who do you want to see, bete? You want to see Rakhee, hain na?" teased Mrs. Verma.

"Don't go on about that, Mummy. I've told you so many times, I don't like her." Mrs. Verma quickly changed the topic.

When we got to the hotel there was a queue nine cars long waiting to get to the entrance. "Hai re, yeh to bhed lagi hai," Mrs. Verma exclaimed. "We should have come earlier." I craned my neck out of the back window to see what was going on.

"Now, both of you stay close to me when we get into the hotel, okay?" We waited an age. Every five minutes the cars moved a few inches. The sweat trickled down our bodies. "Arre, Cyrus, just go and see if one of the watchmen will take our car and park it." Mrs. Verma fretted. The watchman in his red turban and white suit was not impressed by my schoolboy attire. I pointed toward the Fiat, where Mrs. Verma sat smiling in our direction. He followed me to the car where Usha Aunty gave him the keys and a five-rupee note. He saluted smartly and held the door open for her. "Don't worry, madam, I will bring the car to you when you have finished." Why did she give him so much? I could have done with half that amount.

Mrs. Verma took Navnish's hand and I followed them

through the glass door into the air-conditioned lobby. At times like these air-conditioning seemed like a miracle. How was it possible to step from the oven-like heat of the afternoon into this quiet arctic breeze? Mrs. Verma was all flowers, sari, and smiles. She dabbed her face with a little white hanky taken from her handbag. The normally tame hotel was thronged with people. Men in bright bush shirts and safari suits, women in shimmering saris. The occasional foreigner, looking bewildered. Babies, as usual, bawling. Children moaning at their parents. "Mummy, please can I have one Coca-Cola!"

Out on the patio by the swimming pool, security guards in khaki uniforms with laathis in their hands wandered up and down. The swimming pool was cordoned off with a rope. Everyone was looking around for stars or semi-stars, or failing that, someone they knew. I felt a hundred fleeting looks pass apathetically over my face. Mrs. Verma's half-smile flashed in all directions like a lighthouse. Piped hotel music, the James Last Band, flowed incongruously in the background. All around us people greeted each other with great big bear hugs and pats on the back.

Mrs. Verma and Navnish seemed rudderless and I felt bereft, more like an appendage than ever, in this lounge of coruscating blouses and clotted cosmetics. At least my friends would soon link up with their Tabassum. There was little chance of my being recognized here. I tried to stand as close as possible to Navnish, whose sheepishness made him slightly more friendly.

To our right, the crowd suddenly surged forward. We followed like ants. A knot of people made their way through us into the swimming-pool area. In their midst was a lady bedecked in a red churidar outfit with gold braid, dripping jewelry and heavily powdered cheeks. It was difficult to see very much of her but Mrs. Verma whispered in my ear, "That's the new actress." I stretched forward to catch another glimpse but the group had disappeared. We followed in slow procession.

There were a lot of frantic assistants flitting to and fro. "Hey, Ramesh! Cameraman ko bulao na. Hussein, kya kartai re?"

"Hullo, Smita! Dancing ladies kaha hai? Abhe time ho gaya hai. Chulo, chulo, jaldi karo!"

A lady in a pink sari came scurrying past. "Rukmini ka makeup case, Rukmini ka makeup case! Fernandez, what are you doing, yaar! She is getting so angry at me. Hurry up, please!" Then she shot a self-important glance into the crowd.

No sign of Mrs. Verma's friend. We were outside by the swimming pool and the lead actress sat in a little makeup tent in one corner of the set. Perhaps Tabassum was lost in this mêlée. I scanned the unfamiliar faces: it gave me a sense of purpose and I imagined that the onlookers would think I had someone to meet. It was only then that I noticed the huge audience that had gathered on the beach. There were at least twenty rows of people standing around a semi-circular piece of sand, surrounded by rope and security guards. They were looking up at us. I felt a sense of importance. All these people out there and here I was, for once, with the celebrated filmi crowd. They could have come to see me as Junior Mehmood, like the urchin boys who'd milled around our car chanting his name.

As the sun dropped toward the sea and the light dissolved my fantasies, I got bored by all the waiting around. My neck ached, my feet hurt. Occasionally a cameraman would appear, measure the light, and disappear again.

An hour later when the shooting finally started, all I could see was a man with a little black slate and some chalked words. I'd seen this before in photographs but for the life of me I couldn't understand what he was doing in the film. Why did he appear so often, shouting, "Take one, take two!"? Navnish didn't know either. Through the heads of the crowd, I could see a man sitting on a cart fixed to some rails, holding a camera and being pushed up and down by a troop of helpers. There was an ugly, stern-looking woman in a white sari who kept yanking the heroine around by the arm, forcing her through the steps of the dance routine. The unattractive tutor was adept at moving her head from side to side, while holding her hands together in a namaste gesture, then suddenly swiveling her hips and pirouetting with an exaggerated smile. The words of the song come chiming through. Now the ugly dance madam takes Dev Anand by the hand and leans back, then grins coyly and covers the lower half of her face with the end of her sari, while backing away from him, shaking her head and joining in the song, "Na, na, na . . ." When the heroine attempts to copy her, she gets it all wrong and looks like a dressed-up doll with the ungainly waddle of a sow. Madam scolds her and angrily interrupts the routine to change her hand gestures or to show her how to swing those hips in the proper seductive manner. I was startled at how abrupt and aggressive the madam was. It had never occurred to me that the steps and gestures of the song sequences were so rehearsed: it all seemed so fake, like the sound, the dialogue, the music, and the songs, which I hadn't realized were all recorded later and added to the film. When Dev Anand appeared, his face all made up, he looked so much more bloated in real life, standing there with the two huge silver reflectors on either side, the camera right up in his face, I couldn't imagine what he was doing. All I could see were his lips moving. Then someone barked, "Action," which made the crowd go quiet, and "Cut," which sent everyone into a tizzy again. The patient multitude stood on the beach. I'd so much rather have been out there with them. They were the kind of people that I went to the movies with, much nicer than this glittering, perfumed, makeup-caked society lot.

Going to see a picture was so much better than all this shooting nonsense. It was the opposite kind of experience. I loved the darkness and calm of the theater, the comfortable seats, the fact that no one could see me, and the certainty that for the next three hours I could abandon myself utterly to the twisting plot, the double roles, the comic interludes, the classic dialogue, and the thrilling fight sequences at the end. For three hours I could stop thinking about my poor marks at school, my parents' fighting, the lies that blighted my existence, or the tennis matches I should have won. That's why I liked going to the pictures on my own. You never had to worry about the person sitting next to you and what they might be doing or thinking. The presence of someone I knew was always an irritating reminder of the real world. And then there was always a slight shift in the seat, a certain unrest when a sexy or embarrassing scene came on. Once I knew my way round the cinemas of Bombay, I was much happier to be in an anonymous audience. That moment when the lights dimmed and the Indian Board of Censors white page with the name of the film written on it was projected on the screen, no one knew me, and I didn't know them, but for the duration of the film we were pulled together, wrapped up, and spellbound. Out of the vastness of our city we came into this ship of darkness, paid our due, had our fun, and returned once more to our separate lives.

WE DROVE back to the Vermas' house at nine o'clock. I had a quick bite to eat and lied that I was spending the night at Juhu. Our house, with my father and his old dog, though only a few steps away, now seemed like a home I had left long ago.

I walked down to the bus stop on Gorbunder Road. During the day this stand was teeming with commuters. It seemed absurd to be waiting here alone, leaning comfortably against the fat iron railings of the shelter. From the opposite side of the road the Dena Bank sign stared back at me, as did the poster with a woman's face painted pink, advertising Modena Saris, "All Women Are the Same, Modena Saris Make the Difference." How long would I remember this scene, standing here looking at Dena Bank, waiting for the bus? Thinking about this made me feel older than I was.

The 84 Express slowed down just enough for me to jump on board. At this time of night the conductor would often pull the bell twice in quick succession and the bus would roar past without bothering to stop. Three people on the bus: a Koli woman with a huge basket and gold nose ring, her sari hitched up between her legs; and two men with pens in their shirt pockets. Where were they going? Where did they think I was going? I thought of myself tucking in under the covers of my bed on the twenty-first floor while the Koli woman arrived in Sassoon Dock to buy a basketful of the late-night catch of fish. The air felt cold as the bus driver bolted past the empty stops. Two more people got on at Shivaji Park.

We arrived at Peddar Road in twenty-five minutes, which must have been some kind of record. I walked back to the corner of Carmichael Road, where the paanwallah on the corner still had his shop open. I had forty paise in my pocket. I thought I might find something to eat. In the front of his shop I saw a box of Nirodhs. I had no idea what they were though I had seen the advertisements saying, "Hum do, Hamare do" (The two of us and our two children), with the round cartoon faces of mummy, daddy, smiling son, and pigtailed daughter. The model family. I had heard some boys at school whispering about Nirodhs. I asked the paanwallah how much they were and he laughed at me. "They are fifteen paise for three, but you don't need them, bacchu." I was intrigued.

"Why don't I need them? What are they for?" He looked at me as if I were mad.

"Do you want them or not? It's late, I'm closing up."

"Can't I just have one for five paise?"

"No. Fifteen paise or nothing."

"Okay, I'll have them. Give me two packets of Milan supari and one Double Bubble."

In the lift on the way up to our flat I examined the red and yellow wrapper of the three Nirodhs. They looked like large round lozenges, but they were squidgy on the inside. Jeevan, our new servant, opened the door. He was not happy to be woken up. "What the hell have you been doing out till this time of night?"

"Has Mummy come home?" I inquired. He didn't bother to answer and went back to his kholi. The flat was like a morgue. I went to my huge room with its towering view of the city. In bed I ripped open the packet of Nirodhs and found a white powdery balloon all rolled up with a small nipple sticking out of the top. I unfurled a bit of it; it reminded me of one of those plastic curiosities my mother had on her dressing table. There were some very blurred instructions in Marathi that I couldn't decipher.

I stowed the Nirodhs in my bedside drawer. Then I remembered the James Hadley Chase novel I had found on the living-room bookshelf. I opened it at the first page.

18

On the Tuesday, four days before I was to leave for Kerala, my father phoned up the flat at seven in the morning. I was still groggy with sleep.

"I've got a surprise for you, Cyrus. I think I can get you a P form to go abroad by this evening. I'm leaving for Hamburg on Thursday, and if I get the P form, would you like to come with me to Germany for a week?"

"But what about my trip to Kerala?" Delighted as I was by his offer, I couldn't think what the Krishnans would say if I suddenly canceled. "That's what I said to Minoo," said my mother, who was listening in the background. "It's too short notice."

"I'll talk to Mr. Krishnan and explain. You can go to Kerala anytime. The point is do you want to come with me to Germany or not?"

"Of course I do!" I shouted.

"Then get your bags packed for Thursday," laughed my father.

He rung off and I started jumping up and down. "I'm going abroad! I'm going to Germany on Thursday! Will I need a sweater, Mummy? Will it be really cold? Will there be snow?" My mother looked at me with a wry smile. "He's just feeling guilty," she said.

I had always wanted to go abroad. The whole day I was beside myself, grinning at the world. I had often lied to my friends about trips I had made to England and America. I never imagined my stories would come true so soon and so suddenly.

All day I waited by the phone. Late in the evening, by which time I was sapped of excitement, my father's call came through. "I'm ever so sorry, Cyrus. I tried everything I could, but the bloody fool at the passport office just refused to grant a P form by Thursday and I have to be in Hamburg at a meeting on Friday morning. I even tried to telex the Germans, requesting that they postpone the meeting, but the date had been set months before and it was impossible to change."

"But isn't there some way you could get the form tomorrow?" I asked, hopelessly.

"I tried my best, believe me. If there was any way possible I would have done it. I even asked Pandu to offer him something, which I am dead against doing, but the man is just a stubborn bureaucratic swine. He kept saying, 'But what is the necessity to take your son with you on a business trip?' Unfortunately, the senior man Padgaokar, who is very sweet and always does my work, was away, and we couldn't get in touch with him. Next time we'll plan it properly in advance and make sure we get the P form in on time. I'll definitely be going on a trip to America soon. Would you like to do that?" I said yes, feebly, but I could hardly speak for disappointment.

"Cheer up, Cyrus. It was probably best for you to go with the Krishnans. You were really looking forward to it. I'm sure you'll have a good time. Anyway Mummy wasn't very happy about you going. Now, you make sure you behave yourself with the Krishnans, not too much musti, hah?"

"Next time," I thought to myself. The only thing certain about next time was that it would never come.

BEFORE LONG I was on a train, traveling through the night, somewhere in the middle of India. Leaving home on an adventure into the deep south. I was accompanying the Krishnans back to their father's ancestral home in the middle of a forest. Back, far back into the countryside away from towns, shops, bicycles, cars, and people. Down there were coconuts, paddy fields, and water. A lot of water.

The train picked up speed. The wheels revolved and revolved. I could hear the steam driving the crankshafts, driving the massive iron-black wheels: chhhkkk-chhhkkk, chhhkkk-chhhkkk, the sound of rice being sifted and shaken in flat wicker baskets. The fans whirred, sleepers snored, Mr. Krishnan turned and grumbled like a demon spreading menace over the feeble limbs of his fellow travelers. Crumbs of soot flew in through the open window, stinging my arm.

In that moving night, events just gone unfolded before my eyes. My father had come to visit us in our flat. I kissed him warmly, like a traitor. We were all in my mother's camp now. My elder brother, Behroz, was the only one who from time to time stayed with my father in the glass house in Juhu. My sister was too young to understand what was going on, my younger brother behaved as if he were still umbilically attached to my mother.

I was a traitor because I had looked forward to moving in with my mother and Naresh, pictured living in his big house with the tennis court, eating sumptuous meals served by his liveried servants. I was a traitor because I had listened eagerly to my mother talking of their courting, of their romance, of their meetings. The first time something happened between them, in the elevator of the Air India building at Nariman Point, he had pulled her to him and kissed her. She had felt "pleased as Punch." Those were her very words.

I had lapped up her stories, mouth agape, eyes wide with the glow of being her confidant. This was what I had always desired, for my mother to talk to me. Sometimes she even asked my opinion. It didn't much matter what it was. All I cared about was that my advice was sought. Occasionally what I said, which was simply an encouraging echo of her own thoughts, was quoted at my dad or at one or other of her close friends.

I was able to ask my mother all kinds of questions about her past, about my father's past, about their joint misdemeanors, about their dalliances and their scams. My mother told me about her romances with tennis players, princes, champion golfers, movie stars, and a German shipping magnate.

She told me and I listened. I, Oedipus, listened to tales of adult love and infidelity, adult fights and adult madness.

In this train, wending its way to the south, I recalled my father's voice on the day he came to visit us at the flat. They were in my mother's bedroom arguing as usual; I was outside, standing in my customary position by the door. Their efforts at reconciliation had come to nothing. My father refused to budge from his position, my mother had delivered her ultimatum. But this was not a contest. My mother had the upper hand from the start. Not only was she in the right but she had the teeth to prove it. She had the lover—a devoted lover, not some fly-by-night foreigner. She had the flat in Bombay and the children living with her. My father was all alone with the dog in his glass house by the sea. Report had it that he was sitting there, after his years of manic movement, on the balcony looking out to sea, hour after hour, on his own, stroking the dog, draining himself of energy. It was as if too much light shone into his vacant life.

Standing outside the bedroom, I sensed in his words a certain tiredness, a muted pain. As if he didn't mean all the stupid things he was saying. As if he just wanted to give in and start all over again. A bullish pride held him back.

Then something broke inside him and out spilled these hoarse sobs, such as I had never heard before. "Not my children. Don't take . . . my children . . . away from me. Please . . . not my kiddoes. They're . . . all I've . . . got. I can't bear it without my little Shenny." My heart smoldered in its cage. I could imagine my father bent over with tears. He was such a broad man. I could feel him craving for my mother. She was saying something rational to him but I didn't want to hear. My father was crying. He was crying for me, for himself, for us all.

I walked away. I had said earlier to Behroz in the car, "Can I change my surname? I want to change my surname to Kumar when we move into Naresh's house." Behroz didn't say anything at the time, but I knew that he had reported this to my father. I sat down at the dining table, knots of guilt in my stomach.

A couple of days ago, I had learned from my mother that it was Naresh's birthday soon. My friend Glen and I had baked him a cake. I, who had never in my life cooked anything for anyone, baked a brown cake for Naresh's birthday, sent it to him in a box, with a card, and waited with bated breath for his approval. The thought of Naresh's smile, his oily smile, his ugly long face, his hairy nostrils, his horrid angular head, filled me with hate. I never wanted to see him again.

I heard the bedroom door slam, and the clocking of my father's shoes. I see him now from my seat in the train—see him striding toward the living room, his fiery face, his dark suit, his bold orange and blue Sulka tie. My mother's voice came following behind, "You will lose your children! Already they don't care about you." He crossed the living room and made toward the door. Then his eyes fell upon his son. My mother walked into the large space. She saw me sitting at the dining table. The pictures move so slowly through my brain.

"Cyrus even baked a cake for Naresh's birthday!" she

exulted. I don't think she had noticed the way my father's eyes, like darts, had lit upon me. He advanced on me like a primeval warrior. He rushed to attack his son. I could see him coming: his hunched-up body, like a boxer, bursting through several layers of pain. "Cyrus!" My mother's bird-like alarm propelled me out of my seat. I skipped round the table, too frightened to run. My father chased his son, the son who could always run faster than anyone else. "You ungrateful wretch!" he bellowed. "Come here!" Three-quarters way round the gray table the thunder in his voice struck me still. He grabbed me by the arm with the same hand that had held me in loving check.

"Minoo!" my mother's voice rang out in foreboding. For many years I had wondered how strong my father was. I felt a pain in my stomach where an imaginary blow had landed. I felt my body being shaken. "How could you? How could you do that to me!" His voice faltered.

"Let him go, Minoo! Let him go. He hasn't done anything." But my father's hand had already fallen from my arm. He stood there, as if he were looking at this scene in a mirror. Then he turned around and walked out of the door.

From my bum-numbing wooden bunk on the train I wanted to call out to him, stop him from leaving, explain to him what had happened, I wanted to kiss his stubbly cheek.

The wheels slowed down. A gentle rain began to fall. Amber lamps glowed in the distance. Steam rose from the neat squares of water in the fields, mingling with the trailing puffs from the engine spout. I could hear the fans again and the chirruping of birds. A sultry heat gripped the air. Passengers stirred in their sleep. We were approaching a large town. I wiped my nose with the back of my arm.

Our train clattered into the covered part of the station, the noise echoing against the corrugated-iron roof. Ravi, the youngest of the Krishnan boys, stretched out his arms and yawned loudly. "Where are we, Appa?" he asked. There was no answer from the sleeping demon. The piercing cry of vendors streamed in through the window.

"Chaaaiiii, chaaaaiiiiiyyyya, chaaaiii, chaaaaiiiiiyyyya!"

"Samosaaay garaam, garaaaaam samosaaay!"

Ravi looked around. Finding all his family still asleep, he covered his head with his blanket and curled himself into a ball. I stepped down onto the platform in my rubber chapals. Announcements fed through the loudspeaker cackled over the clamor of a hundred voices. Sellers of tea, ice cream, kachoris, chore bhature, coconuts, sing-channa, water, and oranges passed to and fro. I stood in amongst a group of men watching a karahi of bubbling oil as the chole-bhaturewallah dipped two floury breads in with a slotted spoon. He caressed the bhatures from side to side, slid them onto a plate of dried leaves, and topped them with spicy chickpeas freshly spooned from a steaming pan.

Farther down the platform I bought two potato wadas, crisp and golden, lashed with dark ground chilli. My mouth burned nicely. At the tea stall I ordered a cup of chai. Its syrupy hotness soothed my burning tongue.

"Still twenty minutes before the train goes," the shopkeeper said, as I hurried to pay him. In the glass cases of the stall were various jars of sweets, biscuits, and pastries. A south Indian man stood at the counter tucking into a long cone-shaped confection. "How much for that?" I asked, pointing at the pastry. I counted out thirty paise. The pastry was alarmingly sweet. Flaky on the outside and custard-soft within.

Next to the tea stall was Wheeler and Company, the booksellers. At the front of the stall were laid out magazines, newspapers, comics, and books mostly in English. I browsed through *Tintin, Asterix, Phantom, Mandrake the Magician, Richie Rich, Little Lotta,* and *Archie.* Out-of-date foreign glossies: *Vogue, Motorcycle Maintenance, Tennis World, Woman's Own, Life,* and

National Geographic. I wanted to buy my favorite film magazine, *Stardust,* but I was scared Mr. Krishnan might catch me reading it. He despised what he called the "vapid frivolity" of the Hindi cinema. I looked through some of the books. There was one called *The Secret Garden of Pleasure,* several novels by Thomas Hardy, and Samuel Butler's *The Way of All Flesh.* Authors whose names I had seen on my father's bookshelf: James Michener, Anthony Burgess, Italo Svevo, Gore Vidal, *A Guide to Motorcycle Maintenance* by Robert Pirsig. I parted with four rupees for two *Archie*s and one *Little Lotta,* then, glancing up at the station clock, cobwebbed amongst the iron girders of the roof, I hurried back to our carriage.

The Krishnans were still asleep. A couple with a baby had occupied the two empty bunks just below Ravi. Out of the window I could see the platform slowly emptying, the frenetic activity partially abated. People were standing around waiting for the train to move off so they could wave their last goodbyes.

Two coolies in red shirts and dhotis came scuttling along the platform with suitcases on their heads, behind them two large women waddled with exhausted faces scanning the compartment numbers and scolding the porters. The stationmaster blew his whistle, the superintendent came out of his office and waved his green flag, the wheels began, ever so slowly, to roll.

The couple with the baby settled themselves in. They moved noiselessly from task to task, exchanging whispers as they worked. The woman wedged herself in the corner by the window. She covered her baby's head, a glistening ring on its nose, with the pallu of her sari, eased a breast out of her blouse, and pushed her nipple through its gums. Once the baby found its rhythm, the woman stared with vacant satisfaction out of the window.

Meantime, the husband unlocked his attaché case with a tiny key, surveyed the contents all neatly arranged, unwrapped a towel, and laid it on his bunk. From a bag he removed a pair of worn leather chapals. He placed these gently by his feet. Then he leaned over to his wife to ask her if she was all right; she nodded. He returned to tending his feet. Socks and shoes were delicately removed and stowed in a plastic bag. The bare feet crept into the leather slippers. His face showed that they had found their home.

I began a story in one of my *Archie* comics. But before I got to the end, my lids drooped. An easeful light filtered in through the window. As I drifted off into an early-morning slumber, I remembered hopelessly that the Krishnans would not look kindly on me sleeping late. But the train swayed and lulled like a crib. Soon there were no thoughts left to think.

Hours later, eyes shut, I heard the voices of the people sitting around my reclining body. I could tell the voices of my friends. I think they were laughing at me. The sun was scorching one side of my face. I would have liked to break free from the dream I was in, but I was sewn up by sleep, like Gulliver tied down by the Lilliputians.

I recognized Ajay's voice. "Should we wake him up?"

"Yuk!" said Ravi. "Look at the way he is dribbling onto his elbow." I could feel the thread of hot spittle hanging from my mouth.

In the dream, a man is chasing me. I am too tired to climb any farther up the spiral stairs. The steps have come to an end. The gnarled face grabs me by the arm. But now his face is not gnarled, and I recognize it. It's the face of my six-foot-six uncle Soli, the mediator in my parents' quarrels, talking to them, trying to get them to see sense, trying to patch up their marriage. He looks angry, fiercely angry, as when I kicked his son Jehangir in the balls. I wonder who would win in a fight between him and Mr. Krishnan? My burly uncle twice as large as his foe, or the pugnacious pugilist from Kerala? My uncle is dragging me down the stairs. "What have I done, Soli Uncle?" I cry out.

Mr. Krishnan's voice cut short my nightmare. "Ravi, wake him up now. This is ridiculous, it's ten o'clock." Ravi shook my shoulder. I made the most of looking bleary-eyed. The faces that greeted me were all disapproving. "You've been snoring for the last two hours," said Mr. Krishnan. "Go and wash your face."

This must have been the longest journey I had ever made. We had been one day and two nights in the train. I think we must have stopped at more than thirty stations. I wish I was one of those people who can tell you how many stations, big and small, they passed during a journey. I knew some who would even have noted down the names. People who were going to make a success out of their lives.

During the next day we made slow progress. Often the train stopped in the middle of nowhere. No one knew why and no one bothered to ask. A basket appeared at the door of the carriage, a hawker climbed on as if arisen from the dust. He was selling spicy banana chips. A green and black lungi wrapped around his thighs in the south Indian style, he passed silently through the compartment as if uninterested in selling his wares. The attention of the passengers on the train was undisturbed by such occasional forays. Their lives were spread out on their berths and any surrounding space they could occupy, as though they had taken up temporary residence in mini-houses. Like Mr. Krishnan, who seemed as comfortable here as on his living-room divan. I don't think they would have cared if the train decided, on one of its inexplicable halts, to stay there for a few months.

All day I stared out of my window as the train eased itself across a landscape that grew ever more green and lush as we slid southward. Sometimes steel trays of food were brought by one of the waiters in blue uniforms who worked for the Indian Railways Catering Service. These men were very rude and hurried through the compartments an hour before the meals arrived, shouting, "Lunch, dinner. Bolo, bolo, bolo, hah, lunch, dinner.

Vegetarian two rupees, non-veg three-fifty, special five rupees. Bolo, bolo, jaldi bolo." Someone wanted to know what was in the special meal. The waiter was not forthcoming. "Same as the non-veg. Do you want it or not? Don't waste my time."

"How can it be the same as and you are asking so much more money?" demanded the passenger.

"I don't know, don't ask me. I don't fix the prices," replied the irate employee. "I think you get an extra sweet dish. Custard or something. Now, do you want it or not?" The buyer held out a note. "Do you have change for ten?"

"No, I don't," said the waiter and walked off down the corridor, shouting, "Lunch, dinner, lunch, dinner."

"Where does all the food come from?" I asked Sushil. He asked his father. His father said there was a kitchen in the middle of the train doing curries, sambhar, vegetables, and rice in huge, vat-like pans.

"Can we go look at it later?" I asked.

"No," replied Mr. Krishnan.

The boys were under strict orders, and I had to do what they were told. We were only allowed off the train at large stations for a fixed period of time. They did not have any money, so we couldn't buy anything unless Mr. Krishnan decided it was appropriate for the whole family.

The last six hours of the journey were hot and boring. The carriage had emptied of all but a few travelers. We stopped at small stations with strange south Indian names: Varkala, Anjengoo, Kottayam. The vegetation had turned riotous. There were palm trees, banana trees, paddy fields, and mango. Yellows and greens of chemical intensity. The unmistakable smell of the sea wafted through our compartment. I asked Mr. Krishnan where we were. "We are traveling down the coast at the southern tip of India."

"What is the name of the sea?"

"It is called the Lakshwadeep Sea, after the Lakshwadeep Islands," said Mr. Krishnan enjoying the sound of the words in his mouth.

"Didn't Vasco da Gama land somewhere here?" said Sushil.

"No, that is not correct. We passed that part of the coast many hours ago. Vasco da Gama landed further north at Calicut and then went from Calicut to Cochin." The place Naresh came from.

My friends and I listened intently while Mr. Krishnan gave his wise answers.

"How far is it from Nayyar to the farm, Appa?" asked Sushil.

"Not very far at all. It must be some twenty miles. But there is only one bus a day during this time of the year. We may have missed it by the time we get there."

"Hey, Cyrus," said Ajay. "Where's that *Archie* comic of yours?"

"I've told you not to read that rubbishy American propaganda. Show it here," ordered Mr. Krishnan, taking it from my sheepish hand. He was in a good mood; we were all cautiously enjoying ourselves. Too much enjoyment never went down well in the Krishnan family.

Mr. Krishnan flipped through the pages of the comic. "Total and complete one hundred percent rubbish," he said, banging the comic down. Then he rubbed his face with his hands, cleared his throat, stuck his finger in each ear and gave it a wiggle, rocked back on his haunches, and folded his arms with satisfaction. The comic sat by his side. No one dared touch it. Archie, with his cute freckles, Betty, the nice blonde with big tits who adored him, and Veronica Lodge, the rich bitch whom Archie was always chasing.

19

After forty-one hours on the train we arrived at Trivandrum. The roads were wide and the pavements clean. There was hardly any noise, though the streets were ripe with activity. Mr. Krishnan seemed to know his way around the town. I was surprised by the number of posters and hoardings advertising films, more garish even than the ones in Bombay, though I couldn't understand a word of the Malayalam script. Everyone had the same fig-colored skin as the Krishnans. Most of them wore shirts and lungis folded double and tucked up just above the knee. The most popular mode of transport was the bicycle. The buildings were no more than two or three stories high. We turned onto the main road of the town, busy with shops and restaurants. A policeman was standing in the middle of the crossing under a parasol-shaped shelter, dressed in white, with a whistle in his mouth. Everybody was following his instructions. I felt I had entered a new country.

Mr. Krishnan led us to a small eating establishment, the Palathingal Hotel. There were wooden benches to sit on outside, and we were given rinsed banana leaves from which to eat. Before beginning the meal we washed our face and hands with elaborate care. My banana leaf was piled high with rice followed by dal, runny mango-flavored raita, mushy vegetables, curry, and fish. There was no choice of dishes: every two minutes a bare-chested man dolloped out food of unfamiliar flavor and consistency onto my leaf. On both sides of us, men were eating in the traditional style, shaping rice and curry in the palm of their hand, molding it into a compact ball, and flipping the sticky mixture into their open mouths. While they kneaded and squeezed the rice, yogurt, and curry, juice ran down their arms. Their tongues darted skillfully to lick away this juice. My food lay, colorfully arranged—white, red, and yellow—against the lime-green leaf. The curry was fierce, the rice glutinous, and the fish bony. The Krishnans ate with ardor, an intensity I simply could not match. For once, I found it hard to make it through the meal.

"I can't wait till we get to the farm," said Ravi. "Then we can have lovely jackfruit. You don't know jackfruit! It's got sticky yellow bits, like petals. The smell is so sweet. Like perfume!" Ravi swallowed with the effort of his description. The man sitting next to us slurped up a trickle of sweat mixed with the curry that ran down his arm. I was frightened to admit that my stomach hurt and I couldn't finish my meal. I knew Mr. Krishnan hated food going to waste.

"Ajay, would you like some fish?" I said quietly. He looked up from his rice. "You mean you don't like it? Look at all that rice on your plate. Eat up fast, come on."

"No, yaar, I'm not feeling well. You can have it." He picked up my fried fish and popped it into his mouth, scrunching up the bones and swallowing another lot of rice and yogurt to wash it down.

After lunch we walked down Mahatma Gandhi Road to the bus station. Mr. Krishnan led the way like a true patriarch. The family seemed to swagger a little, now that they were in their natural milieu.

I LOVED the journey to Nayyar. The bus rattled along the broken road, a cool breeze rushed in through the open window. The countryside was all fields of rice and coconut trees. Mr. Krishnan pointed out cashew and tobacco plants. We trundled through the parrot-green landscape, with only the occasional honk of the bus and the intermittent conversations in Malayalam babbling in my ear. All of us boys were smiling at the thought of getting closer to our destination. We held onto the seats in front, ready for when the bus hit a bump and sent us lurching into the air, a motion we exaggerated by letting our bodies be thrown.

Mr. Krishnan pointed out a low range of hills. "That is where we are heading. Ponmudi Hills." From time to time the bus was flagged down by travelers and tradesmen. A man got on with a gunnysack full of clucking chickens. Three women with immense baskets of green bananas found a way of fitting them under the seats. Mr. Krishnan had begun to talk to the passenger sitting behind him, asking him questions, nodding, and smiling. These were rural people, with creased leather faces; so dark a black I had seen only on the occasional African face strolling down Colaba Causeway. They traveled short distances, then new people got on. We city-dwellers were objects of curiosity. Our fellow passengers wanted to know who we were, where we were going, what we were doing there. I could tell that Mr. Krishnan took pride in telling them he was going to stay with his mother whom he had come all the way from Bombay to visit.

We reached Nayyar, a sleepy, thatched-roof mud-hut village, at five that evening, hungry and tired. People at the bus stand stared at us quizzically. I felt proud to be at the center of this commotion—a spectacle in their rural lives. To them, Trivandrum was the largest city in the world, a place few had visited but from which came tales of wealth, technology, and everlasting happiness. A wizened old man with spectacles and a walking stick emerged from the crowd.

"Where have you been for so long!" he groaned. "I have been waiting for more than one hour." He had a deep well-like voice with an accent which was a mixture of P. G. Wodehouse and strong south Indian. "How are you, my boys?" he said, turning to his grandchildren.

"You shouldn't have come all the way," said Mr. Krishnan to his father.

"Don't be silly. Next year I will be too old to come. Then you can make the journey on your own."

The boys touched his feet and he gave each of them a one-armed hug. "So this is Cyrus the great!" he chuckled. "Welcome, welcome!" Here was an awkward moment. Was I meant to touch his feet too? Was I meant to sidle over for an embrace? I knew kissing wasn't on, so I just stood there, grinning shyly.

"You won't find it easy, mind. Here we live rough. None of your Bombay-style comforts, eh. Anyway, we'll make a man of you by the end of the holiday. Cold baths at five A.M. Maybe you will be lucky and see a leopard or a bear." What a friendly chap this grandfather was, so unlike his strict and somber son. He was full of contagious laughter; like the Pied Piper of Hamelin, he made you want to follow him.

"Ingé va, Ajay, ingé va, all of you. Come here, yes, you too, Cyrus. Look at what I have brought for you." We crowded around him, I a little less close than his grandsons. From out of his kurta pocket he produced two shining Cadbury's Five Star chocolates. The boys began jumping up and down, gasping their thanks in Malayalam. "Now, share and share alike and make sure your Bombay boy gets some as well," he said, giving one to Ajay and one to Sushil, who began with some self-importance the careful measuring out of equal halves of chocolate-coated caramel.

Mr. Krishnan's father had booked the only taxi in the area to transport us to his farm, a rickety 1962 Ambassador with an old-fashioned steering wheel and pomegranate-red sofa seats. Getting eight of us and all the luggage into the car was no easy operation. It took a good half-hour, many attempted permutations, instructions given to the driver, bags tied to the boot and on the roof, before we were all jammed in one on top of another.

Soon we were ascending a winding road into the hills. These were gentle bends, not like the steep hairpins of the Bombay-to-Poona ghats. There was no traffic to be seen. We passed sloping fields with waist-high bushes planted in neat rows, which the elder Krishnan explained were tea plantations owned, in the good old days, by the sahibs of the Raj. Mr. Krishnan talked in a mixture of Malayalam and English to his father. The setting sun washed over us—a film of dusty orange. Before long, my lids were flickering toward sleep. The Krishnans tried to keep me awake to look at the scenery, but my eyes refused to obey their orders. The night spent awake in the train was catching up with me. Now and then, in a movie I'd been keenly watching, this same sweet slumber had wrapped me in its stubborn arms.

When I awoke we had arrived at the farm: a single bungalow with a wooden verandah and a tiled red roof. After all the build-up, it seemed pretty ordinary to me, surrounded on three sides by open fields of brown and green. At the back of the house was a fenced-in kitchen-garden, and behind that a small wood rolled uphill. I had been expecting astounding vistas and acres of fairy-tale forest.

Mrs. Krishnan came out to greet us, a gruff, short-tempered woman, who immediately gave orders.

"Come on, come in," she said to her son. "Pick up those bags, Ajay. No, no, not that one, the green one. Where is this friend of yours? Is he here or not?" She gave me a cursory look. Her graying hair spread around her head like a lion's mane. "He will sleep with you, Sushil, in the boys' room. Did the taxi man arrive on time? What a surprise. Useless fellow, he is. Ajay, I have made the dosas just the way you like them. Now, all of you go and wash your face and hands and then I will give you some food."

This frightening grandmother turned out to be a wonderful cook. Over the next few days I watched her, with undisguised fascination. Her round face, her commanding eye, the elaborate gestures, and the roll of stomach below the line of her blouse. She was one of those adults who like to have an audience: living alone with her sedentary husband, she had had little opportunity to show off her talents.

She took us round her vegetable garden pointing out the tomatoes, the cauliflower, the onions and ginger. She showed us the fruit trees: mango, banana chikoo, papaya, and jackfruit; and the spices essential to her cooking: cardamom, pepper, cumin, and curry leaves.

But it was the grandfather that I warmed to. He was full of stories, delivered with a glint in the eye and the unharried timing of a raconteur. The four of us sat at his feet on the verandah while he lay back in his easy chair, stroking his well-shaved cheeks with his fingertips.

"You see that rock over there," he said, pointing at a far corner of the field. "I wouldn't go too near it if I were you."

"Why's that?" I asked.

He looked at his grandsons. "Because, my boy, in the shade of that rock lives a black snake."

"How do you know?"

"I've seen it, my friend. If you want to find out, go and take a look. Sit yourself down on the edge and soon you will encounter the serpent. But don't come running to me if you get bitten. The nearest doctor is a good six miles away."

"How come *you* haven't been bitten?" It was possible to be more forthright with the elder Mr. Krishnan than I could ever have been with his stern-faced son.

The old man shook his head from side to side and wagged his finger at me. "A snake is an extremely intelligent creature. It knows its enemies and it watches over its friends. The cobra knows I am here and I know he is there. We respect each other's territory. I never have reason to go near that rock. Sometimes, if it is very hot, I put a bowl of water nearby. After a day or two, the water is gone." Grandfather's eyes wandered to the ceiling. "One time, oh, three or four years back, Kamla's nephew came to stay with us." Ajay and Sushil beamed; I could tell they loved hearing these stories again. "Young Manu had just graduated from college, so he thought he knew everything. I told him about the snake and he said I was talking nonsense. 'Superstition founded in Hindu mythology' he called it. I didn't try to argue with him.

"One evening, just as the sun was going down, I saw him standing by the rock. He was standing still, like a frozen statue." Grandfather held up a steady arm and his eyes narrowed with concentration. "This must have been about five-thirty. I thought to myself, 'Let him be,' and I went inside to read the papers. At seven o'clock the boy was still standing there, in the same position! Night had fallen. I thought to myself, 'I must go and see what's wrong.' So, I took my torch and walked across the field. When I got to within four or five feet of the boy, I could hear Manu, the clever college boy, gibbering, 'Oh my God, oh my mummy! Please, uncle, save me, mujhe bachao.' " Grandfather hammed up the student's fearful protests and we laughed at his acting. "Such was his state," he continued, "that his trousers were all soaking wet."

"Ai, ai, oh," exclaimed Sushil.

"But why was the boy so scared?" I wondered aloud.

"That is exactly what went through my mind as I looked him

up and down. Then I saw the cause of all his crying. The snake had wrapped its black coils around Manu's ankles and was lying there calmly resting on his feet."

"What did you do?" exclaimed Ravi.

"My good friend," grandfather said, turning to me. "I had half a mind to leave him standing there for the night. Why should I get involved?" He gesticulated with his fanned-out fingers. "I didn't want that the snake become an enemy to me and my wife. It could make our life hell. While I was standing there, thinking all these thoughts, and the college boy bleating like a small child, the snake reared its head—I was sure it was going to strike at Manu's calf—but then, slowly but surely, it uncoiled its scaly body and slithered away to its hideout underneath the rock."

"Did it look at you?"

"Why did it go when you arrived?"

"Those are all imponderables," said grandfather, dwelling on the syllables. "We will never know the answers, so there is no point asking. The snake went away and I had to carry Manu home in my arms. The boy did not leave his bed for two days. And after that, he very soon went back to Madras. These are the ways of nature, my friend," grandfather said, shaking his head sagely. "You city-dwellers have no idea." The boys looked at their grandfather proudly as he rested his head back. "So many things have happened," he said wistfully.

"Achachan, tell about that time the leopard woke you up in the forest. Please, Achachan!" Grandfather rubbed his thighs up and down. For a second it seemed as if he was gathering the pictures for this new tale of the jungle, then he sighed. "Another time. Let's leave it for today. You have to go and prepare yourselves for dinner now. Tomorrow I will tell you the story in full Technicolor."

20

Early in the morning on the third day, we set off to shoot birds in
the wood. There had been a lot of talk about wildlife in the surrounding forests and I was full of trepidation lest a langur or a
wolf should spring out of the undergrowth. Grandmother had
made us packed lunches of dosas, spicy potatoes, and coconut
chutney. It was my job to carry the food in a canvas backpack. All
I could think of, enveloped by the misty dawn, was when the time
would come for us to eat the lunch and what it would taste like.
The trees in the wood had tall thin trunks with branches high in
the sky. We walked uphill for hours and I began to feel exhausted,
in the way I used to when we went for our marathon early-morning runs on the beach. Mr. Krishnan strode ahead with the
twelve-bore shotgun strapped to his shoulder, Ajay just behind
carrying the box of cartridges, followed by Sushil, Ravi, and I
trying desperately to keep up.

Before we left the house, Ajay showed us the box of cartridges as if it were a set of rare coins. Chubby red sausages hel-
meted with gold. We fingered them with awe. "Each cartridge has
hundreds of tiny pellets in them," explained Ajay. "Like air-gun
pellets. When it hits the target this little trigger in the cap is
released and the pellets spray all around like a shower. So, with
two of these cartridges, you can shoot many birds. The record is
nine birds with one shot."

"How many has your dad shot at one go?" I inquired.

"Once he shot four birds with one shot."

"But he has shot two many times," added Ravi.

"So that's why it has a double barrel, so you can shoot both
cartridges together and disperse more pellets."

"Yah, but you don't have to use the double-barrel action.
Appa doesn't use it much. If you don't want to, you can just move
the lever and fire only one cartridge at a time." I was thoroughly
confused. "I'll show you later," said Ajay. "Appa has promised to
give me a shot today."

"Me also," piped Sushil.

"Oh, shut up you pipsqueak. The gun will throw you to the
ground with one shot."

The heat of the day was beginning to settle on our backs as
we trudged through the thinly carpeted jungle. I could hear the
chirping of birds in the branches above. In single file we
marched, stepping carefully on the ground lest we disturb the
innocent birds larking beside their nests. I imagined I was part of
a platoon in a Second World War movie, the enemy hidden all
around us, but we, the heroes, had plotted our route and would
gun them down in their camouflaged lairs. Every few moments,
Mr. Krishnan stopped and put his finger to his lips, and the signal
was passed down the line. Then we bent our ears and necks with
reverence, listening out for the call of a partridge or a cock pheas-
ant. Ajay or Sushil would point to the branches of a tree and

sometimes crouch down. Such was the intensity of their demeanor that I was forced to lie and nod in agreement at their sightings. "Oh, yes. I can see it now," I would whisper.

Then Mr. Krishnan would steady himself, eye squinted, iron-gray barrels pointing to the treetops, and all us boys would wait, breaths locked in our beating hearts, for the flash and the crack, the zooming red bullet, the squealing bird falling from its branch, the smoking gun, and the cry of the flock as they winged their way to safety. We waited, Mr. Krishnan took aim, and time ate itself up. But there was no roar of thunder, no bursting flame, no wasted cartridges lying on the ground, no carcass of bone and feather. Just Mr. Krishnan's clucking tongue as he lowered his weapon and the unsuspecting birds continued in their revelry. "No point. It's too far away," he would say. Or, "There's only one bird sitting on its own. It's not worth it." At first I let out my imprisoned breath with relief; I couldn't imagine what might happen when the gun went off, having only ever seen gunfights in films.

My disappointment grew. I began to wonder about the truth of my friends' stories, of twelve and fourteen birds shot in one excursion. I became more inventive with my lies. When one or the other of the boys pointed to the trees and said, "There it is. Can you see it perched on that branch, on the top there?" I would peer in the direction of their finger, only leaves and sky in my vision, and say, "Oh, yah, I can see it. In fact, there are two or three sitting there, can you see? Go on, Sushil, tell your dad to take a shot, they're not moving."

"Appa, look, three birds, there, by the silvery branch," urged Sushil. Slowly, like an accomplished marksman, Mr. Krishnan, the Robin Hood of Kerala, raised his weapon and took aim again. We took our positions like rocks of silent salt. I just wished he would shoot, even if he missed the target, even if there were no birds for grandmother to curry. All I wanted was to hear that gun go off. But there was no telling Mr. Krishnan what to do. He was his own master. He was master of the world. And we followed silently behind.

Lunch finally arrived. We sat on the rocks, munching, lost in the lovely tastes of coriander, coconut, and curry leaves, fresh curry leaves with waxy yellow potatoes, dotted with black mustard seeds. Smoky, spicy, nutty, scented potatoes. The taste of curry leaves made me appreciate the dark canopy of leaves above, the heat of the afternoon offset by the cool sweat brought on by the spices. Sat there in the forest, I realized how important food was in my life but also how much the thought of it tormented me. The thought of having it, of not having it, the taut expectation of its delights, and the sweet torture of eating it.

Mr. Krishnan led us back to the farm using a circular route. He shot three times into the trees. A pellet managed to find the breast of one bird, though Mr. Krishnan insisted that two had fallen out of the trees. I was past caring. The pariah bitch from the farm sniffed every dead leaf in the vicinity to no avail. Our Irish setter would have put Mr. Krishnan's lie to rest.

When we got back that evening I was too tired to think of anything but bed. I insisted on staying in it for twelve hours. The Krishnans jeered at my lily-livered fatigue. The next day at lunch we ate the bird. I was shocked at how tiny the pieces were. There was barely a bite for each of us. It tasted like liver—a dense, dark, bitter meat. The curry seemed infected by it, olive-green and oily, with a peculiar blandness to its flavor. I sang its praises without compunction. While everyone was absorbed in their eating I looked at Mrs. Krishnan's breasts. She was wearing a loose sleeveless dress like a housecoat with buttons down the front. Across from me she sat, chewing assiduously on a tiny bone of bird, and through the opening in her dress I glanced slyly. She had no bra and I had a partial side view of her large brown milky dug as it jigged from side to side with the motion of her eating. I was aware both of the danger and the pleasure of my entrancement. I kept looking away and talking to Sushil or Ajay, knowing that I could always turn around and look again at her delectable bosom. If Ajay knew I was looking at his mother in this way, he would beat me to a pulp. I dropped something under the table and bent down to pick it up. Mrs. Krishnan's legs, her rubber slippers, her fat fleshy calves, her knees, and her dress pulled tightly around her thighs were clearly visible. I came back up quickly. I was surprised that this was the first time I had noticed Mrs. Krishnan physically. It was normal with me to imagine something sexual with virtually every woman I saw. Perhaps it was because she was always so sullen and stout in her ways. I noticed her mouth had relaxed a little; she talked more and even allowed us to get away with things which would have earned the boys a sound hiding in Bombay.

At the end of the meal the two men retired to their respective resting places, grandfather on the planter's chair with the long wooden footrests extended, Mr. Krishnan to the bedroom. The boys helped to clear up, the two women did the washing-up in the kitchen.

The afternoons were hot and still. The adults took to their beds and we were meant to lie down for half an hour. But more often than not we crept out through the kitchen, and played games, chatted, or wandered around in the wood at the back of the house. There was something unearthly about these afternoons. Even our games were affected by the air of listlessness.

The afternoon of the bird curry, Sushil and I sat on our haunches and played marbles on the baked mud of the backyard. Ravi was napping, Ajay couldn't be bothered to play, and lay on a grassy patch reading the comics I had bought on the train. Sushil, the most skillful player of us all, having tired of beating me, was giving me a few lessons on the positioning of my forefinger in relation to the eye-blue marble. It was no good, my finger just wouldn't bend back the way his did, like a bow. I tried to copy his technique a few times and then gave up. Sitting on the ground with my legs pulled up against my chest and my arms swaddling my knees, I watched him play on his own for a while. Then he jumped up. "Let's go and climb up that tree." Oh no, not the tree, I thought to myself. He was referring to the tree near the house which had a thick branch running off the main trunk, six feet from and parallel to the ground. Every evening we went down there and swung from the branch like amateur gymnasts, doing countless chin-ups, rolling over and round the branch like chimpanzees. I dreaded this tree because the branch was mainly used as a test to see who could do more chin-ups and other stomach-turning twirls. I could barely hang from the branch without feeling that my hands and arms were going to be ripped from my body at the shoulder. After four pull-ups I was ready to die; each half pull was an agony of strained muscle and gritted teeth. Of course the two elder Krishnan boys could do many more than me. Ajay and Sushil could do five with one hand and five with the other without any loss of composure. They performed twenty-two chin-ups as if they were bored with the counting. Only Ravi, three years my junior, would huff and puff as he counted past my own pathetic achievement.

"Let's go, na," Sushil urged. "I'm getting bored."

"Ask Ajay to come," I said, trying to find a way out.

"You go, I'll finish this comic and come," said Ajay decisively.

"Okay, wait here, two minutes," I said to Sushil. "I have to go to the bathroom badly." I decided to go round the side of the house to waste time. I walked past Mr. and Mrs. Krishnan's bedroom window. The curtains were loosely drawn; I could see through one-quarter of a pane. I crouched down below the parapet. My eye level was almost parallel with the blue and white checked bedspread on which husband and wife lay. Out of fear, or deference, or my natural inclination to hold back from the desired object, I looked at Mr. Krishnan first. He lay on his back with his hands folded in a cradle of fingers supporting his head. His iron legs were tightly wrapped in a white lungi and his bare chest rippled like chocolate icing on a sumptuous cake. He slept the deep sleep of a strong man.

Mrs. Krishnan was lying alongside her husband, one arm drawn across her eyes, the other resting on her stomach. Her left knee was bent up toward her pillow almost at right angles to the rest of her body. I couldn't believe she could be comfortable with her hip contorted so, like a Kathakali dancer squatting on one leg, frozen in repose. Her housecoat had been unbuttoned to let in some air and fell open about her waist. I could see the inside of her thighs, the lines made by her bottom, and a huge area of black hair growing in between. For a second I couldn't make sense of what I was seeing. The scene on the bed was like a painting, of a woman naked below the waist and above the knees, so clear it could masquerade as an enlarged photograph: tremulous pale pouches of puckered flesh. The heat of the afternoon, the silent resting figures all around, my friends playing in the trees behind the house, and Mrs. Krishnan lying here in a position of luscious fatigue. I looked again at the painting. Surprised at its awkwardness, the pallid sunless skin, the dark crease disappearing into her bottom, the relaxation of every sinew, the narrowness of her waist compared to the bell-like flesh swelling around her hips, the black hair growing in little tufts around the inside of her thighs, fanning out warm and thick and dark right up and onto the first tumescence of stomach. I had no idea there was so much hair, that it grew so far and wide and wild. It was like looking right up inside her body. I was reminded of my mother and what she looked like in the shower. I was reminded of all the other women I knew. Did they all look like this? Like ripe fruit, mossy and blemished, hanging in the warm air. Mr. Krishnan rubbed his nose, turned onto his side, and dropped his hand on to his wife's stomach. Petrified, I crawled away under the window and silently entered the house.

While sitting on the toilet, fear draining out of me, I recalled what I had just seen. The image was ruined by the thought of Mr. Krishnan climbing over her body and flooding her space with his thrusts. I closed my eyes and worked him out of my picture. I wanted simply to sit there in the bare gray of the bathroom and nurse the sight I'd seen, caress it, sink my body into her open thighs. There I sat with my shorts around my ankles, the world's turning weighted in my thoughts.

And I wondered how many years would pass before this scene would yield to the process which steals our images from the light of memory. How long would this image of Mrs. Krishnan's bum remain a photograph in my mind? The words and images of my life were like rush-hour passengers piling into the vast entrance of Churchgate station; I imagined them all jostling and pushing for position, throwing themselves in through the door. And when the train leaves the station most of them have been left behind, like the people I'd met whom I couldn't remember, like the things that I'd heard that I couldn't recall, like the hundreds of minutes and days in my life that were nothing in the calendar of my brain. I resolved, as I poured water down the toilet, to use my notebook more often. I must try and make a record of things. This image especially would be one I would try to fix in my thoughts.

21

"Minoo suffered heart attack. Please send Cyrus home on earliest possible flight from Trivandrum."

I saw the telegram. It lay on the table in the dining room. The first thing I thought when Ajay told me that my father was in hospital was that I was never going to see him again. I walked out onto the verandah and looked at the dumb fields. I just stood there on the Krishnan farm in Kerala and a voice spoke in my head, "You are never going to see your father's face again." I could see the banana trees at the edge of this sun-dried field with their flat green blades. I could hear the grandmother in the kitchen clattering amongst the pots, and the voices of my friends as they prepared for their daily outing, while I waited for the taxi that would transport me to Trivandrum airport. The family dog, the filthy beige bitch, the scrawny-haired, tick-infested mongrel who kept me awake all night with her barking, was scrabbling after some creature in the ochre dust. I stood there and watched her.

I reasoned with myself: "Your dad is not dead, he is only ill. He will recover, that's what everyone is saying. Even if he dies, Cyrus, you will see his body, you will see his face at the funeral. You are going home by plane now, so you are bound to see him in the hospital."

I SUCKED hard on my boiled sweet as we took off from Trivandrum. Plane journeys made me sick. I was fine on car journeys, even when we were coming down a steep ghat, but on a plane my stomach went into revolt and my body's plumbing creaked.

The air hostess came round with a plastic tray of snacks. A vegetable samosa and a small sandwich of decrusted white bread and cheese. I gobbled them down, closed my eyes, and the thighs of Mrs. Krishnan opened before me. I tried to push them away. I should be concentrating on my father's illness. In my trouser pocket there was a ten-rupee note. I hadn't had time at the airport to go into the shop and buy any comics and I had left the old ones for my friends. A boy in our class at school called Kailash swam into my mind.

A well-behaved, quiet boy with big pink lips and a protruding nose. I recalled a Friday afternoon in the classroom, period nine, a few minutes from the end of the day. Kailash was sitting in the middle of the front row opposite the teacher's desk. We had English with Mrs. Silgardo. She had set us an essay and was calling in our books, one at a time, to be marked. I was doing as little as possible of the essay and trying to get Hoshang to play a game of book cricket with me. "No, yaar, we'll bloody get into trouble, Cyrus," he moaned. "She'll make us kneel down in front of the class and stay after school." Just then I heard Mrs. Silgardo scolding somebody in the front row. We all listened because it was rare that a goody-goody like Kailash got a tongue-lashing from a teacher.

"Look at this!" she said, holding up an open page of his exercise book. "Do you call this work? Half a page in this illegible handwriting of yours. And what is this?" she screamed. "Noughts and crosses! Is this what you are coming to school for?" Kailash looked dumbfounded, his mouth open as if he were about to speak. The rest of us were rapt.

"I know the problem with you," said Mrs. Silgardo. "Your mother is too lenient, she should give you a good slapping. I talked to her about your work last month and nothing has happened. I know what I'm going to do now. I'm going to phone up your father." Mrs. Silgardo pronounced the word "father" with deliberation and a hint of satisfaction. "You need someone strict, someone who will give you a good hiding, so you won't forget next time." There she stopped and a hush fell on the class. I was looking at the rise and fall of Mrs. Silgardo's chest in her mauve dress when I heard sobs coming from the front of the class. Kailash was wiping the tears from his streaming eyes. At first I thought to myself, what a weakling, a little bit of shouting and he's broken down. But why was Mrs. Silgardo looking so guilt-stricken? Some of the boys were whispering conspiratorially to one another. Kailash's face was a picture of pain. Sobs breaking in upon themselves, like a stuttering engine. Mrs. Silgardo stood up and went over to him. She was searching for words to speak. The whisper reached where Hoshang was sitting; he repeated it in my ear. "Kailash's father died two months ago."

Mrs. Silgardo softened. "I'm sorry," she said. "I shouldn't have said that. Why don't you go and wash your face, my child? Glen, why don't you take Kailash to the toilets?" This only made Kailash sob louder. He shook his head to show he didn't want to go anywhere. He didn't want to wash his face. He just wanted to sit there and cry his heart out. All of us boys thought of our own dads. Even Mrs. Silgardo thought of her gray-haired pater who lay in his pajamas all day, listening to the BBC World Service in his flat in Bandra. I pictured my father in his dark suit striding down the corridor toward my room to wish me goodnight. And we all imagined, for Kailash, what it would be like to have your father dead.

Later that day Kailash's anguish revisited me. Your father's dead—so what? What it meant, I decided, was that you would never see him again. Never see his face or hear his voice or feel his rough cheek against your skin. Now, as I sat on this plane soaring home through the Indian sky, I saw again the silhouette of Kailash's face on that Friday afternoon at St. Mary's, I saw his stained cheeks, his sore eyes raging at the thought that there was someone out there, this stupid English teacher, who did not know, or had momentarily forgotten, how his life had been mangled. If only, he must have thought, she could phone his dad, write to him to come and see her at the school, tell him to administer a beating to his son. "Cyrus, your father is not dead," I said to myself. "He has only been taken to hospital with a heart attack." Out of the plane's window I could see nothing but thin blue sky.

WE CUT into the dark clouds and dropped down over the city where I was born. The lights of Bombay winked up from the inky blackness where the sea kissed its hot shore. Somewhere underneath me was the house my father built, the bed in which I slept and heard planes like this one roaring in and out of Santacruz airport. The stewardess came round with the boiled sweets and the cotton wool. I didn't turn my head for fear of being sick. Keeping my forehead pressed against the window, I concentrated on the lights below. I knew there was a sick bag in the pocket of the seat, but I tried not to think of that. The descent of the aircraft sent ripples of nausea rising up from my stomach, like the lines of scum left on the beach by the encroaching waves. My head felt as if a belt were being tightened around my temples. I saw lights again, amber lights, I wasn't sure if they were runway or street lights. I thought of lights going out in the monitor strapped to my father's body. I saw my mother's face waiting to pick me up at the airport.

I could see the hutment dwellings that swarmed like pubic hair around the buildings, the jhopadpatis made of gunnysack, bamboo, tin, and cardboard, the film stars' houses just next door, the tea shops, the paanwallahs, the children playing cricket by lamplight, the slow progress of cars, and Mrs. Krishnan's thighs resting like ripe fruit. A woman's voice came through the air as the plane revved its engines. "In a few minutes we shall be landing at Bombay's Santacruz airport. Indian Airlines wishes you a pleasant stay." My ears felt as if the air was being sucked out of them with huge syringes, my head shuddered with constriction. The engines whined, the tarmac approached at last. I thought of my father's heart split open inside his body, like a pomegranate torn in half. A smell of sour potatoes came up my throat. The wheels thudded down, I lowered my head against the seat in front of me; there, next to my eyes, was the vomit bag. "Hold tabs over your ears," it said. The plane taxied toward the domestic terminal. I followed the instructions on the bag and out rushed everything I had eaten that afternoon. With it, the pressure in my head and ears ebbed away. Shame took its place. I wanted to be a suave, relaxed traveler, reading the paper as he touched down, not this retching little boy hugging a paper bag.

22

At the door of the arrival lounge I saw my aunt Zenobia, a round figure of a woman who moved like a heavy and amorphous ball being pushed along the street, swiveling herself forward with the help of her short blobby arms. She was white, like a foreigner, with blue eyes and cropped mousy hair. Her nails curved out like the long talons of a kite: manicured, varnished, and layered with pale pink lacquer.

Zenobia was unpredictable, frightening, and rich. She wore roomy dresses that ballooned over her haunches and ended halfway down her shins. On special occasions her plateau-like chest glistened with rubies and emeralds the size of sweets. As I followed her through the halls of the airport, I noticed her rubber-chapaled feet pointing outward as she walked. Zenobia Aunty could be marvelously generous and thoroughly bad-tempered in the one short space of time. Everyone was scared of her, some hated and envied her, but I was always enamored by her mysterious past—she was said to have been a femme fatale in her college years—her whiteness, the excess of her dining table—you could always count on a five-course meal of exotic foods, lobster, Goa curry, escalopes with cheese and ham, spaghetti with clams, meat pies, trifles, jellies, and zabaglione—and by her perverse sense of humor. She never spoke an uncontroversial word, and most of her statements were theatrical.

"Mehroo, you have put on so much weight," she would say loudly to my mother. "You are really looking very fat today." Offered a drink, she would say, "No, no, no, I never drink outside. No, no tea or coffee, just freshly squeezed grapefruit juice. But you won't have that in your house."

Zenobia lived in a flat on the top of Malabar Hill. A devout Zoroastrian, she said her prayers four times a day, waking at three in the morning for the first session. When evening descended quietly on the prosperous trees of this exclusive hill, Zenobia's Gujarati servants wafted urns of burning sandalwood and frankincense around the flat, perfumed smoke which bars the evil spirits from our lives and purifies the soul. She was to be seen standing on the balcony, saying her prayers, looking out at the Parsi Towers of Silence and the vultures, well fed on the remains of the dead, circling above. Then it would be time for the whisky—the grapefruit juice was all a sham. What she really liked was smoked oysters on toast, dotted with Tabasco and lime and washed down with a large Black Label clinking around in a goblet of ice. These she would consume whilst sitting on an ancient rocking chair and contemplating the dying rays of the sun. The chair groaned beneath its burden.

I loved being part of these evenings on her balcony. "Cyrus, you are a very stupid boy," she would say. "You know why you are such a stupid boy?"

"No," I said, shaking my head and smiling.

"Because you don't read enough. When I was your age I was reading at least ten to fifteen books every week. My father used to have to force me to stop. At night, I used to hide under the sheet and read with a torch." She took another swig of whisky and returned to her meditative rocking. I couldn't imagine Zenobia fitting under a sheet even when she was very young. "What kinds of books did you read, Zenobia Aunty?"

"Oh, I don't remember. All sorts of books, mysteries, religious books, Dickens, Thomas Hardy, philosophy. Enid Blyton wasn't there in those days. But all the time I was reading."

"But you couldn't have read fifteen books in one week. Especially thick books like Dickens."

"Don't cheek me back," she said sternly. "You don't know anything. I'm telling you, we used to read at least one book a day." I laughed. "Where is your sudhra and kusti? You haven't even had your Navjote yet. You don't know any Parsi prayers and you're trying to behave smart. Arre ja ja. If I was your parents, I would never allow such rubbish." Zenobia glowered. "By the time a boy is eight or nine," she said in her sing-song voice, "he should definitely have had his Navjote. After that it is too late, puberty has been reached. I will teach you some prayers. Repeat after me, 'Ashem Vahu, Usta Asti.' "

"I know 'Ashem Vahu' and 'Yatha Ahu Vairyo,' " I said, confidently.

"Ha, you know that at least. Jehangir!" she screamed suddenly at her son, who was sneaking out of his bedroom to go downstairs. "Where do you think you are off to? Have you done your homework? No, you have not done your homework. Don't lie to me. Get back into your room and don't you dare come out till you have finished!"

That's what she was like. She had come to pick me up at the airport because she considered it was her duty, while my father was ill, to look after her sister-in-law's children. The place of the wife was at her husband's side.

•❖•   •❖•   •❖•

THE GREEN Packard stopped at a traffic light. The engine cut off. I was surprised to see Zenobia acting like the taxi drivers who switched off their engines to save petrol. My father told me it was more cost-effective to keep the engine idling.

"Why do you put the engine off?" I asked, turning sideways in the front seat.

"It's not off. The engine is so smooth there's no sound. So you think it's off."

"But how can that be? I can't feel anything."

Zenobia pressed down on the accelerator and the engine burred. "These old American cars are very smooth and comfortable but when they go wrong it takes months to get them fixed. No one really knows how to do it. Our mechanics are useless. It's all guesswork for them." What a car, I thought, sinking my back into the padded sofa seat. It was like sitting in an armchair in her comfortable living room. I looked out of Zenobia's car window, her fleshy pink triceps resting on the door. The pavement on the road into town had been colonized by makeshift homes— pavement dwellings cobbled together with recycled materials collected from rubbish heaps. Brown sheets of cloth, bits of metal, torn shreds of plastic, calendars, books, and hundreds of other discarded artifacts that surfaced like flotsam from the ebb and flow of the city. I was familiar with these settlements: some had been there many years. On my countless journeys up and down and across Bombay I had watched them burgeon. I was told by our driver that many of these streets were controlled by goondas, who rented out space on the pavement for exorbitant sums. They also paid off the police to keep them from demolishing the source of their income.

Zenobia thrust the gear lever up and we shunted forward, behind a crawling BEST bus. The hoarding at the back was for Wills Navy Cut cigarettes. A picture of a man and a woman with the slogan, "Made for each other." I stuck my chin on the bottom edge of the window and surveyed the passing world. I imagined I was on one of those trolleys I had seen at the Sun 'n' Sand film shoot, where the camera is pushed along a short set of rails. It moves along slowly but it sees everything. A group of pavement boys, one of them with a rain hat over his head, was crouched over a game of cards. They were arguing noisily. A man sat on his haunches smoking a beedi. A baby girl was being vigorously washed by her mother; her brown body, covered in lather, glistened in the darkness. A gaunt man in a vest emerged red-eyed from one of the entrances to a bamboo-pole and cloth hut. I had once gone to one of these addas with our driver, Pandu, and taken a pull on a chillum he had paid to smoke. The hit had been so dizzying that Pandu had to carry me back to our house.

The car gathered speed. The scenes and characters flickered past. I glimpsed a boy selling tea in little glasses held together in a wire tray. A girl cried out as her mother beat her around the backside. Then I saw Mrs. Krishnan lying on the bed again, a fecund forest of hair between her outspread legs. I still didn't know where we were going. Zenobia had told me nothing.

"Where is Mummy? Is she in the hospital with Dad?"

"Your mother has taken Minoo to America. That is why I have come to pick you up."

"I thought Daddy was in hospital."

"Yes, he had a very severe heart attack. He was in intensive care at Breach Candy. The doctor said he was very lucky to survive."

"Then what happened?"

"Then what? I told your mother to keep him here and let our world-renowned heart specialist Dr. Gamadia—everyone says how good he is—take care of Minoo. But she wouldn't listen. She heard about some new method of open-heart surgery in Chicago and she bought tickets on the next flight over there. Dr. Gamadia told her Minoo might not survive the flight, but she insisted on going. You know what Mehroo is like—very stubborn. By the grace of God they both survived the flight and now he has got a bed in this famous hospital in Chicago, what the name is I have no idea, and the surgeon is looking after him. Hah, the surgeon's name is Kennedy, like the president. That much I know."

I couldn't control the thoughts that tumbled into my brain, while feeling ashamed of them. America, I thought, lovely country, I've always wanted to go there. Chicago, gangster city, it's in all the movies. Then I thought of my father lying there in a glass chamber, snow covering everything outside. If he died, would I have to go to America? I knew I was not going to see him again.

"Is Daddy all right now?"

"The last news we got from your mother was that he was stable, but they are still deciding whether to operate or not." I didn't like the tone she used when she said "your mother."

"I am taking you to Granny and Grandpa's house now. Then later on we will see what happens. Maybe you can come to my house for a few days. You like to play with Jehangir, don't you?"

"I don't mind," I said.

23

I didn't want to go to my granny's flat on top of the hill. I wanted to go home to Juhu and visit my friends, the Maharani and the Vermas. I wanted to be in my glass room, with my scratchy Polydor record player. I wanted to listen to "Those were the days, my friend" and be sent to sleep by the waves curtaining in over the sand. I wanted to sit on the wall of the house in the middle of the day and look out at the gray sea.

But I had no say. My younger brother and my sister were already waiting at Belmont. Instead of the sea and my neighbors, we were surrounded by the jungle of thorns and black rock at the back of my granny's building, where the peacocks screeched and wild cats streaked in and out of the thirsty bushes. There was something ancient and absurd about this clump of vegetation: a shrubland of little trees, animals, and inhospitable rocks, and unchanged for hundreds of years, somehow forgotten in the furious scramble to develop every empty space in the city. Perhaps all Bombay was like this once.

Here it was that I searched for a vision of my father. For an end to the sulky premonition that had dogged me all the way from Kerala, from the first moment of hearing about his illness. I looked for his face amongst the brittle sunburnt twigs, the crows in the useless, nameless dull green trees. I tried to picture him in hospital or in our house in Juhu. I tried, but nothing appeared, not even a fabricated memory. All there was was the weather-beaten boulders and the animal certainty that I would never see my father again.

In and out of this emptiness, like a broken thread, the tableau of Mrs. Krishnan's outspread thighs wavered in the stillness of a Keralite afternoon. Her puckered flesh exuding warmth and horror: a warmth in which I wanted to bury my face, the horror of finding it impossible to conjure up my father's features while having no trouble at all with the aromatic thrust of Mrs. Krishnan's arse.

EACH DAY there was some kind of news. For all I knew, it was made up by my granny. News of my father's recovery, news of an operation on his heart, news of him in intensive care, news of him eating porridge. It was a long-winded and tenuous business trying to get through to Chicago on the phone, but my mother sent us telegrams and short letters: chronicles of exhaustion, of a life lived from morning to night in the hospital.

I comforted myself with Granny's hot chapatis filled with clotted cream and strawberry jam, the scrambled eggs made to perfection, and the sweet sesame ladoos after lunch. She cooked delicious evening meals too: rus chawal, with its tender goat and coconut milk, khichri kheema; lentil-stained rice with healthy portions of clove and cinnamon-flavored mince, machhi-no-sas, a thick white curry with tails of pomfret. There was a pudding every night: caramel custard, rice pudding, homemade ice cream, falooda, and an opaque pink ghas nu jelly.

My grandfather sat at the head of the table on a large black cane-backed chair with armrests. His six-foot-six bulk silent, his lips folded out, his face furrowed in a frown, he waited anxiously for his food. When it arrived, steaming in oval dishes of white porcelain, he shoveled mounds of it into his wide-open jaws. There was hardly any gap between mouthfuls, no discernible bite or chew, just heaps of scalding rice and mince slipping down his throat. My granny would try to calm him, "Aste, Fali, aste. Please, slow down. Em jaldi na khavanu. It's bad for your heart, the doctor has told you." A few seconds later his plate was bull-dozed clean. The frown returned to his face as he waited for a sec-ond helping. I wanted seconds too, and I tried to race him to the finish but I was never anywhere near. My sister, Shenaz, hadn't even started before his plate was empty. He would never ask for more, but from time to time he shot a questioning glance at my granny, who was busy feeding the children. She forced him to drink a glass of water, after which she carefully laid three or four spoonfuls of rice and mince onto his plate, taking her time and bit-ing her lip as she served. His spectacled eyes followed the silver spoon with desperate impatience. When she had stopped, he looked at the small mound of food on his plate as if to say, "Is this it? Is that all I get?" My granny would say, "Cyrus and Adi want some more as well. Now, don't be greedy, Fali, you've had a lot already. Think of others. Look at me, I've only got the bones to chew." Truth be told, even when there was lots of food to go round, my grandmother preferred to strip the leftover bones with her teeth rather than help herself to another spoonful of rice and curry.

As soon as he had finished, my grandfather decamped to the sofa, conveniently situated behind his chair. Here he stretched out and waited for the relief of a protracted burp or a thunderous

fart. During these emissions the expression on his face showed no
perceptible change. None of us laughed or showed any sign of
surprise.

I DECIDED to go home to Juhu. I took the 4Ltd bus straight after
school and phoned up my granny from the Maharani's bedroom,
saying that I had gone to get some books for school and could I
stay over for the weekend. I told her the Maharani had agreed to
look after me and keep me well fed. She acquiesced with surprising ease. The news from Chicago indicated my father was recov-
ering, she said, and they would probably be flying home within a
fortnight.

I was overjoyed to see my friends. The Maharani hugged and
kissed me, brought out a box of Belgian chocolates, and told me
all the news I had missed. I regaled her with tales of my time in
Kerala, some made up, some doctored. It was like a festival of
light and love and mutual admiration. I felt honored at having an
adult, a Maharani, as my close friend. I stopped caring about
Meera and whether or not I was betraying her by being so close
to her adopted mother.

I spent the whole evening with the Maharani. She changed the
habit of a lifetime and came downstairs to eat her dinner. She
ordered my favorite Rajasthani white curry, and at nine-thirty,
two hours before her normal time, we were seated at the long dining table, Meera and her sister beaming with surprise, the servants
perked up and attentive. In this mood of unfettered enjoyment, my
mouth full of korma and rice, it dawned on me that my relatives
had been hinting at a possible reconciliation between my mother
and father. I realized that my father's illness may have brought my
parents back from the precipice of permanent separation. His
heart attack, I told myself, had reawakened in them the passion for
each other which had been damaged by his deceit. I let myself
believe that my presentiments about my father were nothing

more than morbid fancies. I imagined him alighting from the plane, his broad face pallid but smiling, my mother standing right behind looking proud, the way she used to before all their dreadful fights. Surely now, on their return, we would all be back together in our family home, fighting and bawling across the dining table. I thought of my father's feet mounting the spiral staircase to my parents' bedroom. I thought of him once again clasping my upper arm in his strong fingers and I returned to the phulkas and cauliflower before me with an inch added to my wide smile.

For pudding we ate Alphonso mangoes. Ripe and golden from their straw beds. Nothing can quite compare with the sinking of teeth into the vivid orange flesh of an Alphonso. The scent of marmalade and candied fruit, and a taste like the sweet sharpness of limes are followed by the clean juice running into the mouth. "Food for the Gods" my father called them. The Maharani cut mine in the regal manner: not vertically down the sides but round the belly of the fruit. Then she twisted the two halves with her hands and laid them on her plate like the earth split open at the equator, with the stone sticking out of one of the halves. She showed me how to scoop out the flesh with a teaspoon, using the skin as a handle, whilst sucking on the fibrous heart of the mango. She demonstrated all this with poise and precision, but by the time I had got to the gootli there was pulp and juice all over my fingers and face.

At the end of the meal the Maharani said, "Why don't you just stay the night here? There's no one at your house and tomorrow morning you can have some bacon and eggs with me." She smiled slyly, knowing I could not resist her offer. When she departed upstairs I sat quietly in my chair while Meera and her sisters cleared up. I accompanied them, as usual, when they took the dogs out for their last walkabout of the day. We didn't say much. I helped with the rounding up of the last straggling chihuahuas, calling out their names as Meera used to. I felt like just another member of the Maharani's household.

Afterward, I followed Meera and her younger sister Sivi to their bedroom at the far end of the house, the opposite end from the Maharani's bower. It was in this room that the girls let their hair down, smoking cigarettes, gossiping, cursing their benefactor, and flirting with the boys who were allowed into the house. I had spent a lot of time hanging around here, but most times I was ignored or treated as an annoyance. On this occasion, the one time I hadn't bothered to seek her favor, Meera was acting really friendly. When we smoked a cigarette together in the bathroom, she didn't make her usual scornful comments about my attempts to appear older than my age when I couldn't even inhale properly. Then she pushed me out of the bathroom, so she could change. I sat on the single bed against the wall and flipped through back issues of *Stardust* magazine. Meera came out of the bathroom, applying lotion to her face and neck, in a sleeveless blue-gray top and a white petticoat. She sat next to me, our backs against the wall. She took up a magazine and started going through the names of all the models in the advertisements. My bare arm was touching hers. I couldn't quite believe this was happening. After all those nights of fantasy, my bare arm was kissing hers.

"That's Smita Dayal. What do you think of her? Her cheeks are a bit fat, no? But look at that hair. Hai, it's beautiful, isn't it?"

"Not as lovely as yours," I thought to myself. But I didn't dare say anything lest Meera suddenly turned on me with her razor tongue. I nodded my head in agreement with everything she said, too scared to move in case she noticed how our arms were touching.

"I wish I had nails like these, yaar, Cyrus. Just look at this Jasmine Padiwala's hands! Bloody Parsis all have lovely skin. Your mother has lovely hands as well. She wears too much makeup though and she rubs lipstick on her cheeks, doesn't she?"

"How did you know that?"

"I can tell. You should tell her to stop doing that. It's very bad for the skin." I didn't like people talking about my mother, so I changed the subject.

"What's wrong with your nails? They look fine to me."

"Oh, they go on chipping all the time because they're so thin, even though I put lots of varnish on them. I need more calcium. Let's see *your* nails," she said taking my hand in her palm. "Chh-heeee! You dirty boy! Why don't you cut your nails? Look how long they are. No wonder they get so filthy. Look at that," she said, trying to bend the top of my nail. "Hard, hard, and no white spots at all. That's because you all eat so much cheese." I thought it odd that she just glanced at the pictures in each magazine and got through them in a matter of minutes. When I read *Stardust*, I explored every article with studious diligence, scrutinizing the pictures and the captions that explained them.

"Look at this! Nandini Seth in the Khatau advert. And that sicko Prakash Kapur standing next to her and all. They used to come to Elphi and sit on the bench with us and now they are engaged to each other. Bloody fool she is. She must have got at least twenty grand for this ad. Sivi! Look at this!" she shouted to her sister lying on the bed near the window on the other side of the room.

"Oh, shut up, Meera! I'm trying to get some sleep. Stop your buk-buk, yaar. I'm not interested in some stupid model's fees, okay?" Meera didn't respond to her sourpuss sister. She just smiled at me as if nothing had been said. I was thinking of the hallowed bench at Elphinstone College where Meera and her friends held court, teasing and terrifying any innocent they could lay their hands on. In this other life, Meera was a queen and most of the important people in the college flocked to her throne. She had her henchmen, her slaves, and her ladies-in-waiting. All and sundry were required to pay homage on a daily basis. New entrants to the college had to undergo a set of initiation rites. Those who passed enjoyed her support for as long as she deemed them worthwhile, those who failed were condemned to a life of mockery and shame within the corridors of the college.

"Who sits on the bench these days, Meera?"

"All changed now. It's not like the old days when Bharat and Sanjay and Madhu and Ding-Dong Surdi and Honky Shah would come every morning and we would all go through the day's gup shup. And Raju, sweet little pappu, would keep on bringing us coffees from the canteen. And Bobs, what a darling he was, even though we were always teasing him to death. I got a letter from him the other day, from London."

"And do you still go to the Sterling morning shows and all?"

"So many films we have been to. You should come with us one day. We went to *Irma La Douce* four times. I loved that movie. *Mackenna's Gold* we saw at least three times. And *Soldier Blue*, that's my favorite. The actor in that is so sexy, I could just get lost in his eyes for hours. What a smile he had. Hey, Sivi, what was his name?" she called to her prone sister.

Sivi shot up into a sitting position on her bed, her mouth in a pout, her eyes glazed with semi-sleep. "Oh God!" Meera said under her breath, preparing herself for the tirade.

"Will you shut up and let me sleep. Or get out of here. And take that little brat with you." We stayed sitting where we were. Sivi wrapped her blanket around herself and stomped out of the room, saying, "I've had enough of your rubbish. Just you wait, I'm going to tell Maharani about this tomorrow." On her way out she switched off all the lights. In the darkness Meera and I giggled into each other's ears like a pair of chirping crickets. I felt swept up by her mad behavior. We smoked another ciggie in the dark.

"Come on now," she whispered. "I'm going to lie down." She unfolded the sheet and drew it over her waist, patting the space next to her. "Come here, kuchoo, come and lie down."

I had stayed many late nights at the Maharani's, but tonight I realized no one knew or cared where I was. And now, Meera was beckoning me under the sheet. I lay down, she put her arm around my neck, I snuggled my head against her breasts. For some time we stayed like that. There was something radiant about Meera tonight. It wasn't just that she was being nice to me because my father was very ill: in her arms there was something open and allowing. I couldn't guess what was in her mind, but the arc of her body drew me in, smooth and warm and cool. Part of me just couldn't believe where I was, another part envisaged the removal of clothes, naked bodies, my first penetration.

"You've got goose-pimples all over your arm," laughed Meera. She rubbed them up and down.

"Why does that happen?"

"What?"

"Goose-pimples."

"It just does. I don't know. I think it's when you're cold." Feeling seemed to return to different parts of my body, as I felt the different parts of Meera's body. What part of her was my thigh up against?

"Cyrus, Maharani really loves you, you know. She was so happy to see you tonight. What was it like with the Undu Gundus in their Kerala house?"

"It was quite nice." I was guarded. "Lots of sambhar and idli on banana leaves. And we went on a shoot and shot nine birds. I shot one of them myself. Mr. Krishnan showed me how to do it. He was much more relaxed over there." I think she knew I was lying.

"So, who do you like more, Mr. Krishnan or Maharani?"

"Definitely Maharani. A hundred times more than Mr. Krishnan. He's a bastard, yah. He beats his children so badly, and his wife also. I have heard them screaming so many times." In the moonlight, I saw Meera's face like a lamp. "Does the Maharani still hit *you*?" The question came out before I could stop it. There was a pause, a melancholy expression appeared on Meera's face.

Then she forced a smile. "I don't want to talk about that. I'm really happy today."

"How come?"

"I passed my third level translation tests. I never thought I'd make it, but I did." I remember Meera working really hard for these exams. She had been in a foul mood all through them. "Now I can get a job as a German translator. I've just applied for a scholarship to go to Hamburg for a year."

"Oh, yah, I know where Hamburg is. My father goes there for work sometimes. So what will you do if you get the scholarship? Have you told the Maharani anything?"

"No, I haven't told anyone in this house yet and I don't know why I'm telling you. You've got such a big mouth. Oh, God! Kasam khau, swear on your mother, Cyrus, that you won't say anything to anyone. No one at all." She propped herself up on one elbow and fixed me with her bewitching eyes, throwing her black tresses to one side of her neck.

"I have never seen hair so beautiful," I said. Meera smirked, but her eyes were waiting for my promise. "I swear, I promise, on my mother." Pinching my neck, I said, "I won't tell anybody about it. But how will you go if she doesn't allow you?"

"We'll see about that. Veena and Manju went, so I can go as well. Anyway, come here, you badmaash, with all your questions." She pulled me to her and cuddled me, kissing me softly on my cheek. Then she lay on her back with one arm around my shoulders. I stroked her hair, running my fingers through the silken strands above her forehead. I was Robert Redford in *Butch Cassidy and the Sundance Kid*. Robert Redford was Meera's all-time crush. Around her neck, Meera always wore a fine gold chain and a silver box that hung from a black thread. "Can you take these off?" I said, pulling provocatively at her mala.

"What?" She sounded shocked. "No, I always keep them on." She moved the necklaces to one side as a concession. My fingers edged down her neck toward her breasts. "Rascal," she said. "Barely ten years old and behaving like this." She grasped me by the hair. "You think you can do anything you want?" She sunk my head down on her chest and held me tight. I got one of my hands in and squeezed, glanced up, and said, "They're so soft, like cotton balls."

"What do you mean like cotton balls—that's my arm you're feeling, you silly boy. Cotton balls! Wait till I tell Rajnish about that." I didn't mind her laughter.

"If your arms are so soft," I whispered, "I don't know what your breasts must be like." Meera liked my joke. She pressed my head down, I could tell she still had her bra on so I put my hands around her and pushed them under its fastening. Finding the clasp, before she could stop me, I pushed the hooks together, as I had seen my mother do, and her breasts lost their shape. Meera pulled me up by the chin. "Where did you learn to do that? How did you know that, huh? Even boys of eighteen, nineteen don't know how to undo a bra and all."

"I've done it before," I lied.

"With who?" Meera looked genuinely startled.

"One or two people," I said coolly. "I can't tell you who they are." As I spoke, I tried to slip the bra straps off her shoulders.

"Stop it," she said, pulling my hand away. "You're a bad boy. I don't believe you."

"Come on, Meera," I said growing bolder. "I promise I won't do anything. Just take it off."

"Don't be silly. You're only a baccha, you can't do anything. You're like my kid brother."

"Okay then, if I'm a baccha and I can't do anything, take it off, no."

"All right, but you must promise to tell me about these other girls and what happened with them." Deftly slipping her arms through the straps, she pulled out the bra from under her nightshirt. I thought hastily of who should be in my girl stories and what sort of details I should use.

Once the bra had come off, a new kind of ease enveloped her. She tucked me into her arms and I hung in there limpet-like, stroking her back and the sides of her legs. Her body shivered. We lay like that for a long time, coiled around each other like snakes. Meera enfolding me like an elder sister. Once, when my hand moved high up the inside of her thighs, she clamped her legs around it and snatched it out.

So I told her my stories, larding them up. Sofie in the bathroom, my second cousin Yasmin (totally made up), Mrs. Krishnan's thighs. Some things she was shocked by, but mostly she laughed. Sometimes she would stroke and kiss me fervently, as if I were someone else—a lover she dreamed of having, perhaps. Then she would demand another story.

I remember falling in and out of sleep. "Sleep, sleep now, Cyrus," she said relaxing her hold. "Come on, it's almost light outside." I tried a feeble movement. "Enough, baccha, enough," she said, caressing my head. Later she curled up and turned away from me. Thoughts ran in and out of my wakeful slumber: perhaps Meera would fall in love with me? There would be so many nights like these. I would feel so proud tomorrow. I would smile knowingly at Rajnish and Behroz. I couldn't wait.

I WAS STILL awake when the crows began their cawing. The dawn light silhouetted the shapes in the room: the painting of a peacock fanning its feathers, the bathroom door, the mirror, the wooden dresser, the dress hanging on the handle of the cupboard. The world seemed like somewhere different, peopled by misshapen objects, with Meera breathing, her head on my arm, a pillow clutched to her bosom, like a sleeping child.

24

In the afternoon, I wandered into the Maharani's room, aimless and happy. It was a Saturday. She was sitting on the window bench looking out at the road.

"Are you going out somewhere?" I asked.

"No, I'm just sitting here looking out for those boys. They're trying to come through the gate and steal the papayas."

"Why are you wearing a white sari?"

"One day I'm going to take out my air pistol and shoot them in the legs," she said, ignoring my question. There was a silence in which I noticed that Meera's mother, sedentary as a rule, was hovering around the room casting her eyes at me. I thought, the Maharani will get into trouble if she tries to shoot at those boys. They'll bring in the local gangs against her.

"Are you taking Sheila to Dr. Hatangadi's?" I asked.

"I don't think so. She hasn't vomited today. It may just have been a mild bout of food poisoning. She eats so much rubbish in the compound." The Maharani continued looking out of the window. No words were spoken for some minutes. "Come and sit here, Cyrus," she said patting the cushion next to her. I went and sat down. We were awkwardly placed in relation to one another. An uncharacteristic awkwardness. The Maharani turned her torso toward me. She opened her mouth to speak. Before the first word was uttered I realized something had happened. Was it to be about my night with Meera? Then the words began to fall.

"I know you're a sensible boy, Cyrus. I know you will understand what I'm going to tell you." The white sari, the distant look, Meera's mother fidgeting—I should have guessed. "Sometimes in our lives we have to deal with very painful things. Things happen suddenly. People get taken away from us. It's very hard to deal with at first . . ." The white sari, the faraway look, the awkward silences: how could I have ignored these indications. "Then it gets easier." Was I a "sensible boy"? No one had called me that before. "We learn to deal with these things. Do you understand what I'm saying? I know you do. You are very mature for your age. That's why I'm telling you all this." Yes, I understood. I had understood for a long time, I wanted to tell her, I had known about it all along. From the first moment in Kerala, I knew I would never see him again.

The Maharani stopped speaking. I could tell that she wasn't sure I had grasped the import of her words. Meera was standing by the door. How long had she been there?

"When did you hear about it?" I asked calmly.

"About an hour ago, your aunty Zenobia phoned." The Maharani's voice relaxed slightly. "I don't know the details. He passed away at eleven this morning."

I was so composed, so cool. "Does Bhagwan know? Do my brothers and sister know?"

"Yes, they do. And your aunty Zenobia is coming to pick you up at five to take you to stay with her."

"Can't I stay at Juhu? I don't want to go to Bombay."

"I'm sorry, Cyrus, that's not up to me. I think it would be best if you went with your aunty. There will be prayers in town tomorrow. I'm sure you'll be back soon." She spoke with the restraint and kindness that made her such an important person in my life. "You should do what you feel like. Do you want to cry? Shall I get you a glass of water?" There was a silence in which nothing happened. "If you want, we can leave the room?"

I was making them uneasy. My stillness, my lack of reaction. What could I do? I didn't feel anything. A little discomfited to have them all standing there looking at me, waiting for me to do something. Our easy friendship seemed to have flown out of the window. I looked at Meera, standing by the door, her shoulders and arms bunched up, eyes lowered. "I'll get you something to drink, huh? Do you want a Coke?" she asked.

"Okay," I said feebly. I didn't want a glass of water. I didn't want a Coke. I don't know what I wanted.

"Should we leave the room, Cyrus? If you feel shy to cry in front of us, we can go out," the Maharani said once again.

"No, it's all right. I'm . . . fine." I found I'd injected a fake tremor into my voice.

"You should cry, Cyrus. It's natural. It's good to cry," advised the Maharani. "Let it all out. You mustn't keep it in."

Keep what in? I wished I had the courage to speak boldly, to say, "I don't feel like crying." Instead, I kept quiet, hoping something would happen. The three of them just stood there looking at me, and at my half-empty glass of Coke.

Then Meera came over to the Maharani and whispered something in her ear. Meera's mother joined them. I tried not to listen to what they were saying. Most of it was in Marwari anyway. The Maharani donned her slippers, picked up her cigarettes, and tiptoed out of the room. Meera drew the curtains, surveyed the darkened surroundings, came over to me, and said in the hushed voice of a nurse, "Cyrus, we're going to go out and leave you for a bit, okay? You can lie on the bed if you want to. Do you want to do that? Go on, bacchu, lie on the bed." I did what I was told. I lay on the Maharani's bed, a thing I had never done before.

I felt like an actor who was refusing to perform before his audience. I remembered the nativity play all those years ago at my primary school, my parents amongst the spectators. I had the lead role, but I refused to say my lines and played with my toes instead. Here I was again, unable to act my part, lying on the bed incapable of transforming myself into the Niagara Falls and weeping for the death of my father. I wished I could be like my mother, brave enough to speak her mind, regardless of embarrassment. I would have sat up on the bed, thrown back the curtains, called everyone back into the room, and asked them to carry on talking. Demanded some tea and kachoris, maybe even some bhelpuri as a treat, asked the Maharani to bring out her Monopoly board and entered into a long and absorbing game with Meera and her mother. Instead, I lay prostrate on my stomach, looking at the cream bedspread, daylight blocked out, thinking of nothing except the strangeness of this situation.

I could hear the three of them conferring in the adjoining room. I put my head in my hands. I imagined crying, or pretending to cry, for their sakes, perhaps for my sake, for my father's sake. I had every reason to cry, but no tears could be summoned. I looked into the blackness of my covered eyes. Was this the kind of void blind boys stared into? Tiny singing stars chinked in this emptiness like a miniature sky at night. I felt a hand on my shoulder, Meera's hand. Her consoling voice, "We're all here to look after you, Cyrus. Don't worry, baccha." I kept my head buried and tensed my shoulders. It had been some time since I thought of last night. I saw her breasts again. They made me ill. Even the thought of them. I wanted her to stop touching me. I hated her—her voice, her stupid "bacchu" and "baby." I hated her stroking hand, like a viper wending down my back. The displeasure grew so acute I threw myself into a sitting position and wiped my dry eyes.

"Maybe I should go home now," I said.

IN OUR house there were two things I noticed. The bare-bright strip lights, cruelly fluorescent in the pantry, and the silence. Everyone walked around like ghosts. There were no greetings or discussions, no words. People moved about looking at the floor. My uncle Soli was there, my aunt too, one of my father's favorite people in the world, sitting in the corner, staring at the fusebox. "Bhagwan," I said. But Bhagwan couldn't answer. He was talking to someone, some imaginary person. "Why did you do this? Why did you go away? So soon. I told you not to go. I told you I would look after you. I looked after you so well. Why, Lord, why did you take him away?" Bhagwan had worked for us for nineteen years. In the last few months, while we had been away, he had looked after my father on his own. Bhagwan's chiding questions were uttered as if my father might hear them and emerge from his study. My uncle put his huge bear-arm around Bhagwan's frail shoulders. "Bus ave, Bhagwan, bus. Ai badhu khuda nu hath ma che. It's all in the hands of God." A phrase I was to hear many times in the coming days.

25

My mother wasn't coming back from Chicago for a week. She had to make arrangements, said my uncle. Settle hospital bills, pay for the body to be flown back, and make peace with the city she would never see again.

We drove to town in the Packard. I looked for the familiar landmarks on the journey. The last time I had seen them I was a different person. I had a father. I couldn't face a conversation with my relatives. They were uneasy too. We drove in silence through the noisy night: Khar, Bandra, Mahim, Shivaji Park, Century Bazaar, Worli, Racecourse, Haji Ali, Breach Candy, Warden Road, Nepean Sea Road, up the hill, down the lane that led to their building. I was impatient to see Zenobia's son, Jehangir. Many nights, with my parents out of town, I had spent with my cousin, lying awake in bed and talking. He'd told me about Spinoza's ethics and I'd regaled him with my sexual exploits.

When I walked into my aunt's flat, I had that same sense of change. The paper knife by the door, the bronze horses in the living room, the turquoise sofa, all these familiar objects seemed suddenly transformed. It appeared as if with my father's passing nothing would remain the same as it was. I was orphaned now and every face I encountered reminded me of my new status.

Even Jehangir seemed strangely shy when he came to greet me. I had a quiet dinner with the family; beef Stroganoff and rice. I was hungry and the food was easy to eat, a mingling of tastes from East and West. I asked my uncle where this dish came from. He said Russia. I don't think I had ever had Russian food before.

After dinner Jehangir and I went down to the compound. They lived in a complex of buildings with a huge lawn in the middle, called Hill Park. I had an acquaintance, who was a friend of Meera's, who lived in building B. We had met at Elphinstone College. I put it to Jehangir that we could go and see her.

"Are you sure you want to go so late at night?"

"Yah, man, she stays up late. Meera told me. She knows I'm coming."

"You know her properly?"

"I've seen her two, three times, yaar. And I've talked to her sister, Anu. She's damn sexy, man."

"I think she hangs around in the table-tennis room. She's got braces in her teeth. Cheh, I didn't think she was good-looking." Jehangir always played down the attributes of women.

"Yah, but you haven't seen her sister Sunita," I said.

SUNITA LIVED on the fifth floor. The frosted glass on the lift door had fish swimming in it. We rang her bell around nine-thirty. The servant looked bemused, especially at my shorts. He kept us standing outside while he went in to call Sunita, a doe-eyed girl of nineteen. When she spoke it was as if there were pebbles in her mouth. She had a black bob and round thighs encased in a pair of faded Levi's. Everything she did was at quarter the pace of a normal person. She had a casual lazy air about her. "Hi, Cyrus. Come in, yaar." She offered us a drink. We sat in the living room. "I'm sure I've seen you in the TT room," she said to Jehangir, her head resting sideways on the sofa. He nodded, too abashed to speak. I sipped nimbu-pani, Jehangir had nothing. We sat on a gray sofa set in a room that lacked the signs of everyday habitation.

I asked Sunita about college, about the famous bench. She told me what I already knew from Meera. I surprised her with my insider knowledge. She seemed mildly amused.

"So what are you doing tomorrow?" I said to fill in the silence.

"Uh, I'm going to college in the morning, and . . . then at eleven we're all going to see *The Brain* at Sterling, morning show. Meera's coming as well."

"Really!" I exclaimed. "I've been dying to see that movie. I've heard so much about it. It's where the Statue of Liberty twists its head and looks to the right at the end of the film."

"Yah," said Sunita. "That's because throughout the movie, Gene Wilder, the main character, keeps turning his head to one side. It's really funny. I've seen it twice already." There was a pause, then she said, "D'you want to come? Come, if you want to." I held back for a moment, a tiny polite hesitation, then I burst out. "I'd love to. Should I meet you at Sterling or at the college?"

"If you can make it to Sterling," said Sunita, "then just come to the main entrance, by the steps, at twelve. You'll see us all sitting there."

"You sure you don't want me to come to Elphi? I can wait on the bench," I said, not wishing to allow any chance to upset my outing.

"Don't worry, baba, you won't miss us. Anyway, what time do you get up? I catch the bus at eight-thirty."

"Which bus?"

"One-oh-six, obviously," she said in her soporific voice. I felt like a charged-up battery.

"You better ask my mother first," said Jehangir.

"Yah, yah, I'll ask her," I said quickly.

"That's true, Cyrus. You'd better make sure it's okay with your Aunty and all."

We left soon after and walked aimlessly down Mount Pleasant Road, past Sorento, where my friend Darius Jejeebhoy lived. They had two Christian nannies for him and his sister. Very strict women. Past the cigarette shop on the corner, where I bought a packet of foreign fags for nine rupees. They didn't have any Salem. My aunt had given me thirty-five rupees pocket money, an inordinately generous amount. I was lucky if I got five a week from my mother. We lit up and dragged hard on our Marlboros. Outside the Chief Minister's house, the chowkidar was standing in his customary position, bamboo stick in hand next to his minaret pillar-box. "Ram, ram Kaka!" we teased. "Kai zala. Zopla nukko! Don't nod off, you bastard!" He ignored us, pretending he was like one of those motionless guards standing outside Buckingham Palace.

Our footsteps echoed up the winding road. I felt carefree with my beloved cousin by my side. We pulled the wipers up on the parked cars. Jehangir laughed at my silly jokes and I bent my brain to his sage wisdoms. Jehangir was knowledgeable about books, especially on philosophy and psychology. He told me about Freud's obsession with his arsehole——news I greeted with some relief. Apparently Freud's experiments included the insertion of pencils and candles up his anus. He found the experience pleasurable in the extreme and compared it to the excruciating joy of defecation, especially in childhood.

"I like that word defecation," I said to Jehangir, after he had explained its meaning. "I think I'll say it to my"——I was going to

say "Dad"—"next time I see people shitting on the beach."
Jehangir didn't notice my stutter and I carried on. "Have you
heard that new Deep Purple record, something about Japan?"

"*Made in Japan.* Arun's got it. But it's all the same songs as
Machine Head, only they are live and much longer. 'Lazy' goes
on for twenty-seven minutes. Ian Gillan freaking out on the guitar." Jehangir had a proper record collection, not like my
brother's motley out-of-date stash. His neighbor Arun was a
fanatic. He got all the latest records as soon as they came out,
including rare ones by Zappa, J. J. Cale, and John Lee Hooker.
He lent Jehangir an amazing Rolling Stones album with a blown-
up crotch and a real zip that went up and down on the cover. I was
always unzipping it to see if there was anything underneath.
Arun also had his own electric guitar, which he had managed to
hook up so he could play along with his favorite Zeppelin songs.
I longed to see his collection and hear him jam, but whenever we
bumped into him he was too busy.

"Hey, Jhangu! How many records do you think Arun has?"

"Solid amount, man. Easily into the hundreds. If you
counted his brother Uday's records, they must be over a thousand, easy."

"And he keeps them all in alphabetical order, no?"

"One whole wall is just covered top to bottom with the
records."

"One day I'm going to start collecting records, man."

We got to the bottom of the hill and U-turned up Nepean Sea
Road. A provision store had its iron shutters half down. We
climbed under and bought some Duke's mangolas and perfumed
sponge cake. I saw one of those cream pastry cones I had seen on
the railway station and I forced Jehangir to share one with me.
The cream tasted a bit rancid. Then Jehangir took me through
the back streets of Walkeshwar and we ended up by the sea. I
couldn't recall having been there before. The waves were furi-

ous, phosphorescent against the graphite-black rocks. The whole bay was a frothing mass of white. Water spumed into the air as the crest of a huge breaker boomeranged into the base of a boulder. Salty spray showered our faces where we stood silently watching this fuss. So different from the calms I was used to outside our house in Juhu. The buildings and streets behind us seemed shut away from this maelstrom of water and rock. A few steps, a little slip, and I could be in there being thrashed about like a cardboard box. I saw myself floundering in the surge. I imagined the news Jehangir would have to take home. I imagined my mother hearing it in Chicago.

To the right of where we were standing, a thin concrete walkway ran out to the sea, half its crumbling length submerged. We walked out dangerously far. The water swirled about our ankles. "Wow!" I said taking a few steps back. Jehangir stood well behind me.

"Cyrus, watch out! A wave can come and pull you away. That boy Porus was swept over out here." I went forward a few steps while the ocean gathered its strength. No sound from Jehangir. For the moment a calm hung over the surface of the sea. I could see a pregnant hump of water snowballing toward the walkway. As it approached, the water round my feet rushed off toward it, pulling and sucking at my ankles with alarming strength. I ran back toward Jehangir, the giant wave at my heels. Jehangir, on dry land, wore an irritated expression.

"You behave like a real idiot sometimes."

"I didn't realize the undercurrent was so powerful. Look how wet I am. Oh, shit! The fags are drenched."

"Don't be silly,' said Jehangir. "They've got that cellophane wrapping round them. Give them here." He put two in his mouth. "Actually they are a bit damp, man." It was so blustery that Jehangir used up several matches before he could light the cigarettes.

We sat on a rock and drew in the warming smoke. I felt like I was in a Marlboro Country ad. Jehangir pointed to a couple of cars parked in the darkness on the edge of the bay. "Lovers fucking in the backseat."

"Shut up! How do you know? Have you seen them?"

"Yah, man. Arun comes and hides behind the rocks and watches them. Sometimes havaldars come and make them get out of the car, half-naked and all. In their bras and panties, man. Ha, ha, ha." We laughed at the sound of those sexy words.

On the way back, Jehangir asked me how I felt about my father's death. "I feel fine," I said. "I mean, I don't feel anything right now." I told him about my night with Meera. He was suitably amazed.

"Why didn't you try and do some more? She obviously wanted to, didn't she?"

"I could have, but I just didn't feel like it."

"You're mad. You had a real chance, yaar."

Crows cawed from the trees, trees with large expansive branches and little green droplet leaves. I had never noticed any tree in Bombay except the palm trees in Juhu. I looked up at these overhanging branches and they made me think of a Bombay two hundred years ago, of the drawings in my father's books of pastoral scenes where these same trees shaded the shepherds and their flocks amid the swampy land covered now by the tarmac we walked on.

"What are these trees called?" I asked.

"Don't ask me about trees, man. How come you were allowed to stay in her bedroom?"

I was happy to oblige with lucid answers to Jehangir's inquiries, adding pepper and salt where necessary. He wanted to know more about Sunita's sister. "D'you think I have a chance with her? She's always coming and talking to me when the building gang play cops and robbers. She goes to Queen Mary's with my sister. I think I'll try and patao her in the table-tennis room on Sunday." I was thinking of my film rendezvous with Sunita. Meera would be surprised to see me there. I wished she weren't coming.

"Hey, Jhangu, your mum will allow me to go to the film with Sunita tomorrow, no?"

"I don't know, man." Jehangir shook his head. "Maybe she will. She wouldn't allow me to go. But you tell her your mum allows you to go to films on your own. The problem is I think there are some prayers at the agiary tomorrow and you might be expected to attend."

That night, the room was cold with air-conditioning. There was a lovely purring from the Air Temp on the wall, the sinking mattress so luxurious compared to my hard wooden bed at home, the cottony quilt, the birds chirruping in the trees, Sunita in her bed only a hundred yards away. In the seconds before sleep, I saw my father lying in his hospital bed, eyes open, staring into the Chicago ceiling, my mother by his side.

26

It was past ten o'clock when Jehangir and I made our way grog-
gily, still in pajamas, to the dining table. At our house, even on
weekends, there was no food to be had after nine. Jehangir
ordered breakfast, quick as a wink, causing not the slightest com-
plaint. Their servant, Manu, brought out a plateful of bacon,
toast, and two fried eggs each, sliced white Britannia bread, and
hot mugs of strong tea. None of these basics ever made an
appearance at my home. I was in the midst of gobbling my fifth
piece of bacon, mindful of my impending date, when my uncle
Soli came in.

"Cyrus," he said in a tone that immediately reminded me of
why I was staying with them, "Zenobia and I, we would like to
talk to you." He beckoned me into their bedroom. My parents
never said things like that. "We would like to talk to you." I felt
nervous as I walked into their private room. My aunt was seated

in the corner on a green chair specially shaped to hold her bulk. I placed my bum on the edge of the large double bed. My uncle stayed on his feet, behind him a single gray bookshelf stacked with Time-Life books.

"Jehangir tells us that you have arranged to go to a movie this afternoon."

"I was going to ask you. I'm going with my friend Sunita."

"Who is this person?" chimed Zenobia. "How old is she?"

How dare they ask me all this? My mother never asked me anything about my friends. This behavior made me think kindly of her nonchalance.

"She's a friend," I said. "I know her."

"We know how old she is," said my aunt. "And we don't think it's appropriate for you to be going out with a group of nineteen-year-old girls." With that she pursed her lips, eased back her torso, and rocked decisively.

I found myself staring at my uncle, who was looking at the ground, as if embarrassed by his wife. "Cyrus," he said gravely, "I'm afraid you can't go to the film today. In fact, it is quite likely that you will not see any movies for the next month."

"My mother always allows me to go to the movies," I lied. "Who says I can't go? Meera, the Maharani's daughter, is coming and I've been to see many films with her."

They both fell silent. I was tired of these pregnant pauses. They looked at one another and then at me, as if I were a sick patient. "You have to show respect for the dead," said my aunt.

That burned me. Adults were always creeping up on you by the back door. What they were implying was that I didn't love my father, that I didn't cry for him, that I didn't show I was sorry. Coals stirred in my stomach. "But why does it make any difference whether I go to the movies or not?" I must see *The Brain*, I thought. I will never ever get another chance. I was one hour and a bus ride away from being in the comfortable darkness of a theater, the film flowing like a river of forgetfulness over my eyes.

"Cyrus," said my uncle, "when Mehroo comes back, you can ask her if you can go to the movies. If she permits you, that's fine. But until she returns from America, you are our responsibility and we can't allow you to go."

"But can't I go this time? How will I cancel? Sunita will have bought my ticket."

"If you give me her number I will speak to her and if she has bought a ticket I will make sure the money is returned to her."

I went and sat on the bed in my cousin's room. My bare feet dangled over the tiled floor. My uncle and aunt had lodged an arrow of guilt in my heart. A cramp clutched the back of my neck. The ganga was sweeping the shiny tiles with a black rag. She waddled forward and back on her haunches, wetting and wringing out the swab in a bucket of water. The sound of car horns drifted up from the streets below. I thought I might slip on my shorts, creep out, and take the 106 straight to the Sterling. I didn't want to go to the fire temple for the prayers. I'd show them. If they thought they could keep me from the movie, I'd run away and not turn up for the death ceremonies.

Jehangir's sister Erzan was playing catching-cook, with my sister, Shenaz. I could hear them counting each other down in the living room. Then they ran round the verandah and in through the bedroom and out again, giggling and screeching like mynah birds. I felt furious. How could my sister frolic and yelp when our father had just died? When the two girls came in again, I grabbed my sister by the arm. "Come here," I said. "I want to talk to you."

"What do you want to talk to me about? I'm playing with Erzan."

"Just come here for a second." I led her to the bathroom door. Erzan stood by, looking puzzled. I locked the door and put the seat down on the toilet. My sister sat down on it and I perched on the end of the bath. I had no sense of what I wanted to say.

"Do you know what's happened? Do you know why we have all come to stay here?" Shenaz looked at me with sweet concern in her eyes, eyes I found difficult to meet. "Do you know that Daddy has died? How can you just run around with Erzan, playing and laughing? Didn't you love him? Didn't you care for him?" My wounding words sank in. Once I'd cut tresses of her long hair and the tears had fallen out of her eyes as the black locks dropped from her head.

In the bathroom, Shenaz's eyes turned to glass. She sobbed. I felt awful. And guilty, for having done this to her. I tried to comfort her. "I know you love him." She wailed my father's name unstoppably, and I had no choice but to open the door. Out she stumbled into the living room. Zenobia came rushing out of her bedroom, her voice full of alarm, "What's wrong, Shenaz? What's wrong, maro dikri?"

"Daddy!" wept my sister.

27

At the entrance to the Grant Road fire temple a man was selling sukhar, cigar-shaped sandalwood sticks of various thicknesses, laid out in a box. These were meant to be given to the dusturji, who blessed them and placed them on the ever-smoldering fire. I used to keep the sukhar hidden in my palm, stealing sniffs of its bark-like cinnamon scent. Often, on our way out of the fire temple, my father had to prize the sticks from my grasp. This was after my stash had been discovered in a drawer.

My uncle Soli and I, fingers entwined, entered the main room of the fire temple. The smell of smoking sandalwood filled the hall. The walls were stained ochre and nicotine-brown from the wood smoke rising between the framed portraits of venerable Parsi worthies. These ladies and gentlemen had donated large sums of money during their lives and after their deaths to this agiary. Worshippers paid homage to their munificent souls, bowing their heads and touching the glass cases that housed their glowering faces.

In the central hall was a mixture of devotees and of those who had come to attend the death ceremonies for my father. You could easily tell the two groups apart. Dressed in white, the mourners waited for the prayers to begin. Those dressed in everyday garb looked at us with curiosity. You could see they were thinking, "Who is it that has died? Look at all those cars parked outside. Must be a very rich man. Could be one of the Tatas." I adjusted my skullcap over my flattened hair, combed to one side by Zenobia Aunty. I looked smart. My father would have been proud of me.

I wandered over to my favorite place in an agiary, the kuha. There was always an open space or a courtyard at the back with a stone well. People drew out water here, said a few prayers, washed their hands and faces, loosened their shirts and untied their kustis, the sacred thread worn around their waists. I had no kusti and no sudhra. The Navjote ceremony which marked my initiation into adulthood had, much to my aunt's dismay, not yet been performed. But I used to love watching my father or my elder brother, or some stranger, turning his face to the east—or was it the west?—mouthing the familiar prayers, flicking the sacred string, snapping their fingers three times, looking up to the sky, and rebinding the plaited cord round their muslin vests with reef knots and ritual incantation.

On a table, to one side of the well, were laid small glass beakers with tiny cotton wicks floating in oil. Worshippers used a sandalwood splinter to light up a devo. Flames were lit in memory of a dead relative. Afterward, the devotee left a rupee note under the tumbler.

The courtyard was shot with morning sunlight. Leaning down into the well head, I reached into the abyss as far as I could go. It was dank, moss-smelling, a darkness in which to remember my father. I pulled the bucket up on its rope, heavy with water. When I got it three-quarters of the way up, I let it go again. The steel rim bounced noisily inside the well. A scruffy stubble-faced man came stomping out from a side room. "Hey, chokra, you're not allowed here. Go inside and stop fooling around with the bucket. It's not a toy." His worn rubber slippers, grimy pajamas, and gruffness marked him out as a servant of the agiary.

I waited by the inner sanctum, where the main fire burned, a space only the priests were allowed to enter. The square chamber had two doors at opposite ends, one for the dusturjis to enter from and one at which the fire-worshippers could bow down and pray. On the other sides were brass-barred windows from which one could peer in at the imprisoned flame. The floor inside was marble, in the center stood a huge silver urn overflowing with ashes and bits of wood. A wisp of smoke seeped out from this pile. It was the job of the dusturjis to keep the fire burning, as it had been, day and night, since the inception of the agiary. When we prayed, kneeling down on a raised platform of red carpet, I kept one eye on the paunchy muslin-robed priest, with his white cap and his mask tied behind his ears like a surgeon. He walked with an ancient bear-like sloth, all girth and sliding soporific feet. He stoked the fire, transporting ashes on a steel wedge, so that we could touch some onto our foreheads. Wasn't he worried that the fire might suddenly fizzle out?

"Where have you been, Cyrus?" flustered my aunt. "The prayers have already started." She ushered me into a special room reserved for the event and led me to the front row, where my brothers and sister were already seated. It was like being in a small theater. Rows of wooden chairs, old Parsi ladies wrinkled and fusty, the priests performing the rites in front of us like ancient Greek actors speaking in a tongue few in the congregation could comprehend.

In the midst of the four dusturjis seated cross-legged on the floor, a small fire burned in a silver receptacle. The priests chanted loudly behind their cotton masks. All around them lay trays of food, sandalwood, and ashes. Salvers piled with fruit: pomegranates, chikoos, custard apples, dates, oranges, and bananas. Dishes of rice, rotlas, and maledo. I was especially fond of maledo, a gooey brown semolina and sugar mixture, spiced with cinnamon and nutmeg. But this was no time to think of food.

I tried to concentrate on what the priests were saying. There was one very small man, younger than the rest, with a high-pitched voice and eyes that roamed his brethren's faces for support. The other three were more or less of the same roundness of size and voice. Now and then they cleared their throats or snorted like bulls in a pen, shifting their fat haunches from side to side, ploughing on with their braying prayers, intoned in a cascading cadence similar to what you hear from auctioneers at a cattle sale in a movie Western. The service was coded in the ancient Avestan script, invented in Persia for the purpose of noting down all the Zoroastrian prayers and rituals. It had gone more or less unspoken, except by successive generations of garbling Parsi priests, often from the poorest sections of the community. My father had been impassioned on the subject, having spent a year on Avestan studies at Wilson College in Bombay and some time as an apprentice priest. He had left in anger at the living conditions they had to endure—and the paltry payments for the tasks they were required to perform. It was no wonder that so many of them had to rely on handouts and presents.

Watching them chant for the safe journey of my father's soul, like auctioneers, or like commentators at a racetrack, I couldn't help thinking of the cruel jokes my Parsi friends at school used to direct at these custodians of our faith. We poked fun at their fat Rolex watches, always visible at the edge of their tunic sleeves, their sex-starved ravings—there was no such thing as a woman dusturji and they weren't allowed to marry—and the absurd figure they cut, roaming the Parsi colonies to wag their fingers at naughty boys whose pert bottoms were of more interest to them than their moral welfare.

My friends Hoshang and Khushroo were adept at imitating their prayer technique. Hoshang said it was common knowledge that as they prayed they slipped in lewd comments to one another on the physical attributes of their immediate audience. As I sat listening to these nasal voices seamlessly passing the prayers from one to another like runners in a relay race, I thought of my friends' imitations. "Aaashhheeemm Vuhuuyatthhhaaii vaaairri-ioo look at those dugs atttaaaara attusshh fourth row in the middle shetrrreemchaiii she is worthy of a good bang."

I smiled inwardly at these scandalous thoughts. I wasn't meant to smile. I was meant to sit here, in my first-row pride of place, and meditate upon the purity of fire, letting the holy words of the prophet roll around my head. This fire-watching became an obsession, as the hours went by. I stared deep into the licking flames, lost in the crackling amber and blue.

Occasionally, and in time with the litany, the head dusturji, using a pair of tongs, would pick up a chunk of sandalwood and place it strategically on the fire. Sometimes he would scoop up a pinch of loban, the holy ash, and dust the flames. All this was achieved without a halt to the pace of prayer, which went on mechanically and without a trace of emotion.

The ceremonies lasted all day. My brothers and sister were taken away in the afternoon but I refused to be moved from my seat in the front row. There were intervals in which people came and went, irritating people, some of whom I didn't know, who insisted on crushing me with their hugs, each vying with the other to say how sorry they were to hear the news of my father's death. "Your father was a great man, a very great man," they said. "God preserve his soul in peace and look after your well-being." Then they would dab their eyes with handkerchiefs. Musty smells came from them, mingled with eau-de-cologne. Some of the women had beards, which they rubbed against my cheek. They all seemed sorrier than me, and I resolved never to say sorry when somebody died. A loathing gripped me for these hanky-toting funeralgoers. I walked out onto the verandah to get some fresh air.

There I found my aunt Homai, my father's sister, a pious Zoroastrian, reading from a small prayerbook. She patted the bench beside her. Her torso swayed from side to side, keeping time with her moving lips. Even during the long breaks between prayers, when the dusturjis retired to perform their ablutions and get some food down their throats, my aunt sat outside and read from her prayerbook. It was as if the evil eye of the world would avert its gaze so long as she kept up her prayers, and reading from her book kept her grief at bay. It struck me that everyone to whom my father mattered was holding the pain at a distance. All those who knew him slightly went in for overt displays of grief.

"What are you reading?" I asked Homai Aunty.

"It's our Zoroastrian prayers," she said in a whisper, immediately returning to her suspirations.

"But is it the same prayers as the dusturjis are saying inside?"

"It's the same as that, but the script in this book is Gujarati. Only scholars can read the original script," she said, anticipating my next question.

"What are they saying in these prayers? Can you translate some for me?"

"I don't know exactly what it says, but mainly it's about the path the soul is going to suffer in its journey to heaven. We believe that when the body dies, the soul doesn't leave the body at the same time. It stays for three days, and during this time we have to pray for its safe passage into the sky. Through our prayers to God we try and ward off the evil spirits from entering the soul. Good thoughts, good words, good deeds——that is what we believe. Now shuush, and sit quietly next to me." With that she held my hand in hers and resumed her supplications.

I wanted to ask her how we know that the soul leaves on the third day. I knew that the soul was not something we could see. What was it, then? Had the priests done any experiments to check the facts? Maybe, if the body was in Chicago, it didn't behave the same way as in India or in Iran. I wanted to know if my father believed in this traveling soul. Sitting beside the sunken red eyes of his sister, I felt the pang of never ever knowing what my father's response would be to any further questions of mine.

I took myself back to the front row. The prayers began again. I fixed my eyes with a ferocious intensity on the flames in the pot. The dusturjis fanned the fire; their voices reverberated inside my body. It grew hot, unbearably hot. The chant resounded in my ears like the roar of rakshasas from hell. Frank-incense and smoke turned my skin dry as parchment. The more desiccated I got the more I was determined to keep my place.

In the middle of the second day my aunt took me home in her car. I had a fever and no more resistance to offer. Zenobia made me a hot drink and tucked me into bed. The next day were the most important prayers of the three-day ceremony, but I was stuck between sleep and waking, swaddled and sweating in my sheets.

28

I just wanted to see my mother again.

We were stood waiting for her in the arrival lounge of Santacruz airport: Zenobia, my brothers, my sister, and I. My aunt was acting as if this were her show. I wished she would evaporate into the muggy urine-smelling air. What if my bidding were done? What if I could cause the extinction of those I didn't like by imagining it?

My mother appeared amongst the baggage and the white-capped customs officers. She looked tired but strong, a bit as if she'd just played a strenuous tennis match. Zenobia zoomed into action, bustling around her sister-in-law like a chaperone, ordering everyone to do things, as if my mother were an invalid arrived in a wheelchair. Quite unlike her usual self, my mother appeared resigned to Zenobia's bossiness: a wan look signaled the pointlessness of reaction. We huddled around her like chimps seeking succor from their fatigued provider.

At home, my mother sat down, surrounding herself with piles of letters and telegrams of condolence. From time to time she read out a particularly moving missive. I don't remember her crying until months later. Over and over again she told the story of his death, sometimes in person, sometimes on the phone. As I sat through the day by her side, she went over the medical facts of my father's end: how the doctors failed to diagnose his problem at first, his lack of appropriate symptoms, the surgeon's diligence, how he appeared to have regained strength after the open-heart operation, his hopes for the future, his sharp descent into death. He died peacefully, she said, holding her hand. One morning, his face serene, he spoke his last words, as she attempted to feed him a bowl of porridge, "I'm behaving like Shenny, making a fuss about eating my breakfast."

Friends were keen to apportion blame: foreign country, American doctors, the flight, the food. But my mother stalwartly argued that everything had been done. American doctors were "the best in the world." It was simply that his kidneys failed at the last. "These things are all in the hands of God."

IT MUST have been the second or third night after her return. I heard voices outside my bedroom window. One of them my mother's. Peering through the glass, I could see two shapes in the dark walking slowly toward the garden. I slid open the window and crept onto the balcony. Who was my mother talking to at this late hour of night? On all fours, I followed them round to the front of the house. The garden was lit by a full moon and a porch light. My mother walked her friend down to the sea wall. I couldn't hear what they were saying but now I could see who it was: the aquiline nose, the tall body, the thin face. I should have guessed. I had no desire to remain a spectator.

A little later my mother came into my bedroom. I had settled in under the sheets. She switched on the stark strip light. In her pale blue lightweight pajamas, her hair slightly disheveled, she stood by the door. "What was Naresh doing here?" I demanded.

"I wanted to talk to you about something. He just came to pay his respects. Naresh was an admirer of Minoo's. Anyway, I've told him, categorically, that I don't want to see him for at least six months."

"Did he agree to that?"

My mother clicked her tongue. "What does it matter? What's happened has happened. It's not his fault."

"Are you going to go back to him?"

"I don't think so. I don't know. I'm not thinking of that right now. I wanted to talk to you about something else. Something your father said to me before he went into the operating theater," she said, moving to the foot of my bed. "When he was on the trolley, about to be wheeled into the theater, he looked into my eyes and said, 'I don't know if God will give me another chance, Mehroo. If he doesn't, I feel so sorry, not just because I caused you so much pain, but because in doing so, I suffered so much myself. I was so unhappy while we were apart. If God does give me another chance, I intend to make it up to you.' " Her voice trembled. "Of course, he came out of the life-threatening operation smiling and all. We were so hopeful. I phoned you all up the next day, remember? He was sitting up in bed and laughing, saying, 'When will I be able to have a steak and a glass of red wine?' The sunlight was streaming in through the big windows, even though there was six feet of snow outside. I really thought everything was going to be all right. I really thought he had made it. But then, you know what happened. They tried everything. They even put him on a kidney machine, but it was too late. And then, that afternoon, Dr. Kennedy, the chief surgeon, came up to me and said, 'I'm ever so sorry, Mrs. Readymoney.' " My mother dropped her head. The doctor's words meant so much to her. "I just want you to remember your father's last words before he went into the operating theater. 'By doing what I did,' he said, 'I was hurting myself.' " She pointed to her heart, emphasizing the word "myself." "Even your father, who was a very proud man, recognized that when you behave badly, you do no one more harm than yourself."

What could I do about this? What had I done wrong? How was I to know that when I spurned my father he might suddenly disappear for good?

AFTER MY mother had gone, I thought of the house in Kerala. The banana leaves and the fields of rice, the Krishnans and their grandparents. It all seemed like a movie I had been in a long time ago. The Krishnans were back now, but I could hardly bear to visit them or to look at their faces, their unchanged, unhurt brown faces. They would be upset with me because I hadn't written to thank them for their hospitality. And they'd feel I was being unfriendly by not going to see them.

I thought of Kailash, as he used to sit in my fourth standard class, the class I had been missing from, the class to which I was returning tomorrow. I thought of his thin face, his ostrich neck, his long dark eyelashes. I wanted to befriend him, go and sit next to him. I wanted to cry my eyes out in front of everyone as he had done when Mrs. Silgardo accidentally taunted him.

I couldn't remember when last I had cried noisily, with sobs and halted breaths. And now I was beginning to feel the need to cry, not just for the world outside but for myself. To maintain my sanity, to be able to say something to someone, to be able to say something to myself. What I desired was unpremeditated, broken-backed howls, as on the occasion when I returned from the Maharani's and found Bhagwan railing against God. Or the time I saw my elder brother Behroz sitting on the Arne Jacobsen chair in my dead father's study, weeping at his big black and white face staring sideways out of the blown-up photograph on the shelf.

There sat Behroz, facing the framed picture, tears dropping from his girly eyes. My father stared back at him with his black unblinking pupils, his square jaw, his hanging jowls, his handsome tailor-made jacket, his brushed-back hair, his small forehead, his thick eyebrows like fat centipedes curved on his brow. I saw my brother, I heard the voice of his thoughts. "Why are you not here anymore?" it said.

29

On Wednesday morning my mother drove me to school in the open-top Standard Herald bought by my parents on their honeymoon. It was a rare treat to be driven to school by my mother. All the more because she had informed us that the car would have to be sold very soon. She talked about her plans, she spoke about the importance of my schooling, about starting a small business to keep the family finances afloat. She hoped, she said, to keep many things the same as when my father was alive. My mother said she didn't want to turn into a white-sari'd widow who'd retreat to vegetate in a back room. As we approached Byculla, she reminded me that D'Mello had allowed me to stay on because he knew that I was soon to be sent to a boarding school near Delhi. Any slips in my behavior and they might still throw me out.

"Your father didn't want to buy the air rifle you had asked for but, when he heard that you had passed the entrance exam for boarding school, he picked up the phone in the hospital and made the order. I'm going to keep it locked up if I hear any bad reports from your teacher. Do you understand, Cyrus?"

"When is the air gun coming?"

"It should be at the warehouse in the airport. We'll go and pick it up on Saturday."

"Is it a Daisy with a telescopic sight?"

"I don't know all that. Minoo chose it from the catalogue. All I know is that it was much too expensive. You better look after it. That friend of ours in New York, Bill Stoddard, his son shot the daughter by mistake and now she's blind in one eye."

"How did it happen?"

"I didn't want to ask the details. You've got to understand, it's not a toy, you have to be careful with it. Anyway, I don't know what you want it for. What are you going to do with it, huh? Silly boy," she tutted.

My mother was finding her voice again, reclaiming her position of assurance and control in the family. We stopped at the lights on the U-turn into Nesbit Bridge, the final ascent toward the school. I remembered the horrific sight of a dying man, felled by a water-carrier truck, lying on this corner four years ago on my first day at the school, a fountain of blood gushing spasmodically from his throat. "Ashem vohu, vesta masti," my mother had immediately prayed.

At the gates of the school, everything looked the same: the mountainous gray steeples, the banyan trees in the brown playground, the beggar boys looking agog at our car as it bumped over the speed-breaker and trundled across the playing field. Chaunt, the seller of imli and budhi ka bal, shouted my name. I waved, climbing nervously from the car. The bell had gone five minutes ago, most of the boys were in the first lesson. The building was quiet, apart from the occasional sound of a teacher's voice lecturing.

When I entered the class, everyone would look at my mother in her Western clothes. She would stride straight up to the teacher, unfazed by the stares of forty-five ferret-eyed children. We walked up the wooden stairs, my mother's heels clacking on the untreated wood, shaved smooth by generations of running feet. On the curved landing at the top of the first flight of stairs, a question popped out of me.

"When will Daddy's body be coming back?" My mother looked at me with mild surprise. I asked again, "His body is being flown back, isn't it?"

"Cyrus, I thought I told you, you aren't going to see the body."

"What do you mean?"

"I had him cremated, in Chicago."

"What does that mean?"

"When someone dies," my mother said in a level voice, "there are many things you can do. You can bury them, the way the Christians and Muslims do, or you can feed them to the vultures at Doongerwadi, which we Parsis do. I've never liked that way. Or you can burn them, as the Hindus do and, nowadays, some people in the West."

"But I thought that's what we were going to do after the body was brought back."

"It's very expensive to fly the body back, Cyrus."

"How did you burn the body?"

"It's all done in a machine. The body just goes in and then in two minutes' time it comes out and the ashes are collected." This couldn't be right. She must be making some mistake.

"Listen to me," said my mother. "Before the cremation I invited a few of Daddy's close American friends from his Yale days and we had a Christian ceremony in a small church with hymns and beautiful flowers. Then I decided it would be much better if I had the ashes enclosed in a nice marble urn and flown back to India."

"I always thought, when you talked about the urn, that his body was coming back in one."

"No, sweetheart. The urn is a marble kind of box, like a container, like a saancha, like one of those tiffin carriers." I had to compress what I had imagined to be a coffin-sized container into the confines of a lunch box. There was something else. The reality of extinction. No room in me to absorb this. Something frantic was going on. My mother could feel it.

"Darling," she said, taking my hand, trying to find my lowered eyes. "When the urn comes back next week, we are going to have a small gathering in the garden, just close family for tea, and then I've arranged for a boat to take us out on the sea in front of our house and we're going to go out in it and scatter the ashes. Because Daddy loved the sea, loved going swimming in the sea."

All the way up to the class I kept seeing that house in Kerala, the balcony where those fateful thoughts had come to me: the stupid fields, the flat banana leaves, the mongrel bitch scratching in the dirt. I was so angry with my premonition for turning out right. How could I have seen into the future like that? Would this kind of thing keep happening to me?

I CAME home and went straight up to my room. The school day had been reassuringly familiar. Mrs. Silgardo and D'Mello offered their sympathies and inquired after my mother. My friends found it easier to behave as though nothing had happened. In the lunch break I joined in a game of itty-kitty with Horace, Hoshang, and Raju. I had a hot kheema-gootli and a bottle of flavored milk from the canteen. I told Horace about my air gun. "Bring it into school, man. We'll go to my compound and shoot some pigeons. My brother Neville is a damn good shot, he'll show you how to aim and all. He shot a kite once, huge bastard," he said, using his hands to indicate the bird's proportions.

"It never died, mind. You can't shoot them with an air gun, you need a big rifle or something."

"Yeah, but mine is really powerful. It's a two-two," I said, thinking to myself, "No way am I bringing the gun anywhere near Horace's house. Once his brother gets his hands on it I'll never see it again."

Lying there on my bed, I thought of my friends at school, who could still go home to their fathers. I summoned images of my father as if I were watching a flashback in a Hindi film: the night he stroked me as I slept, the time he chased me round the table at the flat, his Pantene-smelling hair and Braun electric shaver, his rough cheek when he kissed me at the end of a long day, the night we had spoken on the telephone, when the trip to Hamburg fell through. I tried to remember the last time I saw his face. I rewound various incidents, very fast, then very slowly, like a private eye hunting for clues in a library of tomes. I knew it had to be there somewhere. I recalled that I had chosen not to stay the night with him when I went to the shooting at the Sun 'n' Sand with Mrs. Verma. I could remember him coming to see us at the flat in town, but I couldn't separate the various visits. Confusingly, I had all these imaginary shots of him in a hospital bed to sieve through. I found myself dragged into memories I had forgotten, happily detained by incidents stretching back to the time before my mother took us away to the Usha Kiran flat. Behroz and I used to play a game where he would name a moment from the past and I could fill in all the very smallest details of what had happened, who was there and what we all ate. I could remember the ingredients and courses of meals I had eaten five years ago, even the mundane ones. But where I was, what I was doing, where my father was, the last time I encountered him, just wouldn't come to me.

"Don't panic, Cyrus," I thought. "Just go through every day of the last three months, one by one, backwards and you're sure to hit upon the moment."

It must have been then that my sister, Shenaz, walked into my room. I didn't see her come in. The evening light had darkened. She switched on the tube light. "What are you doing lying here in the dark?" I was still guilty about the way I had accosted her at Zenobia's flat, but she showed no sign of holding it against me. I wiped my blinking eyes to combat the harsh fluorescence. "What's wrong?"

"Nothing," I said. "I was just thinking." She came over and sat beside me. Then she gave me a hug and I put my arm around her mounds of black hair, the same black hair I'd brutally scissored over some petty squabble involving scrambled eggs. My father had been furious when he saw the jagged ends of his shorn daughter's hair. She was another bit of my father, another bit of me, bold and smart, and older than her years.

THAT NIGHT the moon shone in through the massive pane of window onto my bed. I marveled at its whiteness. How could anything real be so round, so shiny, such a strange lantern hanging in the sky? It must be a fake, like that Man in the Moon. But when I looked closer I could see the ridge of his nose, the eyes, the mouth, the peculiar curving cheeks.

30

On Saturday the gun arrived. In the afternoon we threw the powdery remains of my father in the nearby ocean. That night I placed the rifle, in its olive-green case, beside me on the bed. I woke early on Sunday, pulled my red swimming trunks on, and went downstairs, firearm strapped to my shoulder. Scorpio, the Irish setter, was lying in his habitual somnolent state in the corner by the door. He raised his head and flailed his bearded tail, before laying them down again in exhaustion.

I sat on the living-room sofa and flicked through the morning papers. I checked out the comics in the *Illustrated Weekly*. I tried to follow an article by Minoo Masani, a friend of my parents, called " 'Garibi Hatao' Does It Work?" This was Indira Gandhi's slogan—"eradicate poverty." A photo of her in a cream sari, her gray plume stamped on an unsmiling face, decorated the piece. I didn't like her, but I couldn't see anything wrong with her slogan.

I gave up reading. Too many big words—"promulgated," "stultifying," "embryonic." Bhagwan brought me a cup of tea and sat down to talk.

"So this is the rifle Daddy bought for you."

"Look, I'll show you," I said pulling the gun out of its canvas case.

"Oh, maru baap! For God's sake, hold it carefully. I don't want to die just yet."

"Don't worry." I laughed. "It's not loaded." I unlocked the barrel and showed him the empty hole, with the spirally grooves running down into the barrel.

"What do you put in there?" he asked.

I prized open the sweet tin in which the iron pellets lay, each one shaped like a pea-sized hourglass. "You put one of these in here," I explained, slotting the ammunition home with my thumb. "Then you shut the gun and it's ready to fire."

"And what's this?" Bhagwan asked, pointing to the telescopic sight.

"That's where you look through to aim at something. It makes it easier to see the object you want to shoot. There's a little cross in it to help you pinpoint the target."

"Hah, now I understand," he said, nodding. "Acha, what if you're aiming at something and you miss? Suppose you hit some poor innocent walking past, they might die!"

"No, no. It can only kill birds or small creatures like that. You can't kill a human being with this pellet!"

Bhagwan took the gun in his hands. "Hey, don't point it at my stomach!" I said, changing the angle of the barrel. "It's got a pellet in it."

"Tell you what." His face lit up. "You show me how to use this thing and I'll slaughter all those filthy rats that scamper around the house." Cradling the butt, he ran his palm over the smooth mahogany of the stock. "See what a kind man your father was, even on his deathbed he was thinking of you. He left everyone something, you know. He left me a lot, Cyrus."

"What will you do with the money?"

"There's so much to be done. I've got to build a pukka wall on my house in the village. The monsoons this year have ruined the structure. I've got to give my wife and my sons a little bit, and your mother says she's going to start a savings account for me. She'll always look after me, won't she?"

"Of course she will. Arre, what about your son, Ghelo?"

"Forget about him. He's a useless good-for-nothing fellow. Keeps losing his job. I found him an employer in Peddar Road. Cowasjees, good Parsi family. He was working for them as a driver and getting a handsome salary, much more than I get. Then he went home on leave and came back ten days late. Naturally, they sacked him." Bhagwan sighed. "It's hard for him, poor blighter. He's got a young wife and a son living with my wife in the village. He has to see them sometimes, doesn't he?"

"Why can't they come and live with him in Bombay?"

"No room, Cyrus. No space anywhere these days. Everything is so expensive. You can't find anywhere without five thousand rupees deposit. And employers don't allow families to live in their homes. Anyway, we'll see. Something will turn up." He cleared his throat and bent his slight frame forward. "Come on now, I can't sit here the whole day wasting time. Go for a swim. It'll get rid of the sleep from your eyes."

I needed something to shoot at. I walked out into the garden, gun in hand. A couple of sparrows were frisking on the lawn. I looked around: gray water, blue sky, wispy clouds, two men shitting by the water, beach littered with coconut bark, rotting flowers, scurrying crabs. I pointed my telescopic sight at the bum of one of the defecators. All I could see through the eyepiece were sun-flecked waves. Somebody shouted from the beach. "Hey, Dilip! Come and see what's going on here." His friend came running up to him and they both looked up at me with faces of astonishment. I best go in, I thought, before a crowd gathers.

I went upstairs to the balcony and climbed the iron ladder onto the flat roof of the house. Here, high up amongst the water tanks and the air-cooling tower, surrounded by trees, I was hidden from the view of neighbors or passersby. I found a shaded spot by the overhanging almond tree and lay down on my belly. Pushing the butt against my shoulder, I surveyed the world through my telescopic sight. All I could see were blurred leaves and bits of sky. I twiddled the eyepiece. It didn't seem to make any difference. A crow perched on a branch swam into view. I steadied my aching arm and it was gone. Though it appeared much smaller, with my naked eye I could see the bird clearly still sitting on the branch. Once more I tried to find it in the sights of my telescope; its head loomed momentarily in the glass, but the slightest wobble in my arm and the quarry was lost again. It seemed so simple in a movie when a hunter aimed his cross at a target. Why was this operation proving so difficult? Perhaps I needed something larger and closer on which to focus. I walked around the terrace, looking over the parapet for a shootable object. At the back of the house, directly below me, lay a discarded car wheel. The sound of the pellet striking the steel rim would confirm that I had hit the target. I placed my right foot on the edge and aimed the barrel. My foot came into view. I moved the rifle outward and now I could see the magnified sockets of the inner rim. I steadied the cross on one of these holes and pulled the trigger.

A tiny explosion, more like the snap of elastic, accompanied the shot. At the same time, a searing pain raced through my foot. At first I thought I had been seized by an appalling cramp. I collapsed backward onto my bum and let the gun fall to the floor. On looking down, I found, to my horror, the iron pellet hanging from a mangle of skin and blood on my second toe. I leapt up, swearing, hopping like a demented frog round and round the terrace. It felt like someone was poking an acid-dipped needle into my toe. I reached down and ripped away the bloody pellet. Somehow, I made it down the iron ladder, thinking how much better off I would have been to have remained in bed, like my brothers and sister.

My injured toe was bathed in a basin of antiseptic fluid and the local doctor bandaged it, with a soothing smile. The pain had been unimaginable but surprisingly short-lived. The gun was locked away by my mother, "until I am satisfied that you are responsible enough to use it," she strictured.

The next morning, I took the telescopic sight to show to the Maharani. She placed an orange on a table ten feet in front of her and examined the fruit, squinting through the telescope. She spent a good half hour, turning the knobs and moving the fruit. Then she pronounced her verdict.

"Yup, I see what happened. This is a very powerful scope. Come here." She made me look through the eyepiece at the enlarged orange. "Can you see those black felt-tip marks I have drawn on the orange?"

"Yes," I said, as I usually did when I couldn't see what other people were trying to show me.

"When you look through the telescopic sight, you are looking out over the top of the gun. The trajectory of the pellet starts well below what you are seeing out of your scope. The pellet and the sights meet at around seven feet beyond the end of the barrel. You were seeing the tire through the telescope, that is correct, but the gun was pointing at your toe." She smiled, like a detective who has just solved a puzzle. "Never mind, Cyrus, you will survive. These things happen."

Printed in the United States
5895